A Golden Life

A NOVEL BY

JEANNE HARDT

James —
True love
never dies . . .

Jeanne
Hardt

"Jeanne Hardt masterfully blends a touch of sorrow with heartwarming characters and humorous life lessons. *A Golden Life* is truly a wonderful story that will pull at your heartstrings and tickle your funny bone. I loved every page!"

Monica McCabe, author of *The Jewel Intrigue Series*

* * *

"With honesty and heart, warmth and wit, Jeanne Hardt weaves an utterly unique story filled with fantasy and romance. *A Golden Life* is a magical and highly entertaining read!"

Darcy Flynn, author of *Hawke's Nest.*

* * *

"*A Golden Life* is one of those wonderful stories that will tug at your heartstrings while making you laugh out loud! A grieving widow meets a cast of larger-than-life heroes that, with a dash of magic, form an amalgam of true love. Jeanne Hardt shows us hope in the wake of loss and the healing power of a soulmate's last wish. It's a beautiful read!"

D.B. Sieders, author of *Lorelei's Lyric*

I'd like to dedicate this book to my husband, Rick, who is my hero and the love of my life.

Chapter 1

Writer's block.

Someone should come up with a four-letter word for it.

"Damn," Traci muttered. It was as close as she could get. In twenty-five years of writing she'd never experienced it.

Until now.

Her inspiration died. She'd buried it with Jack. How could she be expected to write?

She sat in her favorite spot—a cream-colored, L-shaped leather-soft sofa that cradled her old bones. *Old.* At fifty-eight she might as well be eighty. Why did everything start hurting when she turned fifty? She'd always grinned and bore it—not about to complain when Jack had experienced much worse.

At least all her vital organs seemed to be fine, though her heart disagreed. A doctor's diagnosis would show no problems with it, but what did they know? No medical instrument could display this kind of brokenness.

Her laptop perched where any laptop should be, perfectly balanced on her lap. And her fingers were positioned on the keys, ready to turn a blank white page into something spectacular. Her *golden* book. The fiftieth book in her writing career, and the one her agent had begged for the last six months.

She propped her bare feet on the coffee table. Had Jack done it, she probably would've smacked him. Somehow now, it gave her comfort. Then, every bit of comfort faded when her eyes shifted to the dust-covered remote control. A painful pang twisted her insides into a now-familiar knot.

The silly device had been his favorite toy. He'd flip from channel to channel and drive her crazy. She'd give anything for that now.

The house is too quiet.

She'd love another chance to ask him to turn down the TV. Was that too much to ask?

Stop feeling sorry for yourself.

She had to quit looking at that little black plastic reminder. If she didn't get her mind off Jack, she'd never get any work done.

How did that get out here?

One of her many books lay open on the corner of the coffee table. Troubling, since she had no recollection of bringing it from her office. Another folly of aging. The mind went on spontaneous vacations whenever it chose.

She lifted the book and closed it, then took it back to its assigned place on the bookshelf next to her other accomplishments. This one had been there a very long time. It had been her first.

But why was it on the coffee table?

After excusing her absent-mindedness to something forgivable, she returned to the living room and got comfortable once again with her computer.

Blank page. It used to excite her to consider all the possibilities. Dread had replaced joyful anticipation.

What sort of hero would captivate her readers this time? A prince? A sexy pirate? Or why not someone completely off the wall, like a slum lord who redeems himself?

God, no. What's romantic in that?

Whatever she chose had to be *golden*. A book destined for greatness. It had been rumored that she'd be honored at the national romance writer's convention this year. A lifetime achievement award presented to her for all her success. It seemed meaningless without Jack to share it.

It'd be a heck of a lot easier to just throw up her hands and say, *I quit.* But she'd never been a quitter. Besides, no matter how miserable she was, she didn't like to let anyone down. Especially Vivian.

Bzzz ...

"Crap!" The vibrating cell phone jerked her from her thoughts, and the laptop nearly dropped to the floor. The thing buzzed across the smooth surface of the glass coffee table as though it had grown legs and its own mobility.

She didn't need to look at the caller I.D. to know who it was. Only a handful of people had her number, and the only one who called her this time of day was Vivian. If she asked her again how she was coming on the new book, Traci swore she'd scream.

"If I don't answer it, she'll think I'm dead and send the police," she mumbled and picked up the phone.

She took a deep breath. "Hey, Viv."

"Good morning, Traci. Am I calling at a good time?"

An agent who'd been with her from the start of her writing career and hated to interrupt her creative process, Vivian always asked the same thing. Of course, right after Jack died it had also been followed by, *how are you doing?* She knew Vivian cared about her well-being, but right now the looming deadline was more than likely the reason for her call.

"It's as good a time as any. I'm just sitting here staring at my laptop."

Silence, except for a trace amount of Vivian's breathing coming through. "No luck?"

"Uh-uh. I can't—"

"Traci." Vivian cut her off short. "I'm in Gatlinburg. Why don't you meet me for lunch? I think it might help you to talk *in person*."

Vivian's in Gatlinburg?

Completely unexpected. Vivian never left L.A. this time of year. She hated the cold. And even though Traci's curiosity had been piqued and she hadn't been out of the house in over a week, she found it hard to say *yes*. Life was much easier remaining sealed inside her comfortable home.

"Traci? Are you still there?" The concern in Vivian's voice seemed genuine. She wasn't just an agent, she was a friend. If she'd flown all the way here for a visit, it'd be rude not to accept her invitation.

"Yeah, I'm here." She couldn't suppress a pronounced sigh. "Of course I'll have lunch with you. How about Calhoun's?"

"Perfect. Let's meet at eleven and avoid the noon rush."

After another confirmation of time and place, Traci ended the call. She had two hours to get ready. With any luck she'd be there on time.

* * *

Light snow dusted the ground and made the curving road from her mountain home a bit of a challenge. But she was a capable driver with a black SUV that could go anywhere and on any surface. She'd wanted one of those cute little sports cars—preferably *red*—but with Jack's guidance, practicality had won. Once they bought it, they'd spent hours in the grocery store parking lot learning how to handle it on snow. That knowledge wasn't needed today. Once she got closer to town, the snow vanished.

Being early October, tourism had started to pick up due to the changing colors of the leaves on the mountain trees. And after Thanksgiving, traffic would be bumper to bumper again, and she'd become a hermit in her log home. That had actually been the norm for her in the year since Jack died. She preferred handling grief without having to face people constantly telling her how sorry they were.

It bothered her that Vivian had come to town. Truthfully, the fact it *bothered* her disturbed her even more. She should be elated that her friend had flown clear across the country to see her. Especially considering what day loomed ahead. Still ...

She hates the snow. She must be checking up on me.

Phone calls weren't doing the trick, so maybe she felt the need for this personal visit. After all, Traci had never been late on a deadline in their long collaboration. Vivian probably believed that a gentle, understanding nudge could motivate her. And if that didn't work, Vivian had always threatened drastic measures but had never had to act on them.

Considering the situation, Vivian might follow her home, put her in a chair, turn on her laptop, and then stand over her until she had at least typed a page or two.

That's the last thing I want. I can't write under pressure.

When Traci arrived, Vivian waved to her and motioned to a table. Normally, two gray-haired women would get little notice, but everyone knew Traci. They were kind enough to give her privacy. However, tourists would often recognize her and ask for an autograph. She wasn't as big a success as the other local pride, Dolly Parton, but she came in a distant second.

They gave each other a quick hug, then took their seats. Guilt instantly followed. As long as they'd been friends, Traci should've been grateful for Vivian's visit.

She smiled apologetically at Vivian. Hopefully she'd forgive her for not being more enthusiastic about her unexpected arrival.

Vivian wore a perfectly matched navy blue pantsuit with accompanying jewelry. She had to have just come from a salon because there wasn't even one hair out of place. Perfectly curled, shimmering gray locks framed her pretty face. She'd aged well and though she had crow's feet, had no other noticeable wrinkles.

"You let *your* hair go gray," Vivian said with a tilt of her head.

"Yes. And the hair color industry's stock plummeted." Traci forced a smile. Jack had told her for years she should *go natural,* but she'd never been ready for it. Now it didn't matter. Six months ago, she had her stylist cut it extremely short so it would grow out to her true color. She wore a hat for weeks—not that she needed to. Only a handful of people saw her. It was finally at a length she could live with, barely touching her shoulders.

"I like it. You and I could be sisters." Vivian's face brightened. She then turned her attention to the waiter, who'd approached their table.

He took their drink order, then walked away. Traci had been tempted to get something stronger than sweet tea. She sighed. *Too early in the day.*

"He was handsome, wasn't he?" Vivian asked.

Traci hadn't paid him much attention. After thinking about it, she nodded. Thick dark hair and a nice smile. She hadn't noticed his eyes. They were most likely brown.

"Maybe he'd model for your next cover." Vivian wiggled her brows.

It sure didn't take her long to bring up the book. The woman never beat around the bush.

"I don't know what the book will be about, so the cover's the last thing I want to consider right now." Traci didn't mean to sound harsh, but the change in Vivian's expression confirmed she had.

Vivian fidgeted with her silverware. Her perfectly manicured, red-polished nails clicked against the metal. "The publisher's pressuring me. We're running out of time. Your contract is for a January release. That means you only have—"

"I know. Two months to write the best book I've ever written. I hope you didn't fly all the way here to tell me that. If so ... you wasted your money." Years ago she never would've been so harsh. When Jack died, some of her graciousness had been sealed in his casket.

Vivian extended her hand across the table, and Traci took it. She squeezed and looked directly into her eyes. "Traci, you know I care about you. I want to help you. I know tomorrow's the anniversary of Jack's death. I didn't want you to go through it alone. With Jason in Europe, I knew there was no one else."

A sad thing having no friends except an agent who lived on the opposite side of the country, and an only son who was an architect like his father, studying in Europe. Her friends were her books and the characters in them. She'd never needed anything or anyone else. Jack had always been there when she wanted someone to talk to.

"I appreciate your friendship more than you know. But honestly, tomorrow I want to be alone." She didn't want anyone to see her blubber like a baby. No matter how good of a friend Vivian was, she wouldn't make her witness a pathetic woman wallowing in self-pity. "I'm going to buy a bottle of wine and sit on my sofa and drink every bit of it."

"Mogen David?" Vivian chuckled.

"Of course. I've always said there's nothing like it." She'd been teased relentlessly about her fondness for cheap wine. She'd tried the expensive brands, but always came back to Mogen David. In the early years, she couldn't afford anything else. Now, cost wasn't an issue. She simply liked the taste.

She sensed a presence over her shoulder and turned to face a pretty young girl with long, kinky blond hair. The girl nervously worked her bottom lip, trembling like a frightened rabbit.

She held a book, and Traci craned her neck to read the title. *Deceptions,* book one of the *Southern Secrets Saga.* The series that started her career. And by coincidence, the same book that had appeared mysteriously on her coffee table that morning.

The girl swallowed hard and looked as though she might buckle at the knees. "You *are* Traci Oliver, aren't you?"

"Yes, I am." With a warm smile, Traci tried to lessen the teen's discomfort.

"Would you please sign my book? My mom gave it to me when I turned seventeen." She extended the paperback copy, and Traci gladly took it. "Oh … and please make it out to Gabby."

"Gabby?"

"Yes, ma'am. It's Gabriella, but everyone calls me Gabby." Gabby relaxed and flashed a mouthful of shining, silver braces.

Vivian handed Traci a pen, and she opened the front cover and signed: *Gabby, may your life be your greatest adventure … Traci Oliver.*

She returned the book to the girl's quivering hand. "Do you have a favorite character in this book?"

Again Gabby chewed her lower lip. Not a good thing to do with all that metal in her mouth. "I like Michael." Her cheeks flushed brilliant red.

"As a baby?" The book had been the first in the series, so Michael wasn't grown yet.

"No." Gabby giggled. "As a man. I read the whole series. I wish he was real."

"So do I," Traci sighed. That's what she loved about writing. She could make her men exactly what she wanted them to be. Michael Fletcher was exceptional. He took after his father, Andrew, her first and favorite hero. No real man could come close to matching his qualities. Not even Jack. At least not in the *looks* department.

Gabby walked away after a few more giggles, and for a moment Traci forgot her troubles. She even received a cheerful wave from a woman she assumed to be Gabby's mother. But when she returned her attention to Vivian, all her problems stared her directly in the face.

Knowing Vivian cared about her personally was one thing—and no doubt she truly cared—however, the unfulfilled contract perched on their shoulders like a lead weight.

"She was sweet," Vivian said. "And you were gracious. Just as you always are. I don't think I've ever seen you refuse a fan."

"Why would I? If I didn't have fans, I wouldn't have a career. *And* they were kind enough to see me through that horrible book you made me write."

Vivian's face twisted, and she seemed relieved when the waiter returned to take their order. When he walked away, she splayed her hands wide and huffed out a large breath. "You'll never forgive me for that one, will you?"

"No." Traci laughed to ease her friend. After all, Vivian had just called her *gracious*. She might have been kind to the girl, but to Vivian she'd been borderline *rude*. "I understood why you insisted on it. Scottish romances were all the rage, and for some unknown reason they still are. I did my best. I just didn't know the difference between Scots and Irish, and my fans threw it in my face. To this day I can't figure out how I managed to get a *negative* one-star review."

Vivian covered her mouth with her napkin, attempting to suppress laughter. "Do you know how many people burned that book?"

"No. But I'm sure they kept the cover. Out of all my covers, *Crimson Kilts* had the best looking man on it. There's something irresistible about a bare-chested man in a kilt."

"With dark, wavy hair that touched his shoulders and muscles that could wield a sword like no other." Vivian fanned her face. "I had the cover blown up and framed. It's in my office."

"Mine, too." Traci shook her head. Jack had never objected to the countless *pin-ups* in her workroom. He'd proudly called them *successes* and had been the one who'd had them made. *Crimson Kilts* could've ruined her. Thankfully, her fans never gave up. Would they now?

After needling Vivian a bit more about her reason for coming, Traci picked at the chicken salad the waiter had set in front of her. Having no appetite caused her to drop twenty pounds. Her doctor said it was normal to lose weight when grieving. Even so, she didn't want to waste away to nothing. Then again, perhaps she did.

"Maybe I should stop writing altogether." Traci said the words without really thinking about them. Truthfully, they probably popped out because she *had* been thinking about it non-stop since Jack died. She had plenty of money, so she didn't need the income.

Vivian choked down the water she'd just sipped. "Don't say that." She held up a hand. "And I'm not telling you this because I'm your agent. You're *meant* to write. It's part of you."

"I suppose. But I honestly feel like that part of me died right along with Jack."

"No. You're wrong. You'll get through this. You always said you found writing to be therapeutic."

Therapeutic, yes. When she'd been happily married to the greatest man on the face of the planet, and the only troubles she'd had to deal with were those of fictitious characters. No book could give her the type of therapy she needed now.

She stared at her plate, then scolded herself again once she realized her face had frozen into a frown. She used to be an enjoyable person.

Vivian patted her arm, then smiled at her with the loving expression of a friend. She got her talking again, and Traci finally managed a genuine smile of her own.

Vivian told her about a new client who she hoped would be as successful as her. Or even *close* to her success would suit her. It was a risk taking on a new author, but

Vivian had good sense about them. Though, even if she never had another success, she could retire comfortably on the commissions from Traci.

Their partnership benefited both of them. Vivian had believed in her when no one else wanted to give her a chance. Traci almost gave up more than once. Jack pushed her on. He gave her the encouragement she needed to find Vivian.

The waiter handed Traci a dessert menu. "Of course I want dessert," she said, and winked at him. *Where did that come from?* Maybe Vivian was the therapy she needed.

His eyes widened, and his cheeks matched Gabby's.

She returned the menu to his hand. She hadn't even needed to see it. The desserts here were one of the reasons she'd suggested this restaurant. "The triple fudge cake, please."

"One of my favorites," he said and turned to Vivian, who shook her head and patted her belly.

"Bring two forks," Traci added, and he hurried away. Even in her grief, she could manage to eat sweets. They were her comfort food. "I didn't mean to embarrass him. Do you think he knows how handsome he is?"

"Of course he does. I'm sure he has mirrors. We'll keep him in mind for that book cover."

"And if I decide to write about fluffy animals?"

"Don't tease me. I could never sell a *fluffy animal* book. You'd have to find another agent."

"That will *never* happen." No, she wouldn't want anyone else representing her. But if something didn't come to mind soon, she might have to write about *something* fluffy. Something safe. Something that wouldn't rip another hole in her heart.

* * *

Jason had tried to get Traci to sell the house after Jack died. She couldn't do it. It was their dream home—one Jack designed from a silly idea she'd had. She wanted a hexagon-shaped house with a garden in its center. It had to be made out of cedar logs and set on the most beautiful piece of wooded property in the Tennessee Smoky Mountains.

A real estate agent had told her it would sell instantly, but Traci wouldn't leave. Regardless of the reminders around every corner of her life with Jack.

She set the bottle of Mogen David on the coffee table and untwisted the top. No cork. That alone made her chuckle. How many times had Jason teased her about this? She found it convenient. No need for a corkscrew.

What the ...?

Her breath caught, and then she froze in the middle of the room. Once again, *Deceptions* sat atop her coffee table.

Her heart pounded as she reached for the heavy, wrought iron fire poker. Someone had to be inside the house. But how? Her home was a well-secured fortress with a high-tech security system. If someone had come in while she'd been gone, the alarm would've been activated and she'd have been notified.

With a dry throat, she walked from room to room wielding her weapon.

"I'll hurt you!" She hoped she sounded convincing. Somehow the notion of having nothing to lose increased her bravery. If someone was inside she'd give them something to think about—right upside their head.

She checked under every bed and in each closet, but came up empty. No sign anyone had come in.

Maybe she'd only *thought* she'd put the book back in its place that morning. It had to be the answer. She decided to leave it lying on the coffee table—almost afraid to touch it.

Probably the same thing I decided this morning. I really am losing my mind.

She returned the poker to its place and grabbed the bottle of wine.

Might as well lose a few more brain cells.

Being a special occasion, she poured a good amount into a crystal goblet. On any other day she would've used a cartoon character glass that she bought on one of her many family trips to Disney World. Tonight was different. She'd be toasting the memory of the man who held her heart.

Having taken time to build a fire, it popped and crackled with warmth. The fireplace was the focal point of the room, made of specially selected stones crafted perfectly together by the finest mason they could find. It gave their home that rustic feel they wanted. They refused to use gas logs. The smell of burning wood topped her list of favorite things—Jack's, too.

It happened here. One year ago today, while flipping from channel to channel, Jack clutched his chest and moaned with pain. She'd been sitting beside him typing away on her laptop, but threw it to the side. Something had been different from the other times he'd said he had a pain. This time, his face contorted.

She'd grabbed the bottle of nitro pills and called 9-1-1. The second she placed the tiny pill under his tongue, his eyes rolled back into his head, and he flopped over and fell from the sofa. Even if the ambulance had arrived the moment she punched in the numbers, they couldn't have saved him. Massive coronary.

Her eyes filled with tears. It seemed her body always had more to shed. She lifted the glass and stared into the flickering fire. Almost time. At eight minutes after seven it'd be precisely one year. This year the 10th of October happened to fall on a Friday. A night they used to call *date night*.

How fitting ...

She stood from the sofa and moved onto the thick Persian rug in front of the fire. Unable to sit cross legged, she sat with her knees bent and focused on the flames. Normally she'd sit on the hearth and let the warmth embrace her, but she became mesmerized by the flickering light and faced it instead.

With a long, slow guzzle she downed the glass of wine, then scooted the bottle close and filled it again. A good head start. She had two minutes to go and a lot more wine.

Another glass down the hatch. Mogen David went down smooth.

Truthfully, *one* glass made her a bit fuzzy. She'd not been a drinker—so to speak—*ever*. One had always been her limit if she wanted to carry on a sensible conversation. In her entire life, the only time she'd gotten drunk had been when her son thought it would be *funny* to fill her full of pina coladas—just to see what would happen. They'd tasted like Kool-Aid. Talk about going down smooth ...

One more minute. Another refill. *How many was that? Jack ...*

Eight minutes after seven. She tipped the glass and drained it. *Fuzzy* didn't describe her well enough. She felt light as air.

Knock-knock-knock.

What? Her head jerked toward the front door.

The goblet fell through her fingers and shattered on the hearth. Her heart pounded. She had to be mistaken —no one could be at the door.

Knock. Knock.

She gasped. *How?*

Her electronic gate had a pass code she changed monthly. *The only way in.* Had someone climbed the fence? Maybe the same someone who'd messed with her book.

Of course, it must be Vivian.

She relaxed for a brief second.

Did I give her the new code?

Aside from the fact she'd told Vivian she wanted to be alone tonight, and they intended to meet again tomorrow, Vivian was the only logical explanation. Jason was still in Europe.

"Traci!" *Knock. Knock.* "Traci, please let me in. I've come to help you."

She swallowed the stone lodged in her throat. This male voice couldn't be Vivian, and it came nowhere close to Jason's tenor.

Since her legs were quivering out of control, she placed her palms against the floor, then pushed herself onto her knees before she attempted to stand. With her eyes on the front door, she didn't notice what she'd knelt into. A shard of glass sliced her knee.

Damn ...

Staring at the remnants of what used to be an expensive wineglass, she assumed she must be dreaming. Either that or being drunk had caused her to hallucinate. The wine had a kick.

Might as well play along.

Unfortunately, this illusion had blood trickling from her knee. At least it wasn't gushing.

She pulled her thick white robe tight around her body. Her bare feet padded over the wood floor. The room tilted to the left, so she compensated by leaning to the right.

Another knock pushed her on. Blinking twice, she looked at the image from the security camera.

The waiter from Calhoun's?

No, this *gorgeous* man looked somewhat older. *And hotter.* Something familiar about him perplexed her, but without a doubt she'd never met him before.

"Traci," he persisted. "It's very cold out here. Please let me in. I want to help you."

What did she have to lose? If he was a serial killer she'd join Jack. That couldn't be all bad. Except he might do horrible things to her before killing her. Horrible, *painful* things.

Hmm ...

She checked the image again. Black hair. Incredible dark eyes. Gorgeous. Kind face.

Her hand rested on the doorknob.

Why not? I have nothing to lose.

Chapter 2

I'm going mad.

Traci had never been brave enough to open the door to a complete stranger. But the warmth from the wine made her bold, and his good looks certainly didn't hurt.

He stood on her door stoop, shivering. *No coat?* She wasn't the only insane person standing here.

His mouth formed a large smile and exposed perfectly straight, white teeth. *Chattering* teeth, but straight nonetheless. "May I come in?" He rubbed his arms briskly.

Good Lord, his feet are bare.

Had circumstances been different, she might have thought him a homeless man, yet she'd never seen one of them with perfect, clean teeth. She blinked hard. His live image was even more impressive than his face on the camera. He stood at least a full six inches taller than her, had a dark complexion and a chiseled face with features that looked a bit ... *Indian?*

He wore a lightweight, cotton shirt and tan pants. Unlike any khaki she'd seen from the Gap or elsewhere. They looked hand sewn. And why had he dressed so poorly in the cold?

"Traci?" He cleared his throat. "Please? I'm freezing. I can't help you unless you allow me to enter."

He spoke like an educated man. *Definitely not homeless.* Maybe just a little down on his luck. She might have to recommend that he go to a modeling agency. With a face and body like his, he could get work in a heartbeat.

After taking a step back, she motioned him in, then once again tightened her robe. All she had beneath it were a white tank top and pink panties. He *absolutely* didn't need to know that.

He closed the door behind him, then stopped on the throw rug in the entryway. With a slow twist of his head, he glanced around the room, then nodded toward the fireplace. "May I?"

"Oh—Of course." She managed to find her voice. Her head pounded. How many glasses of wine had she drunk?

He walked tall and proud with his shoulders back and head held high. Once he reached the fire, he turned his back to it and sighed. "Much better ..."

Maybe for him.

For Traci it was anything *but* that. Why was he so at ease in her home, and why did he keep calling her by name as though they knew each other?

She staggered toward him, doing her best to remain upright. Her legs felt like putty. "Who are you and how do you know me?" As far as she could tell, she didn't slur her words.

He started to say something, then shifted his attention to her legs and stepped away from the fire. "You're bleeding." He knelt down beside her and pushed back her robe, exposing her bare knee.

"Don't touch me!" She jerked the robe closed.

He held his hands in the air. "I'm sorry. But you know very well that I'm a doctor. I can help you. It appears you need a bandage."

"You're a doctor?"

"Of course I am. Don't you recognize me?"

She thought about all the doctors she'd seen the last time she had her check-up. This man would never be forgotten. None of the doctors at the local clinic looked anything like him. Most were gray-headed like her. This man looked too young to be a doctor.

"No, I don't recognize you. Where do you practice?"

He chuckled, as if she was playing a game. "Mobile City Hospital. But you already knew that. Are you feeling poorly? Your eyes look rather odd."

Vivian, how could you?

"Mobile City Hospital, hmm?" She shook her finger at him. "Vivian put you up to this, didn't she? Did she give you the code to the gate?"

"Who is Vivian?"

"I can't believe she went to all this trouble. And—how did she find you? You look exactly the way I pictured Andrew. And I had *quite* the picture painted in my mind. You're even better looking than the man who posed for the cover."

He tipped his head, studying her face. She preferred studying his. *Incredibly gorgeous.*

"Traci, I *am* Andrew. Doctor Andrew Fletcher."

This could be fun. She'd play along. After all, what could it hurt? She'd opened the door, now she needed to find out where Vivian had come up with him and what she intended for her to do with him.

"Okay ... *Andrew.*" She giggled. The wine made it easy. "If you really want to fix my leg, I have some bandages in the medicine cabinet in my bathroom."

"Very well. Take me to your supply cabinet." *Take me to your supply cabinet?* Such a good actor. He must have studied the time period, which explained his clothing. The exact things Andrew wore in the beginning of *Deceptions.* Clothes representative of the early 1870s.

"Very well." Trying to sound as proper as him, she tittered and took his arm, then led him down the hall to the bathroom. His bicep bulged with an enormous muscle just like Andrew's in her book.

He constantly turned his head, seeming to take in everything around him. He appeared genuinely intrigued by every item in her house. When he turned the light switch on and off several times, she couldn't keep from giggling. "You're very good at this. I hope Vivian paid you well."

"You keep speaking of Vivian, yet I don't know who she is. However, I want to take this opportunity to thank you for Claire. She's made my life worth living."

"Oh ..." Traci teetered and bowed low. "You're very welcome. Both of you made living *my* life a great deal more comfortable. I should be thanking you." She played along, using her most proper English. In her state it wasn't easy. And all the while she fought back a case of hiccups.

She removed a bandage from the cabinet and handed it to him, then lowered the lid on the toilet and sat. The man studied the porcelain as if he'd never seen one before. She tapped his arm and brought his attention back to the bandage.

He looked at the thing, more perplexed than ever. "What is this?" He turned it over and over in his hand.

"A bandage." *Man, he's good.*

"I don't understand. How does it work?"

Playing along, she took it from him and tore away the paper packaging. "You see, you peel back these little tabs, and then it sticks to the skin."

"First I must wash the wound." He glanced around the room. "I see the basin, but where is the water pitcher?" She flipped on the faucet and he pulled back, wide-eyed. "You don't have to pump it?"

"Nope." *Okay, this is getting a little old.* "You can stop anytime. You've done a great job, and I'll be sure to recommend you to my friends. You model, don't you?"

His brows drew in. "I don't intend to *stop* until I mend your knee." He grabbed a washcloth that hung on the towel rack beside the sink, dipped it in the water, then knelt on the floor. Once he washed the blood from her leg, he blew on her skin to dry it. "At least the bleeding has stopped."

She couldn't take her eyes from his lips. The tender way he'd helped her made her quiver, and his warm breath somehow gave her goosebumps.

He dabbed at the cut with the dry end of the cloth, and then—after examining it like a boy would a new toy—placed the bandage across the wound.

"It sticks all by itself ... amazing," he mumbled, then rose to his feet. "Let me help you." He extended his hand.

How many times had he said he wanted to help her? Even before she'd let him in, he'd said he'd come for that reason. Before he'd been aware she'd been hurt. So what did he mean?

She placed her hand in his, and they returned to the living room. He helped her take a seat on the sofa, then wandered around the room. Watching him entertained her. Maybe she should've been afraid of him, but oddly felt comfortable. Probably due to intoxication.

I'm going to regret this in the morning.

He looked closely at all her trinkets, then gazed out her floor-to-ceiling windows. This time of night there wouldn't be much for him to see. Probably only a few trees illuminated by her exterior lighting.

He moved on, taking his time examining the cedar walls. Seemingly more interested in them than anything else in the house, he ran his hand over the wood and shook his head. "I've never seen such finely crafted logs. And your furnishings are remarkable. Can I assume you've made a good living?"

Now she understood. *He's here for the money. Probably hoping for a good tip.*

"You know I have. How much do you normally get for your performance?"

"My performance?" He crossed the room and sat beside her.

"Yes. How much are you paid? Do you rely on tips to make your rent?"

"Traci." He reached out and took her hand. Instinctively, she almost pulled it free. The look in his eyes kept it there. "You're aware of my finances. You made my life what it is." His thumb rubbed across her skin.

"I'm too old for you." She choked out the words. The way he'd touched her gave every indication he expected something more than monetary payment. The comfort she'd felt left her, replaced by a large pit in her stomach that didn't set well with the wine.

He patted her hand like a parent would a child. "You're not *that* old. You still have a lot of life left. That's why I'm here. You're hurting, and I know you're lonely."

Oh, God. This is worse than I thought.

"Are you a gigolo?" She'd *never* forgive Vivian for this.

"A what?" The confusion in his eyes seemed genuine enough.

"Do you expect me to go to bed with you?" Boldness would set things straight. She had to make it clear. "Do you want sex?"

His eyes popped wide. "*Sex?*" Though his brows wove as if he found the terminology foreign, when he pulled his hand away and inched across the sofa, she assumed he understood. He crossed his arms over his chest. "Have you forgotten I'm a married man?"

"Oh ... yeah. Claire, right?"

"Of course I mean Claire. You brought us together. I would never stray from her." He frowned and shook his head. She'd definitely offended him. Either that or his acting was improving by the minute. Or maybe the wine had worn off, and she was seeing him for what he was. No doubt he needed to be on the big screen. One day, he'd probably win an Oscar.

She lifted her chin to match his confidence. "Well then, tell me why you're really here."

"To help with your grief. I knew you needed someone to talk to."

Yep. Vivian put him up to this.

"Tell me about your husband," he said, then leaned back on the sofa and waited. His demeanor softened, and he unfolded his arms.

If only he *was* Andrew Fletcher. The kindest, most giving man she'd created. He had Jack's heart and looked a bit like a twenty-something Taylor Lautner. Eye candy—as the industry called him. But, Andrew's *heart* made him attractive. She could tell Dr. Fletcher anything.

"Jack was everything to me." The words easily left her lips. "We built this house together. Those cedar logs you admired were my idea. I always wanted a log house. And when I saw the atrium at the Opryland Hotel in Nashville, I wanted my own. So, the house circles a garden with its own fountain and waterfall. There's a glass dome at the top that gives it sunlight. I can see it from any room in the house—except the bathroom."

He smiled and nodded. "I'd like to see it. However, I imagine it's too dark right now. Besides, I want you to tell me about *him* ... not the house."

"Jack ..." Just saying his name made her heart ache. "We met here—in Gatlinburg that is. I was a waitress at one of those pancake houses. You know ... they're everywhere." She chuckled, but then got caught up in the memory and softened her voice. "I grew up here. Thought my life was boring until I met him. He was in town working on a project for some rich developer. He was an architect. I served him pancakes and coffee, and the rest is history."

"I see. What made him different from any other man you encountered?"

Unsure why this man cared at all about her and Jack, it still felt good talking about him. She'd kept so much inside for a very long time that letting it out had been a welcomed release. "He took a genuine interest in me—cared about what I thought and felt about things. Not just what I looked like in my waitress uniform. And ... he made me laugh."

"How?"

A hard one to answer. She found humor in so many aspects of Jack—parts only she saw. "He was older than me. I had to teach him things. It's hard to explain ... I helped him become more comfortable with himself."

"You loved him very much, didn't you?"

"With all my heart." She wiped away tears and sniffled. She must look a sight to this handsome young man. A poor old widow woman with gray hair, a skinned knee, and a broken heart.

He scooted closer to her and pushed a strand of hair off her face. "I never imagined you gray." The light touch of his finger made her tremble.

"You never imagined *me*? I don't understand."

"I honestly didn't know what you would look like. All I ever knew were your thoughts, which became *my* thoughts." He grinned, once again flashing those beautiful teeth. "In many ways we're a part of each other."

The way he spoke made her stomach knot. She wished she hadn't drunk so much. At this point, almost anything could happen and she didn't want to do something she'd regret. It was silly to even consider something with this man. She was old enough to be his mother. In fact, she believed him to be younger than Jason.

"What do you want from me?" The words tripped over her lips.

"Only to help you." He cupped his hand against her cheek. No longer lightly trembling, her body shook almost out of control. Jack used to touch her the same way.

"Please tell me honestly—did Vivian send you?"

He shook his head. "As I told you, I don't know Vivian." His fingers caressed her face in a gentle way—not asking for something *from* her, but rather giving something *to* her.

He leaned in. "I can see you're tired. You've not been sleeping well, have you?"

"Uh-uh." The concern in his eyes warmed her, and his tender demeanor soothed her.

Standing, he extended his hand. "You don't have to be afraid of me."

For the second time, she placed her hand into his, and he helped her stand.

She wavered.

Damn wine.

Without hesitation he encircled her waist with one arm and led her down the hallway. She nodded toward her bedroom.

What am I doing letting this stranger take me to my room?

A stranger, yes, but someone also oddly familiar. Gulping, she stepped through the doorway, and he pulled the door shut behind them.

The lock clicked.

Chapter 3

Traci's heart skipped a beat.

Why did he lock the door? And when did it start raining?

It wasn't just a simple light rain pattering on her rooftop, more like a storm. A torrential downpour accompanied by high wind that whistled through—*cracks in the walls?*

Her walls didn't have cracks, so how could they be whistling? And why was it so blessed hot? She must have set the thermostat too high, and with the fire in the other room her bedroom had become stifling.

And for some reason, it was darker than normal. Her nightlight must have burned out.

She turned to flip the switch on the wall next to the door.

"Ow!" No switch plate. Rough wood met her hand and pierced her skin with a splinter.

"What's wrong?"

The voice of *Andrew* almost made her angry. This had gone too far. She'd never drink again.

"I got a sliver." She nursed the tip of her finger. She needed light to remove the stupid thing.

"I'll help you."

Somehow he'd gone from being directly behind her to the far side of the room. Light grew brighter from something he held in his hand. She stared at the object.

Where'd he get that?

A hurricane lantern cast dim light around them. The room it illuminated wasn't hers. So where was she? Nothing made sense.

He stood in front of her and lifted the light to take a look. "Can you hold this with your other hand while I try to remove the sliver?"

"Sure." The moment she shifted her attention from the tiny piece of wood stuck in her finger, she nearly fell backward.

When did he take off his shirt?

This incredibly buff man, who looked exactly as she envisioned Andrew Fletcher, had bared his chest. Her throat became dry as a brick.

The lantern light flickered like a throwback from a disco. She couldn't keep her hand still. How long had it been since she'd seen so much flesh in her bedroom? But, this wasn't her bedroom. Or was it?

The only logical answer ... It had to be a dream.

If she was lucky, it would be a happy dream and not turn into one of the many nightmares she'd had lately.

"There," he whispered. "I got it." He followed his proclamation by taking her sliver-free finger into his mouth, and then drew it out slowly. She almost dropped the lantern.

"Thank you," she said, with a dreamy sigh.

He took the lantern from her hand and set it on some kind of wood furniture. It didn't matter what it was. In this incredible dream, all she intended to focus on was the handsome doctor.

"The storm is much worse," he said. "I know it's improper for me to be here, but I wouldn't want to be anywhere else." He moved toward her.

Lightning flashed and lit up the room through a side window. Her surroundings were simple. A wood thingy that must be some kind of a dresser, and a bed.

A bed.

A sexy, shirtless man and a bed.

She fanned her face, then reached down to tighten her robe.

What happened to my robe?

In place of her tank top, panties, and robe, there was a *dress*. A floor-length, cotton dress with buttons down the front and a scooped neckline. Even in the dim light, she noticed cleavage she'd never had.

My boobs are huge!

What a dream ...

He caressed her cheek with his hand, then pulled it back and stepped away from her. "Claire, I'm sorry. I didn't mean to take advantage."

I know this scene.

No wonder she had large breasts. She'd become Claire, and they were in the scene where she and Andrew had first made love. The storm had brought them together and made him put aside every bit of his gentlemanly manners and enter the home of a single woman.

She'd returned to the dream that had started it all. The one that inspired her first novel. It was well worth a re-run.

I can go along with this. It might be fun.

She racked her brain. It had been years since she wrote this one and many, many love scenes ago. After thinking hard, it popped into her head, and she knew what to say.

She placed her hand against his lips. "No, don't say it. I want this, too." She suppressed a giggle. It was kind of a corny line.

His lips formed a warm smile, then he moved within inches of her.

Yes, I got it right!

At first, she wanted to raise a victorious fist in the air, proud of herself for remembering her own words. But since she knew what came next, she prepared herself for a kiss and licked her lips. He took her face in his hands, then covered her mouth with his own.

Oh, my Lord ...

It'd been over a year since she'd felt a man's lips. And these particular lips were exceptional and hungry for much more.

Her heart beat stronger as the kiss went deeper. Every bit of humor this ordeal brought on vanished. She hadn't been kissed like this in such a long time. Poor Jack could do little more than hold her in his final years of life.

For a dream, it sure seemed real. Wet, warm, and able to send her heart into a spin reminiscent of a whirling carnival ride.

Somehow she not only had Claire's body, but her energy as well. There were no aches and pains, with the exception of an aching desire to take this as far as possible. Was it wrong to want this man? How could it be wrong with someone imaginary? She'd had many fantasies about her heroes, and Jack often teased her about them. Still, she'd never strayed from him. For thirty years he'd been her only lover.

Jack ...

As Andrew's arms drew her in even closer, she allowed her hands to glide down his back. She touched the firmest, finest, *manliest* body—ever. No dream in her memory had been this good. Even the first time she'd dreamed it. Then, she'd been only a witness. Now, she'd become a participant. Able to feel, taste, and savor.

The moment he ended the kiss, she moved her mouth to his chest, drawn in by his young and inviting skin. She placed tiny kisses there, and her breathing quickened.

Her actions intensified his. Running his hands through her hair—which happened to fall all the way to her butt —he tipped her head back and went in for another kiss. Breathless and fervent. He then moved his lips to her neck, and with gentle suction made his way down. The heat of his breath skimmed across the swell of her breasts.

Oh ... crap ... Why does it have to feel so good?

Reaching behind her, he untied the bow, then worked the buttons on the front of the dress.

Ha! That writing contest judge was wrong. I knew Claire could make a dress that buttoned down the front and tied in the back.

She quickly dismissed her literary victory and concentrated on his mouth and where it had headed.

Her body quivered as he pushed the dress from her shoulders, and it dropped to the floor. The lantern light allowed her to see his face. Undeniable desire burned in his eyes.

A plain, cotton chemise covered her breasts. No bras in 1871. After taking an enormous breath, she took hold of the bottom of the garment, lifted it over her head, and tossed it onto the floor. And then, she couldn't help but admire her own breasts. Round, full, and firm as rocks. Just as she'd written them.

His eyes were glued to her body, and he no doubt wanted to touch her—and she wanted him to. Truthfully, she'd been tempted to touch herself. Her body had never looked this good.

Well aware of the next step, she slipped off the odd little panty-like thing on her lower body and lay down naked on the bed. He watched her every move. Proud of her new, perky body, she propped herself up on a few feather pillows and allowed him to see all she had to offer.

The bed cradled her atop a comfortable down-filled mattress. Woodsy but fresh. Claire had always been an efficient housekeeper. The sudden concern over the cleanliness of the dream had her stumped. She'd disregarded the storm outside, and that should've been an even bigger concern than possible dust bunnies. As hard as the wind was blowing it could likely take the roof off. But since it wasn't real, she didn't have to worry. What she needed to do was to forget everything except the man who was about to undress at the foot of her bed.

Breathe, Traci, breathe.

Lightning flashed and brightened the room. Andrew should've been named Adonis. No man had the right to look this good. Tall, dark, handsome. The epitome of the perfect hero. Could she bear what came next?

She closed her eyes. It might be better if she didn't look at it. A rustling of fabric confirmed he'd removed his pants.

Unable to help herself, she popped one eye open. Right on cue, the lightning flashed again, and there it reigned in all its glory. Ready for action. Every hero she wrote was well endowed. Why not? The power of the pen could do anything—or *keyboard* to be precise in the modern world.

And just like Claire, she gasped and trembled as he knelt on the bed between her legs. His hand moved over her body, as though memorizing her flesh, and his tender touch turned her entire being into putty. Her eyes closed completely, relishing the sensation, and her heart beat strong, anticipating ...

Oh, Jack ...

He lowered himself onto her, and she held her breath. As Claire, this could possibly be painful. Claire had been a virgin in this scene. Traci, on the other hand, had experience. She knew what to expect. Hopefully her knowledge would keep her from having to endure first-timer's pain. But even Claire had felt little discomfort. Traci had seen to it that Andrew was a gentle lover. Every woman deserved to have a good experience the first time.

"I've waited for you all my life," he whispered. "There's nothing to be afraid of. I won't hurt you, Claire." His body pressed against hers. "I'll *never* hurt you ..." He kissed one of her eyelids and then the other, and finally kissed her lips. *So gentle.* His hunger had transformed into complete love.

She relaxed even further and melted into the bedding. Grasping his back, she savored his entry. No physical pain whatsoever, yet something sharp wrenched her heart. How long had it been since she'd made love? Kissing was one thing, but this ...

She held him even tighter. Nothing would spoil it for her. For the first time in many years, she allowed herself pleasure.

* * *

The low hum of the drapery drawing back on cue from its automated timer stirred her. Then the bright light from the window brought her *fully* awake.

Traci sat upright in bed, then flopped back down against the pillows.

My God, what a dream ...

She sat up again. *Why am I naked?*

With both hands, she lifted the blanket and looked down at herself. Sagging breasts. *Her* sagging breasts.

She ran her hand through her hair. It stopped at her shoulders. Why would she think it would be any other way? Last night had been a glorious dream—one that still had her tingling.

How many times had they done it? She scrunched her eyes tight and attempted to visualize each luscious encounter. It had to have been at least five. Maybe more. Andrew Fletcher had been young and virile, and because she'd been Claire, she, too, had been able to go on without stopping.

Thinking about the one time she'd taken the lead, she grinned. Claire had never done any of *that* in her books.

Andrew sure seemed to enjoy it.

Had she slept at all? Of course she had. How else would she have dreamed?

Her cell rang and snapped her from her thoughts. The distant sound came from the living room. For some reason she'd forgotten to put it beside her bed last night. Most likely Vivian, but it could be Jason. She hopped from the bed.

Where's my robe?

Ring number four. She didn't have time to find her covering.

She grabbed the doorknob. *Locked?* Why would she lock herself in her bedroom? Luckily, she'd turned her ring volume to high, or she'd never have heard the cell.

Three more rings and it would go to voicemail. She unlocked the door and flew to the phone. Last ring.

"Hello?" With one hand, she held the phone to her ear, and the other hand covered her left breast. Miles from anyone, yet she still felt uncomfortable standing in the middle of her home stark naked in front of the enormous windows.

"Mom?" *Good, it's Jason.* "You sound out of breath."

"Hey, hon. I was in the other room. I ran for the phone." She sat on the sofa and covered herself with a fleece throw.

Much better.

"I should've called yesterday." He sounded just like his dad. "But I was tied up in meetings. You know how crazy the time difference is. Is this a good time for you?"

Now he sounded like Vivian. "Any time you call is good. How are you—and how's Amy?"

"We're fine, but we're worried about you. Did Vivian make it in?"

"She told you she was coming, huh?" He probably asked her to come.

"Yeah. But *I* should've been there for you."

She couldn't have asked for a finer son. Jason had never given either of them trouble—even in his teens. Now, he wanted to take care of her. *So much* like his dad. "I understand why you couldn't get away. You have deadlines. And I know more than most people about deadlines."

"Still ..."

"Jason, I'm fine. I have good days and bad, but I don't want you to worry about me. *I'm* supposed to be the one who worries about *you.*"

He laughed and warmed her to the core. "I have good news."

She said a silent prayer. He and Amy had been trying for years. Could that be his news? "Yes?"

"I'm coming home for Thanksgiving. Just me. Amy's going to Connecticut to see her parents, but we decided it was a good idea for me to come to Gatlinburg. I'll only have a couple of days, but I figure it's better than nothing."

"That's wonderful!" Traci tucked the blanket around her body and went to her desk. After flipping her calendar to November, she marked the date. "Though you know I'd love to see you both, I understand why she wants to see her folks. It'll be great having *you* here." She stared at the date. "Wow ... the twenty-seventh. Thanksgiving's late this year. Still, that's only seven weeks from now. I can't wait to see you."

"You too, Mom." His voice became a whisper. "Are you sure you're all right? Because yesterday wasn't a good day for *me*. I couldn't have gotten through it without Amy."

"Yeah, I'm okay. But promise me something."

"What?"

"Be sure you don't go even one day without telling Amy you love her. I thought your dad would be here forever. But ..." She swallowed the lump in her throat.

"I know, Mom. You two had something special."

Tears welled in her eyes. "Give yourself a hug from me —and Amy, too. I love you, Jason."

"I love you too, Mom. I'll call again when I have my flight schedule."

Their conversations had always been short and sweet. On the phone. In person, they could talk for hours on end. Maybe they kept it this way to ease the pain of being apart. Good thing he wasn't with her last night. She'd be sure to lay off the wine when he came home. No more crazy hallucinations for her—especially in front of her son.

"Talk to you later," he added, before saying "goodbye."

She cradled the phone in her hand and pushed "end call." Then she traipsed back to her bedroom.

Her bunched robe rested at the foot of her bed, but not alone. Her tank top and panties lay beside it. She didn't remember taking them off. Why did she? She always wore them to bed. She hadn't slept naked for at least ten years.

It had to have been the wine. There couldn't be another explanation.

She threw on the robe and returned to the living room. On the edge of the coffee table, sitting beside *Deceptions,* sat the notorious bottle of Mogen David, with only a scant amount remaining. Shards of glass covered the stone hearth.

My knee ...

She pushed the robe to the side. The bandage was still in place.

Right where Andrew put it.

No—right where *she* put it. No way had Andrew Fletcher been in her home *or* in her bed.

All she needed was a good hot shower, and she could wash away the dream. She had a great tale for Vivian.

Chapter 4

Traci chose Calhoun's again. Not only did it have convenient parking, it sat right on the edge of town. It kept her from having to go all the way into Gatlinburg, and she definitely didn't want to go into Pigeon Forge and fight the heavy traffic. When she was younger, it excited her to see all the people. Back then, it wasn't quite so busy. Now, it had become one of the most popular tourist destinations in Tennessee.

Today she wanted something more than salad and dessert. Even though it surprised her, she actually had an appetite.

"You're having ribs?" Vivian shook her head. "I thought you said they were too messy."

Traci eyed the waitress, who shifted her gaze between her and Vivian. "Yes, I want the ribs. A full rack. And extra napkins." She grinned at the young girl, who took the order and bustled away.

Both she and Vivian looked around the restaurant for the other server. They finally spotted him from behind, waiting on a distant table. When he turned toward them, Traci realized how much less attractive he seemed today. Since she'd spent the night with *Adonis*, it would be hard for *any* man to compete.

She found herself giggling and caught a wary eye from Vivian.

"You drank a lot last night, didn't you?" Her friend shot her a reprimanding look that reminded her of her mother. The first painful death she'd had to deal with. She'd been too little to remember her father's death, but her mother's passing was as fresh as Jack's.

"Yep," she replied, lifting her chin. "Nearly the entire bottle." She glanced around the room, then leaned toward Vivian and lowered her voice. "I had the most incredible dream."

Vivian's eyes narrowed. "I assume it wasn't a nightmare?"

"No." Traci took a deep breath. "Do you think it's wrong to dream about a man other than your husband?"

"Oh ..." Vivian leaned back in her chair. "One of *those* kinds of dreams. Maybe *I* should take up drinking Mogen David."

She didn't know the half of it. Dare she tell her *everything?*

Traci unwrapped her silverware and placed the heavy paper napkin on her lap. Then, she took a sip of sweet tea.

Vivian's eyes were on her, but then she nodded toward the good-looking waiter, who'd walked by them. "Was *he* in it?"

"No ..." Traci's belly fluttered with an excited sensation she hadn't felt in some time. "The man in my dream was ..." How could she effectively describe him? She swirled her hand through the air, as if stirring up her thoughts. "He was *fantastic*. In fact, he was Andrew Fletcher from my *Southern Secrets* saga."

"The half-Cherokee doctor?" A sly grin covered Vivian's face. "Your first hero."

Traci nodded and took another drink. "He was amazing. And he seemed incredibly real."

"That girl—Gabby—must have gotten you thinking about that old book. Then the wine set the mood for a romantic encounter. I wish *I* had dreams like that."

Traci considered what Vivian said. Part of her wanted to rush out and buy another bottle; the other part screamed a warning. She didn't want to become reliant on wine for a night of good sex. Imaginary or not. If she intended to complete her book—or even start it—she had to keep her mind clear.

She cradled the cool glass of tea. "Honestly, Viv, I feel a bit guilty. After all, it was the anniversary of Jack's death. I should've been dreaming about *him*, not Andrew."

"Guilty?" Vivian shook her head. "This is the first time I've seen a real smile on your face since before he died. Jack didn't want you to stop living. You aren't betraying him—especially with a fictitious character. And even if you find another man to share your life, it wouldn't hurt Jack. More than anything, he'd want you to be happy."

"No one will ever replace Jack." And she didn't even want to be talking about the possibility.

Vivian reached across the table and took her hand. "I know. But don't be so hard on yourself." She squeezed, and then sat back. "I'd give anything for a night with Andrew."

Traci managed a chuckle. She shouldn't have been so hard on Vivian when she'd only been trying to help. Still, her feelings were quite raw where Jack was concerned.

"So, he was better looking than the waiter?" Vivian wiggled her brow.

It couldn't hurt to tell her a little bit more. "Yes, much better. Do you remember when *Twilight* came out, and I told you I thought the actor who played the werewolf would be a good fit for Andrew if we ever got that movie deal?"

Vivian nodded. "But you said he was too young, and he'd do better as Michael in the later books."

"Yes. Well, he looked like the guy, but twenty-something. And his body ..." Heat filled her cheeks. No, she couldn't go on. Talking about it made it even more real and intensified her guilt. The whole thing was silly. It didn't actually happen, and she'd have done better not to bring it up at all.

"Same kind of rippled chest?" Vivian wasn't going to let it drop.

"Yes. Smooth, dark ..." *Real.*

Traci's mind drifted. Thoughts of Andrew's warm flesh and hot kisses flooded her brain and wrenched her stomach, taking her back to last night's activities. When Vivian finally came back into focus, she realized she'd been staring at her.

"Traci?" Vivian jiggled a single finger toward her. "What's that on your neck?"

Traci ran her hand around it. By the look on Vivian's face, she expected to find a spider or something worse crawling on her skin. "What? I don't feel anything."

"I swear you have a hickey."

Traci cocked her head and rolled her eyes. "Yeah, right. You're teasing me now."

"No, I'm not. If you don't believe me, go look in the mirror. I think you have more to tell me." Vivian folded her arms across her chest. "No wonder you're feeling guilty. A dream, huh?"

Vivian had been known for a practical joke every now and then. And even though Traci believed her friend had been toying with her, she stood from her chair and made her way to the ladies room. She glanced one time over her shoulder at Vivian, who hadn't stopped shaking her head.

A hickey? Right ...

She passed several ladies exiting the bathroom, and for some reason felt the need to cover her neck. Once inside, she shifted her eyes around the small room to make certain she was alone, and then approached the mirror.

Oh, God!

Her neck hadn't looked like this since prom night. How could she not have seen it when she got dressed that morning? A purplish-red hickey the size of a half dollar decorated her neck like a well-placed tattoo. She shut her eyes, unable to look at it. A vision of Andrew's lips cascading down her skin filled her mind. And the gentle suction—or not-so-gentle suction—brought everything to light.

He wasn't real!

Horrified, her hands shook. She braced them against the sink and looked again, but then a young girl entered the room, interrupting her.

Traci's hand flew to her neck, and she turned away from her.

How could she face Vivian again? What if there had actually been a man in her bed? It would explain why she woke up naked. Maybe the wine caused her to imagine the setting and the fantastic set of boobs, but if she'd really had sex last night …

No. I couldn't have.

She needed a scarf.

After a deep breath of courage, she returned to the table. A plate of ribs waited at her spot, and sitting beside them were the requested *extra napkins.* She took her seat, grabbed a napkin, and then formed it into a mock scarf as though it was an accessory she wore every day. Somehow she'd play it down.

Vivian broke into laughter. "So, who was he?"

Traci lifted a large portion of sauce-slathered meat from her plate and took a bite. What would she say?

Vivian calmed and waved her hand. "Never mind. It's none of my business. You just shouldn't have told me you *dreamed* him. You're a grown woman. Even if you want to have a one-night stand, that's your business. But, I know you well. You're not the *one night* kind of girl. I don't want you to be hurt."

She couldn't let Vivian get the wrong impression. A one-night stand was out of the question. "It wasn't like that," she finally said, then wiped sauce from the corner of her mouth with one of the many napkins.

"As I said," Vivian sighed. "It's none of my business. Your book, on the other hand ..."

Good. The subject changed. No way could she explain to Vivian what happened last night, because she didn't know herself. She never thought she'd prefer talking about her unwritten book. But, anything had to be better than trying to explain the sucking evidence on her neck.

"I still don't know what to write. I promise I'll try."

"That's my girl. And since it seems you're headed in the right direction, I'm afraid I have to leave this afternoon. Jim misses me."

Jim. Husband number three. At least this one had been good to her and had already lasted longer than the other two combined.

"I'm glad you came, Viv. Even though we had very little time together." She smiled at her friend. "I'm sorry I don't have something for you, but it was kind of you to be here for me. Jack always liked you. He said you were one in a million."

A sad smile on Vivian's face tugged at Traci's heart. "*Jack* was one in a million. Life isn't fair sometimes."

No, it wasn't fair. It was what it was. Traci had to cope with it, or die herself.

* * *

Traci should've come here yesterday, but couldn't bring herself to do it.

She sat on the bench perched in front of the White Oak Flats Cemetery sign. Most of the graves were old—from the 1800s—with a few fresh ones. Amidst all of the Ogle family plots, one Oliver could be found. It took some hard work to get the plot here, but Jack loved this old place and it was where he'd wanted to be. Fond of architectural structures, he'd also been an avid history buff who found cemeteries intriguing. Of course, the study of history had also been a part of his architectural learning. Along with his genes, he passed on that love to Jason.

A bouquet of red roses rested in her cold hands. They wouldn't last long in this weather, but she couldn't come here empty-handed. A guilt offering? Maybe.

Even with no one else about, she couldn't seem to move from the bench. What would she say to him?

I cheated on you with a fictional character?

It made her feel even worse that she'd enjoyed herself. She'd let herself go, and it felt wonderful to be held again. To be loved, kissed, and caressed, as though no other woman existed.

A thorn pricked her finger, and she instinctively put it in her mouth.

The sliver ...

She examined where it had been. A tiny rise of skin covered the spot.

A good psychiatrist could be in her future.

After making a great effort to push herself from the bench, she trudged slowly up the steep hillside to Jack's grave. She knelt down and placed the flowers at the base of the headstone.

Jack Oliver ~ Loving Husband and Father
He was so much more.

"Jack ..." Her voice came out in a gravelly rasp. "I miss you."

Tears were inevitable, and she dug into her coat pocket for a tissue. When she couldn't find one, she pulled the paper napkin from her neck just in time to stop the trickle of tears.

She plopped to the ground and leaned against the cold stone. "I'm sorry. I feel like I betrayed you."

Wind whistled through the branches of the trees that skirted the property. She shivered and hugged herself. Then, after staring blankly through water-filled eyes, she ran her finger along his engraved name. "Tell me what to do."

Closing her eyes, she thought back to one of their many conversations. "When I'm gone," he had said, "I'll understand if you marry someone else. I don't want you to be alone."

The memory was as clear as if he'd just spoken the words. Her response was even clearer. She'd told him she didn't want anyone else, and she'd rather grow old alone if she couldn't have him. Yes, he'd been almost ten years older than her, and they'd known he'd most likely die first. It had just happened too soon. She thought she'd have him for at least another twenty years.

"I wasn't ready!" She slapped her hands against the granite. Tears fell fast and hard, and she didn't try to stop them.

For over an hour, she sobbed by his grave and shivered in the cold. When her tears finally stopped and dried, she stood. Her legs ached, and it took her a moment to get her balance.

"I need to write, but I don't feel like it. And if I fail as a writer, what's left for me? I can't go on like this. What should I write about, Jack?"

If only he could answer her. He'd always listened silently when she told him about a plot idea or asked his advice on an interesting way to kill a villain. Then, once she'd laid everything out, his turn came. He'd come up with some great ideas.

Her heroes looked nothing like Jack, but each one held a piece of him. Andrew had his heart. Maybe that's why the night had been so special. From the moment Andrew cupped her cheek with his hand, it brought back memories of Jack. From then on, making love to him had been easy. Possibly *too* easy. In so many ways, she'd made love to Jack, not Andrew.

After knocking her forehead against the stone a few times to remind herself it was only a dream, she leaned her head into the wind and prayed she'd hear Jack's voice. The breeze skimmed her bare face like icy, prickling fingers. There were no words—only the memory of long-ago conversations that tugged at her heart and tore away a little bit more.

Chapter 5

The week passed by uneventful. Light snow drifted down from the sky. Nothing stuck. Normally it wasn't until late November that it accumulated at her home. At least the flurries gave her an excuse to stay inside, curled up by the fire. Besides, she wasn't about to go out again until the hickey faded from her neck.

Unable to write, she chose to read. She liked to keep up with other authors and see what creative ideas all her fellow writers had. Believing herself never to be too old or wise to learn something, she kept reading.

She'd only read one erotic romance in her life. Some people liked that sort of thing. She preferred the traditional romances. She craved the emotion and the feelings that drew the characters toward each other's hearts, not their body parts.

Of course, she liked sex as much as anyone. However, writing anything explicit pushed her beyond her comfort zone.

Early on in her career, she'd been told that if she'd just *sex up* her books, they'd surely sell. She couldn't do it. Yes, her characters had sex. Usually on the wedding night. Not always ... but almost.

They were stories she wasn't afraid to have her mother read. She'd read every book Traci wrote, up until the day she died. At least she'd lived long enough to share in her daughter's success. In fact, she'd been more excited than Traci when she got her first publishing contract. She spread the news like wildfire and pre-sold books to all of her friends.

Traci pulled the copy of *Deceptions* from the bookshelf. She'd let it lie for a few days on her coffee table, but then braved putting it back on the shelf. If the silly thing found its way there again, she might have to throw it out. She still thought the entire incident had been a bit spooky, but decided not to dwell on it. There were other things that demanded her attention.

Her shelves spanned an entire wall in her office, with rows that ran from the floor to the ceiling. Her hand fanned across the cover. The artist's rendition of Andrew wasn't perfect, but *close*. Jet black hair and eyes as dark as night. They were the most important features.

Her heart fluttered at the sight of him. Even though it had been a week, the memory of his hands on her body remained. His strong, but gentle, hands. No sensation from a dream had ever lasted this long.

She shook her head. *Stop doing this to yourself!*

Once again, date night had arrived. It didn't take her long to decide that tonight she wasn't about to open a bottle of wine. Reading would be safer.

A huge grin emerged on her face as she read:

He caressed her cheek. "I've waited for you all my life. There's nothing to be afraid of. I won't hurt you, Claire." His body pressed against hers. "I'll never hurt you ..." He placed a feather-soft kiss on one eyelid, and then the other, then kissed her lips with tenderness, causing her to melt into the bedding. She grasped his back; his words gave her all the reassurance she needed. And as their bodies joined together, she freed her passion.

She sighed.

Yes, Claire. I freed mine, too.

Writing historical fiction had limited terminologies for sex. Especially when it came to satisfaction. Actually, Traci liked that she didn't have to write some of the words she read in contemporary romances. Namely the words that referred to male body parts. Much easier to skim around them. With every love scene she wrote, she made a point of keeping them tasteful, yet also wanted to paint an accurate picture of what they were doing. Still, it never hurt to leave some things to her reader's imaginations.

Her favorite love scene happened in this same book—and not between Claire and Andrew.

Poor Gerald. Claire's second choice, but first husband.

From the corner of her eye she spotted Jack's reading glasses lying on her desk. He'd hated wearing them. Then the older he got, the more they sat on his face. He'd complained about how hard it was to keep them perched on his nose and frequently pushed them upward. A habit she bestowed on Gerald Alexander.

Yes, Jack. Even Gerald had a little of you in him.

She hurriedly flipped through the pages until she found their scene. Claire and Gerald. A typical romance would never have a heroine with more than one lover. Probably why it took her so long to get a book deal. But, this book was special, and so was Claire.

The only bad thing about reading one of her old books? She always wanted to edit it. Having learned a great deal since she wrote *Deceptions*, she had to grin and bear the silly mistakes she'd made. Well, they weren't really mistakes, simply early writing.

She found the spot:

She'd positioned herself in bed with the blankets pulled up around her. Her hair flowed over her shoulders and onto the blankets. Would he like what he saw?

He shut the door and crept toward her. She patted the spot beside her and he went to her, but rather than climbing into bed, he sat on the edge.

"What's wrong, Gerald?"

"Are you naked, Claire?" He pushed his glasses up on his nose.

Knock-knock-knock.

She slammed the book shut, and jerked her head around to look at the clock.

Crap! Eight minutes after seven.

This couldn't be happening. She wasn't drunk, and she couldn't be more awake.

Knock. Knock.

Her heart pounded. Then, a slight tinge of excitement crept from her belly. What if Andrew had come back again?

I'm going crazy. Andrew Fletcher did NOT come to my house last week!

She set the book on the coffee table, then walked to the door. Unable to push aside her high hopes of who might be waiting on the other side, she raked her fingers through her hair as she went. She tightened the same white robe she'd been wearing the week before, then held her breath before she looked into the monitor.

No, it can't be ...

She looked again.

Gerald?

Her heart sunk, then she scolded herself for being disappointed. That psychiatrist had just become a darn good idea.

"Traci? You in there?" His heavy, southern accent hung in the air and penetrated the heavy wood door.

Yep. Gerald Alexander. Stout, chubby cheeks, curly blond hair, and that horrible habit of pushing his glasses up on his nose. Someone had to be playing a trick on her. First Andrew, and now Gerald?

Vivian would be the only one capable of orchestrating such a thing. But why would she? Was she trying to soothe Traci's aching heart by hiring men to woo her into bed? And why in God's name did she send someone who looked like Gerald? No man could be sweeter, but he was no lover. Not that heavy, awkward men couldn't be good in bed, he just wasn't her type.

Tomorrow I'm changing the pass code, and I'm not telling a soul.

"Traci," Gerald persisted. "It's right cold out here."

She glanced one more time at the monitor, only to see him push his glasses up. Great acting job once again.

Where is she finding these guys?

If Vivian hired him, then he wasn't likely to cause offense or damage her in any way. Then again, even though Andrew didn't *kill* her, he wasn't exactly harmless. After all, they'd spent the night together, and he didn't even stick around long enough to thank her. The only reason she wasn't angry about it was that it had been one of the best nights she'd had in a very long time.

Her hand hovered over the doorknob.

"Dang, Traci!" Gerald fussed. "I reckon I'll freeze to death out here. There's sleet comin' down."

Fine.

She opened the door.

He seemed shorter than she'd imagined. After the tall, good-looking Andrew, little, plump Gerald was a letdown. It wasn't right of her to be so hard on the poor man. After all, he deserved a chance to give as good a performance as the other actor. Not every man had been blessed with the looks to play the lead romantic roles. Some had to succumb to being sidekicks or simple secondary characters.

He stood there staring at her, soaking wet.

"Come on in," she said, and took his arm. "Go get warm by the fire."

"Thank you." He lowered his head and looked away. "You ain't properly dressed." With his head bent downward and shoulders slumped, he made his way to the fireplace.

Her face heated. Andrew hadn't been bothered by her attire. Maybe—being a doctor—he'd seen it all. Gerald, on the other hand, was a simple blacksmith who knew nothing about women.

What's wrong with me?

These men were *not* real, they were actors. She had nothing to be embarrassed about. Of course, if she believed *that*, then it meant she'd had sex last week with an actor. A complete stranger.

Ugh ...

She took a seat on the sofa, then covered her lap with the throw.

Like Andrew, Gerald had no coat. He wore heavy coveralls over a long-sleeved flannel shirt. And luckily for him, he had boots on his feet.

He rubbed his arms and shivered in front of the fire, but wouldn't look at her.

"You're Gerald, right?" Maybe she could get him talking, and he'd slip and let her know who hired him.

"Yes'm. Gerald Alexander." He chuckled. "You knew that, didn't you? You're just testin' me." He finally looked her way, then seemed to relax when he saw she'd covered herself.

"That's right, I'm testing you."

Might not be a bad idea. We'll see just how well he studied his part.

He pushed his glasses up. "Did I pass?"

"Not yet. I have more questions." She thought hard. "What's your uncle's name?"

"Henry."

"And, how did Henry's sons die?"

"In the war, ma'am. Terrible thing."

"Yes, it was."

She had to come up with something even harder. A tiny tidbit no one but a fan would know. She wrinkled her nose, then shook her finger at him. "What did you lose when you died?"

His eyes became as wide as saucers. "I ..." He gulped. "Died?"

Damn. Of course he wouldn't know.

What gave her that idea? If he was an actor, he'd most likely have been required to read the whole series, so he'd have to know the answer. But, if in some godforsaken weird reality he *was* Gerald Alexander, he wouldn't know. And if he figured that one out on his own, it made him an even better actor.

I'm insane. That's all there is to it.

The man's chin vibrated.

No, please don't cry.

"Miss Traci ..." He sniffled. "Tell me I didn't die." While he waited for her answer, he wrung his hands.

"You didn't die." She shook her head. "It was a trick question."

He let out a long breath and wiped his brow with the back of his hand. "Miss Traci?"

"Yes, Gerald?"

"I'm real cold. You wouldn't happen to have sumthin' dry I could wear, would you?"

Even though Gerald was plumper than Jack, one of his large sweatshirts would probably fit him. "I'll get you something." She left him at the fireplace and scurried down the hallway.

In a year's time she'd not been able to get rid of Jack's things. They still hung in the back of her walk-in closet. Being a bit befuddled, she tripped over a pair of shoes while reaching toward Jack's section of hanging shirts.

Just as she pushed aside a few long-sleeved, cotton dress shirts, the lock to her bedroom door clicked.

Total darkness.

* * *

Traci's heart jumped. After a quick blink of her eyes, she opened them wide and found herself in bed with a quilt pulled up around her. Long brown hair flowed across her shoulders and onto the heavy blanket.

She scrunched her eyes shut again and breathed slow, deep breaths. The scent of recently lit candles filled her nose, and when she turned her head and breathed in a face full of her own hair, it smelled like honey.

Claire.

She shifted her weight, and the bed squeaked.

God, no ... I'm in Gerald and Claire's room in Uncle Henry's house.

She was on the pine bed Gerald made for Claire as a wedding gift. The one he didn't tighten properly, and therefore it creaked so badly it accompanied their wedding night ritual like a violin not properly tuned and played by a three-year-old.

Dear Lord, please take me somewhere else.

She knew this scene better than any other. As a brand new author, she'd read it to her writers group and trembled all the while. They'd laughed in all the appropriate places and gave her the encouragement she needed to press on.

Nothing to laugh about now. If she didn't do it as written, would her book change? She couldn't take that chance. Something weirder than fiction was happening to her, and she'd have to buckle herself in and go along for the ride.

She cleared her throat, mustered her courage, and then patted the spot beside her.

Now dressed in flannel pajamas and no longer wet, Gerald crept toward her. He pushed up his glasses, then sat on the edge of the bed. Being she'd just read this chapter, the lines remained fresh in her mind.

"What's wrong, Gerald?"

"Are you naked, Claire?" Again with the glasses.

Dear, dear Jack ...

Realizing she didn't quite sound like Claire, she decided to feign a southern accent. It seemed more important with Gerald than it had with Andrew. Come to think of it, why hadn't Andrew commented on the fact that she sounded nothing like Claire? Had he heard her differently? Regardless, she wouldn't take that chance with Gerald. "Why yes, I am, Gerald. I thought you'd like it, this bein' our weddin' night an' all." Okay, maybe that was a little too much. She'd have to lighten it up a bit.

He scratched his head. "I don't reckon I'm ready for you to be naked. I ain't never seen a naked woman in all my life."

Just you wait. Claire has great boobs.

"Want me to put my gown on, Gerald?"

"Yes, I would. Thank you, Claire." He expelled a large amount of air.

Okay, here goes.

"You're a very sweet man, Gerald Alexander." She leaned in and gave him a kiss on the cheek, allowing the blanket to fall and expose her breasts.

His eyes opened wider than when he thought he'd died. He stared at her breasts with a suitable, gaping mouth.

She jerked the quilt up to her chin. "I'm sorry, Gerald."

He grinned, then took the cover and pulled it back down again. She'd played her part perfectly, and so did he.

"What are you doin', Gerald?" She batted her eyes.

"I decided I like lookin' at 'em. They're nice."

Yes, they are. I wish I could keep them.

And just like in the book, after he decided he liked her being naked, he stood from the bed. With his back to her, and as discretely as possible, he took off his pajamas and climbed in beside her. They lay there doing nothing.

He shifted, and the bed let out a loud squeak.

"The bed squeaks, Gerald," she said. She wanted to giggle, but knowing what came next kept her quiet.

"Reckon I didn't nail it quite tight enough. I'll fix it t'morra."

"What about tonight? What if Uncle Henry hears us?"

"Don't worry 'bout Henry. Remember, he's deaf as a post."

No, he's not.

She'd written him to have *selective* hearing. Just like her son had when he was little.

They both remained silent and motionless for much too long. And just like Claire, she had to take the initiative, or they'd never get through their wedding night. The song from *The Graduate* popped into her head. *I'm Mrs. Robinson.* If she combined the ages of Claire and Gerald, she'd still be older. But, Gerald had to learn.

"You can touch me if you like, Gerald."

He turned on his side to face her with an accompanied squeak.

Oh, yes, the glasses.

"Let's take those off you." She removed them from his face. Not exactly how it happened, but close enough.

"But ... I wanted to see you."

"You don't need to see for what we're gonna do." Not quite as it had been in the manuscript, either. If she didn't concentrate, she'd mess everything up. This was completely weird, and more uncomfortable than anything she'd ever had to do. Still, she'd see it through. Maybe she could move things even faster than Claire had, and get it over with.

She slid her hand into his thick curls and with a thrust of her body, locked herself beside him. Without waiting for a response, she kissed him like she knew he'd never been kissed before. His body shook, but responded as she'd hoped.

"Take me, Gerald," she rasped, even though Claire never had. She jerked him over on top of her and grabbed his overly large rear end.

"Oh, Claire." He gasped and kissed her more enthusiastically than she'd ever dreamed Gerald could. She'd sparked something in him. She had Mrs. Robinson beat, hands down.

Hmm ... did it go in?

Gerald wasn't as gifted as Andrew in this department. She'd been cruelly unfair to write him with such a miniscule attribute.

Then, she felt *something,* and he started moving. And with every thrust, the bed squeaked. The rhythm section for the *Mrs. Robinson* tune, as grating as it might be.

The lyrics strolled through her brain. She scrunched her eyes tight, and hoped Jesus still loved her as much as he loved Mrs. Robinson.

The tune played over and over in her head, until Gerald shuddered above her, groaned, and collapsed onto her body, bringing down his full weight.

He raised his head and grinned like a happy drunk. Then, he rolled off of her and fell asleep.

Traci climbed out of bed, then tiptoed to the dresser where the candles were perched. The simplicity of this life had its appeal. No wonder she enjoyed writing about it. After blowing out the candles, she returned to the bed and climbed in as quietly as possible.

She folded her hands atop her belly and stared upward into the darkness. As she listened to Gerald's contented snore, she smiled. It hadn't been so bad. He was a sweet man with a gentle spirit, and she'd just gifted him with a night he'd never forget.

She had a new respect for Claire, and a better understanding of the people she'd created. If she had to write it all over again, she'd change one thing. Claire's grief would've been much stronger. All of the times she'd written about death, she'd just *assumed* how someone would react. Living through a death had been research she'd rather not have done. Why couldn't she and Jack have gone on forever?

Tears welled in her eyes, but cradled in the comfortable bed, exhaustion took hold. She turned her head to the side and smiled at the adorable man. Sound asleep.

Good idea. She'd rather sleep than feel sorry for herself.

She closed her eyes.

Chapter 6

Even before the draperies opened, Traci woke.

Alone.

She gazed around her bedroom. Exactly how it had looked before Gerald's arrival. Completely normal.

Normal? The word shouldn't be in her dictionary any longer. Nothing about her life seemed ordinary anymore.

Throwing back her covers, she jumped from the mattress onto the wood floor. Expecting the usual jolt of pain from that first-of-the-morning step, she tensed. No pain.

Odd.

Without a second thought, she walked naked into the living room and lifted *Deceptions* from the coffee table. She scanned the wedding night chapter that she'd altered last night.

"Whew ... it's still the same."

Since imaginary men had been sharing her bed, why not think her actions could change the course of a printed book? She plopped onto the sofa, grateful nothing so preposterous had happened.

Gerald had been sweet. A little like Jack in that respect. She should've never told him he'd died.

But everyone dies ...

Her laptop lay on the end table beside the sofa. Though it probably needed to be charged, it should have some life left. She wasn't ready to write, but definitely had to do a few Google searches.

After a sluggish startup, she tapped the colored icon.

Spin, spin, spin ...

Her fingers flew.

Books on paranormal activity

Since she hadn't been under the influence of alcohol or asleep, what other explanation could it be? The search brought up terrifying images, from ghosts to demon possessions. Horrific, ugly things. Her experiences were anything but that.

She'd go a different direction. Hating to even type the words, she closed her eyes and did it blindly.

Symptoms of insanity

She swallowed hard. With the exception of the family history and drug and alcohol abuse, her symptoms fit the bill. Unless an occasional fling with Mogen David could be counted as abuse.

If that's the case, I'm doomed.

HALLUNCINATION, INCREASED ENERGY

You can say that again...

AGGRESSION, DELUSIONS, THOUGHTS OF CONSPIRACY

Yep. I believed all along Vivian had a part in this.

Shaking her head, she closed the laptop. She knew better than to trust everything she read on the Internet, but more than one site had listed the same things. She had to face her grief over Jack's death, and she believed in time she'd learn how to cope with it.

Why all this? No one told me his death could make me crazy.

She grabbed her cell and autodialed.

"Hello?"

"Hey Karla, it's Traci. I hate to bother you on a Saturday, but could you see me today?" Somehow she managed to keep her voice from shaking.

"You sound upset, Traci. Are you hurt? Should you go to the emergency room?"

"No—no I'm not hurt. But, I need to talk to you. I think something is seriously wrong with me."

"I'm free after lunch. Come by the clinic around one, and I'll tell them to let you right in."

"Thank you, Karla."

She hung up the phone and went to her room to get dressed. How would she approach this? Every time she thought of a new way to say it, it sounded ridiculous.

She pushed herself out the door and climbed into the trusty SUV.

Time to go bare my soul.

* * *

Just two years older than Traci, Karla Peterson had been her OB/GYN since Jason's birth. She knew Traci's body better than anyone aside from Jack. Even though gynecologists weren't *psychologists*, she trusted her. She definitely didn't want to go to a *stranger* to have her head examined.

Instead of an examination room, an assistant led Traci to Karla's office. Traci sat in a fine leather chair facing Karla's tidy oak desk. Her heart thumped as she waited for her friend. Again, her mind whirled, coming up with ways to tell her what happened.

The hickey had vanished, erasing the evidence of her encounter with Andrew. Since she'd showered that morning, she'd washed away everything left behind from Gerald. Nothing physical remained from her trysts. She'd have to stand on her word alone.

"Hey, Traci," Karla said, entering the room.

Traci stood and hugged her. So petite. Clean and crisp in her white doctor's coat. Her short gray hair had streaks of black. Very stylish.

Karla sat behind the desk and folded her hands atop it. She'd become the professional doctor, waiting for her to speak.

I wish it was that easy.

"Thank you for seeing me," Traci said, with a smile. A good way to start.

"I'm *glad* to see you. I've been wondering how you're doing." Like Vivian, Karla cared about her personal life. She'd been there at her side during Jack's funeral.

Traci pulled a pen from a coffee mug that read: *I'll fix whatever ails you.*

Cute.

She didn't need to write, yet somehow having the pen in her hand gave her courage. She rolled it around in her fingertips. "I think I'm going crazy." There. She'd put it out in the open.

Karla leaned in a bit closer. "You lost your husband. You're still going through your grieving process."

"Does that process include having sex with fictional men?" She tightened her grip on the pen.

Karla's head tipped to the side, then she leaned back in her chair. "Fantasies?"

"No, more than that. They come to my house."

"Fictional men come to your house? You mean like— male prostitutes in costume?"

Traci closed her eyes. Spitting it all out in the open came easy. *Hearing* everything that came out of her mouth made her realize just how ridiculous she must sound. If their roles were reversed, she'd probably have herself institutionalized.

She shouldn't have come here. All she needed to ruin her career were rumors she'd gone batty. Then again, maybe she'd get a spot on the front of *The Enquirer.* It might not hurt. She envisioned the headline.

RENOWNED AUTHOR HAS SEX WITH HER FIC-TITIOUS CHARACTERS AND SWEARS THEY'RE REAL!

Traci opened her eyes and looked directly into Karla's. "No, they aren't prostitutes. At least I don't think they are. They're more like actors."

"Actors who willingly have sex?"

Was that really so hard to believe? "Yes. They pretend to be characters from my book. The first one I wrote."

Karla looked upward. "The first one? You mean your saga? *Southern Secrets,* right?"

Traci nodded.

"Andrew?" Karla appeared eager and leaned close.

Again, Traci nodded.

"I'd give anything for a night with Andrew," Karla sighed.

"That's the same thing Vivian said." Traci threw up her hands. "This is absurd! Don't you hear what I'm saying? I've been having sex, *real sex*, with characters from my book. Andrew even gave me a hickey!"

Karla covered her mouth.

Please don't laugh at me.

"Traci ..." At least she didn't laugh. "This may be a way for you to cope with your grief. I saw you six months ago and feared for you. You weren't eating, and your health was deteriorating. Today, you actually have some color in your cheeks. So whatever you're experiencing must be doing some good."

"I don't know ..."

"Have they hurt you?"

"No."

"Then stop being so hard on yourself. Fantasies are normal. If they help you through Jack's absence, then that's a good thing."

"But how can they be real?"

"They're as real as your mind makes them. And if they're truly actors playing a part, I hope you're taking precautions."

Precautions were the last thing she'd considered. They were hard to come by in 1871. "You know I can't get pregnant."

"I'm not talking about pregnancy. I know it's been a long time since you've been in the dating world. Don't forget there are many different types of STDs. Unfortunately, they're very common." She handed Traci a pamphlet.

Ugh. Traci didn't want to look at the words blazing on the cover. She stuffed the thing in her purse.

"Do you need an examination?" Karla gave her that *doctor's* eye.

"No. I'm fine. They were—*imaginary.*"

Karla's smile turned wary. "If you change your mind, just call for an appointment. I can always squeeze you in."

"Thank you." Traci started to stand, then sat again. "You don't think I'm crazy, do you?"

Karla shook her head. "The fact you're talking about it assures me you're not. All I ask is that you take my advice when you decide you're ready for sex." She opened a desk drawer. "Take these with you."

Traci extended her hand, expecting sedatives or something similar. Instead, she closed her fist around several packs of condoms. As long as she'd been Karla's patient and friend, Traci couldn't stop the heat that rushed to her cheeks. She whipped around and strode out of the office before Karla noticed.

She'd made up her mind. From now on, she wouldn't say another word about this to a single soul.

* * *

The days ticked by. Traci managed to get out twice during the week to visit Jack's grave, and she even made a trip to the grocery store. Lots of fruit and vegetables, but she splurged on a case of Pepsi. Now that she'd dropped weight, it wouldn't hurt her. For years she'd stuck to water and made every attempt to keep herself slim. It got harder and harder the older she got. Splurging felt good.

And now, another Friday had arrived. She resigned herself to the idea that someone might come knocking at her door again. What would it hurt to be ready for him this time? Whatever *him* it might be. Andrew would be her first choice, but there were others that could prove to be interesting. If this was how she'd heal, she might as well make the best of it.

She thumbed through the dresses in her closet. The black cocktail dress would do. She hadn't worn it since the New Year's party three years ago. This kind of stretchy dress always seemed to fit well, no matter her weight. It clung to her curves, giving her a satisfying view from her reflection in the mirror. *Mostly* satisfying. She longed to have Claire's upper body.

It was only five o'clock, so she fixed a piece of toast and ate a banana, then paced. Her stomach fluttered too much for a full meal.

What am I doing? How can I expect someone to knock on my door just because they have for the last two weeks?

She attempted sitting for a while. The hands on the clock moved even slower when she remained idle. She loved that clock, an antique her mother had given her. It sat atop her mantel. It chimed on the hour and dinged on the half. Over the years she'd become used to the sound and hardly noticed it, now she longed for the seven chimes. Once they struck, she'd only have to wait eight more minutes.

Maybe a little more makeup.

She hurried down the hall to her bathroom and leaned close to the mirror. Flashbacks of Andrew here with her increased her anxiety. A little more color on her cheeks and a bit of lip gloss. Nothing more. None of it really mattered. After all, she'd probably be Claire again. Claire never wore makeup.

Returning to the sofa, she sat and picked up a book she'd been trying to read. It had been written by an author friend, but every time she started a page her mind wandered—wondering who'd be knocking on her door. She flipped to chapter two.

What's this?

The postcard she'd gotten in Rome hadn't lost any of its appeal. She'd used it as a bookmark because she liked it so much she didn't want to tuck it into a drawer to be unseen forever. The Colosseum had been more majestic than she'd ever thought it could be and screamed at her to write about it. Six months later, *Beneath the Gladiator's Blade* hit the bookstores. Jack had boasted that his architectural road trip gave birth to one of her best novels.

She laid the postcard on the coffee table, then rested her feet to the side of it and tapped her toes, nervously biding the time. No stockings—bare feet. The remote enticed her. No, she didn't want to watch TV.

She hopped up and paced again. Six-thirty.

Damn.

What if she moved the hands on the clock to eight minutes past seven? *No.* She'd be taking too big of a risk. She had to relax and wait.

Okay, off to the refrigerator and a cold Pepsi. Drink and pace.

I'm getting good at this.

Another trip to the bathroom. This time to pee. Her nerves were shot. After washing her hands, she misted her body with Sensuous perfume. Ready for anything. She could easily pace away the next thirty minutes.

It's probably good for my thighs.

Positioning herself by the door, she watched the monitor. With every minute that ticked by, her heart beat faster.

Come on eight after …

Her heel tapped the wood floor. The countdown closed in. She looked away from the monitor long enough to glance at the clock. Any second now …

KNOCK. KNOCK.

She jumped. It sounded like a battering ram, not a fist.

Moments ago, the screen had been blank, but as she peeked into the monitor, she nearly fainted.

Jerking around, she plastered herself against the door to steady her breathing. In her mind she heard their cries, "Death to Magnus!"

He didn't die. He stood, living and breathing, on the other side of her door. Bare chested—*already*—and wearing that cute little skirt thing that covered his diaper. Of course it wasn't called a *diaper*, but a subligaculum. It took her forever to learn how to spell it. And spell check didn't recognize it as a word.

His wavy hair barely touched his shoulders, and he had that ever-present three o'clock shadow thing going on.

She glanced toward the coffee table and the notorious postcard. Had she willed him here? And would she become Alexa if she took him to her room? Alexa, the beautiful, raven-haired daughter of Roman elite with skin as white as milk.

Or something like that.

Why did she expect another visitor from *Southern Secrets*? This was completely unexpected, but not bad. *Beneath the Gladiator's Blade* was a great adventure. One that took her readers to ancient Rome and the tension of the arena.

It seemed *her* adventure had just begun.

"Traci." The deep bass voice of this man-of-a-man boomed through her door. "I'm unarmed. Let me in."

Unarmed?

He must have checked his sword at the gate.

The gate no one had the pass code for, except her. This sealed the deal. These weren't actors, they were something more. She intended to open the door to find out how much more Magnus could be.

After smoothing her dress and primping her hair, she swung it open.

He towered over her.

Did I write him seven feet tall?

She scanned his body up and down, and with the exception of his diaper and skirt, all he had on were sandals. His huge arms had to be about the size of her thighs, and his six-pack abs would make him a prime model for one of those exercise machine commercials.

So now that he'd planted himself on her entry rug, what would she do with him?

He pushed the door shut. "Your home rivals the emperor's."

"Thank you." Her hand nervously twitched as she held it to her chest.

Oh, my Lord.

He strutted across the floor the same way she'd imagined him walking into the arena. Shoulders back, head held high. His little skirt flapped as he walked. She knew what lay beneath it. Boy, oh boy, did she ever—nothing like Gerald Alexander.

"Do you have wine?" he asked. He folded his arms across his chest, making the muscles stick out like a neon sign saying, *ready and able.*

"Yes. It's Mogen David. Will that be okay?"

"I don't know who he is, but as long as it doesn't taste like horse piss I can drink it."

She gaped at him.

Oh, yeah ... this one's a little rough around the edges. Good looking, but tough.

She hardened her jawline and stuck out her chest. *I'm no wimp, buddy.* "It's good. You'll like it."

Whipping around, she fled to the kitchen. Her wine rack had been well stocked with her favorite brand.

Concord or blackberry?

It probably didn't matter what flavor. He wasn't a wine connoisseur. A week ago she'd sworn she wouldn't indulge again. A lot had changed since then. Besides, she had a feeling she'd need a bit of encouragement. She grabbed the blackberry.

A fancy wineglass? Nope. Not suitable for this lug of a man. She found a large beer stein and poured it full. For herself, she used one of the infamous cartoon character glasses.

"Here you go," she said, handing him the mug. "Bottoms up!" She giggled, then stopped when he looked at her as though he found her *insane*.

Been there, done that.

She backed away and stood behind the sofa.

He took several large gulps, and then belched. Not wanting to be outdone, she let out one of her own. The Pepsi helped.

He grinned at her. "You're different than I imagined."

Oh, here we go again. He's going to tell me he's surprised I have gray hair and am completely unladylike.

"I am?" She sighed.

"You're short."

Okay, so she'd been wrong. Her belching didn't offend him, and he paid no mind to her gray hair. "I'm not *that* short. I'm five-eight. You're taller than I thought. How'd that happen?"

He puffed out his chest. "You never specified my exact height." He smirked. "You made me great. I appreciate that. Height has its advantages in the arena."

"And ... what else did you like about ... what I did for you?" Did she make sense?

He downed the wine and set the stein on the mantel. In two large strides he stood within inches of her. Scent of manly man drifted into her nose. She let out her breath in slow sputters.

"I don't want to talk about me," he said, peering into her eyes. "I want to talk about you. Sit down."

She wasn't about to argue with this giant, so she plopped down on the sofa in one effortless thump. After fidgeting with her dress and smoothing it as much as she could, she looked up into his face. *Way* up.

He sat beside her, making it easier. "You seem uneasy," he said, narrowing his eyes.

"You're ... *big*. And I've never met a gladiator before."

"Of course you have. You created me." Another belch.

When she and Jack visited the Colosseum, he never would've dreamed a character like this would have come out of that trip. She hadn't told him one of the reasons she'd made Magnus a belcher was because of him. They'd had a belching contest on that trip after a night of wine tasting. Nothing refined about their relationship. They knew how to have fun.

"You really should say *excuse me*," she said, primly. "It's the proper thing to do."

He chuckled. "*You* didn't say it."

He had a point. But, she'd been trying to prove herself. "I ..."

"Never mind. How are you faring?"

"Huh?" It wasn't the type of question she expected from a man like him.

"With Jack gone. Are you doing well?"

"You know about Jack?"

He nodded. "I know all your thoughts. You've been in my head, and I've been in yours." He winked.

"Oh." Nervously, she gulped. Whenever Jack winked at her, it had always led to the bedroom.

"So tell me. Has time made it easier?"

His eyes softened, and her nervousness subsided. "Each day's a little better. But I can't seem to fill the hole in my heart."

He put his hand against her cheek. Rough skin, and powerful enough to squish her head if he'd wanted to. "It will get better. I promise you."

"How do you know?"

He stood and wandered close to the fireplace. Then, he spotted the postcard and picked it up. "When did it turn to ruins?"

She stood beside him. "Long after you were there. After the fighting stopped and people became more civilized."

He grunted. "Civilized?"

"Oh. I promise you. People have great respect for what you did in the arena. Why do you think I wrote about you?"

"I like you," he said, with a kind of scary-looking grin. "You gave me many talents. Even more important than knowing how to wield a sword, you gave me the ability to be a good lover. And, I like it."

It? He must mean sex. But, because of his loyalty to Alexa, it couldn't be possible he'd come on to *her*.

"That's nice." Her nervousness returned, evident by the quirky little laugh that came out of her before she could stop it. "I like it, too. With Jack."

In a flash, Magnus's heavy hand landed on her back, and he pulled her against him. He bent down and sniffed her neck. "You smell good."

"It's Sensuous," she squeaked out. Her knees were giving way.

"Yes, it is." In one quick swoop, he lifted her off the floor as if she weighed nothing and carried her to the bedroom. She lay limply in his arms and didn't attempt to stop him.

The lock clicked.

Chapter 7

The strong arms of Magnus encircled Traci's body, but her room had disappeared. Her back pressed hard against a rough, stone wall. The low roar of a distant crowd surrounded her. It rumbled through the air with excited fury. How many bloodthirsty people filled the arena?

Daylight had replaced the darkness of the night, and they were in a dusty corridor. The passageway that led to death or victory. A decaying, musty smell burned the inside of her nostrils. Many forgotten souls haunted this smelly horror chamber.

And like a rose in the midst of a field of dying weeds, she couldn't be more out of place. Her dress was now a pristine white garment, and her hair fell to her waist. Alexa's hair.

"We don't have much time," Magnus said. His sweaty body had a fresh wound from a blade that had sliced a deep gash across his chest.

I know this. He just fought Artemis, and they're sending him out again. What did Alexa tell him?

After scanning her brain, it finally came to her. "Don't go out. We can run away together."

"No. They'd find us and we'd both be killed."

He framed her face with his monstrous palms, then kissed her, long and hard. Oddly, he tasted like Mogen David.

"I don't want to lose you," she rasped. Her chest tightened with a sense of dread, knowing full well what he'd face in the arena. *It's all too real*. Frightening, yet stimulating. Did her readers feel this way when they read it? Did they feel his pain?

"Then, let me leave you with a part of me."

He reached under his skirt flap and freed himself, then lifted her dress and picked her up off the ground. With skill, he tore her undergarment, then cupped her bottom with his enormous hands and held her firm.

He plunged into her as though sheathing his sword, and took her with an intensity she'd never experienced before. Since she knew they'd not be discovered, she set herself free and matched his hunger. Gladiators were always left alone to gather their thoughts before a fight. In *her* book, that is. And right now, nothing else mattered.

He squeezed her bare tail with his strong hands, and his mouth covered her neck. She'd have more marks with this one. Still, she wouldn't stop him. He moaned and groaned, sucked and thrust like tomorrow would never come. Probably because he knew it was a possibility.

Somehow he grew even more intense—almost animalistic—yet she gladly endured it, and let him carry on until he finished with her.

And with the screams of the distant crowd, he pressed her hard against the wall. With a scream of his own, he released, and she followed. She dug her nails into his back, then kissed him with a newly found devotion. Yes, he'd been rough, but she'd never forget him. Quick, yet oh so memorable. His penetrating eyes revealed his love for her.

Karla would be furious. But when would she have had time to use protection? And where would she have found any in this filthy corridor? In the book, he'd impregnated Alexa in this scene. A pivotal part of the story.

While catching her breath, Traci chuckled. *No worries about that one*. Her childbearing years had come and gone.

Slowly, he set her down on the dirt floor. A small amount of pain shot through her back. Possibly an abrasion from the wall. His powerful thrusts had done the damage. Regardless of the discomfort and their awkward sexual position, she wouldn't have refused him.

"I love you, Alexa." He threaded his fingers into her hair. "I intend to win manumission."

It would take many battles for him to gain his freedom —and unbearable pain. Why did she put him through it? Knowing what he'd face, tears came to her eyes. She forced herself to breathe and pushed out the words. "You shall do it." She placed her hand over the wound on his chest, and held it there. "Take my love with you into the arena. I'll be waiting for you." Her heart beat strong with a strange sense of deep dedication and loyalty to him. Were these Alexa's emotions or her own?

He held her close, kissed her a final time, and walked away—tall and proud.

She fought the urge to follow him. "I love you, Magnus!" Alexa hadn't said a word once he'd started to leave, but Traci couldn't help herself. She didn't want him to go.

He paused only briefly, but didn't look back. She closed her eyes, then everything turned to darkness.

* * *

Wow.

Traci rolled over and hit the remote on the drapery. She didn't want to get up. The heavy, chocolate-brown drapes inched together.

Lying back, pain shot across her shoulder blades. She sat upright and turned on the lamp beside her bed. Still in her black dress—not naked this time. Tiny speckles of blood dotted her white sheets.

I need to get out of this dress.

She reluctantly set her feet on the floor, then lifted the clingy fabric up from the bottom. As she reached her shoulders, it pulled and stung. She winced, yanked it free, and threw it on the floor. Her bra joined it.

She craned her neck to look at her back. She couldn't see the damage done, so she went to check it out in the bathroom mirror. Straining just right, she saw the marks with fresh blood from where she'd stripped away the dress. It must have disturbed the small scabs that had formed over the abrasions. The rock wall left the deep scratches. It scraped through Alexa's gown.

What about my dress?

She lifted it from the floor. The back looked as though an angry cat had had its way with it. Then she spotted another small bundle of black cloth and picked it up. A long strip of fabric that had once been her panties—torn by Magnus's mighty hand.

Stranger and stranger.

Bare and wide awake, she returned to the bathroom for a shower. The water stung her tender back; still she had to get it clean. A weird fungus growing there would be impossible to explain.

Yes, Karla, I got this in ancient Rome. What do you think it is?

She washed thoroughly with antibacterial soap, cleansing away every trace of Magnus. Then, out of nowhere, something pierced her heart. She knew the feeling. Guilt took its hold.

Friends often shared their encounters with men. Not *detailed*, but enough to make Traci aware they were having sex with men they never intended to marry. She'd even based some of her characters on them. Not everyone she wrote had been a *wait-'til-the-wedding-night* virgin.

How'd they do it?

She lived in a generation where people did what they pleased. Maybe she'd missed out on the promiscuity gene. Or, Jack's death was still too fresh, and she wasn't ready. More than likely, it had something to do with her faith and being brought up to believe sex should be shared in the marriage bed. It had been easy. Until now.

And truthfully, it *was* happening in their bed. Just not with Jack. It could never be with Jack again.

Tears added to the water cascading down her face.

God, I'm confused!

Was it a prayer or cursing? Maybe a little of both.

This would be the perfect time for a conversation with her mother. But—like Jack—the only conversation possible would be one-sided at her grave. She wasn't about to travel to Maine only to have a chit-chat with a plot of dirt. Not now. Possibly in the spring.

The water turned cold, so she shut it off and grabbed a towel. It must have been a long shower because she had an efficient water heater. Time had slipped away from her.

Since she'd previously concentrated on her back, this time when she looked in the mirror her hand shot to her mouth to suppress a scream.

Magnus had just earned the title of *leech*.

I should've remembered that about him.

Circling her neck were purple love bites—as her mother used to call them. His intensity would leave her marked for at least a week. Another good reason not to travel. Though the cold weather warranted a turtleneck— the attire kids used to laugh at in school. Everyone knew what lay beneath that folded cloth.

I'm staying home.

She had enough groceries to get her through until next Saturday. There wasn't really any other reason to venture out. She'd become good at being a hermit. Still, could she endure another Friday night?

* * *

It took Traci two days to stop beating herself up over the encounter with Magnus. Why should she feel guilty about something completely imaginary? It couldn't be anything else. She'd simply had realistic fantasies that left marks and abrasions. And yet, they were illusions. Nothing more.

Magnus had been more than bold—*adventuresome*. Jack had those qualities. Unlike her, Jack had been willing to make love in places other than their bedroom.

Like the time they got lost on a road trip. They were in the middle of nowhere on a dusty road, and he thought it might be *fun* to have sex in the car. Worrying they'd be seen, she had ruined everything. It had been silly for her to fret about being caught out there. Why couldn't she just let her hair down and enjoy it? Jack did.

I shouldn't have been so uptight.

Regret—she'd been told—was part of the grieving process. A large mountain she'd have to trudge her way over. The biggest chunk of that mountain? Time. Why hadn't she spent more of it with Jack? Believing there would always be one more day with him, she put trivial things first.

Jack should've been at the top of the list. No matter what.

She popped the top on a can of Pepsi, took a large swallow, then belched. It made her chuckle, which was probably a good thing. Getting too far into a self-pity wallow couldn't be healthy. Why had it been so easy to burp in front of a seven-foot man in a skirt? Maybe because she knew him well, and his barbaric attitude would never frown on it.

No, it was because I thought of Jack and our belching contest in Rome.

They were never too *stuffy* to have fun. Friends were supposed to be like that, and Jack had been the best friend she'd ever had.

Chapter 8

Traci's back felt much better. She'd treated it with antibiotic ointment just in case. Thankfully, she didn't have to explain it to anyone. The abrasions would be gone soon, along with the purple ring around her neck. They'd vanish the way every man had when the sun came up.

October had also disappeared before her eyes.

Why did Halloween have to fall on a Friday night?

Jason loved Halloween. Memories of his assorted costumes made her smile. Being a cowboy had been his favorite, but he went briefly through a stage of scarier getups. Not so pleasant, still a good memory all the same. And no, she hadn't named him after one of those horrible B movie villains.

He'd always encouraged her to dress up, too. However, tonight she wasn't about to. She wasn't in the mood. No black cocktail dress and definitely no Halloween costume. The weather was suited for flannel pajamas and her good old white bathrobe. If Mr. *Whoever* didn't like it, too bad.

She didn't have to worry about trick-or-treaters coming to her door. They never ventured down her mile-long driveway. Even if they did, they couldn't get through the gate.

Only imaginary people get through my gate.

It seemed she'd accepted her situation for what it was. Her brain created illusions that her body enjoyed. Why fight it?

The only movies on TV were horror films, so she decided to kick back with a bowl of popcorn and a Pepsi and watch one of her favorite movies, *American Dreamer.* When she thought back on what inspired her to write her first novel, at times this movie came to mind. Hardly any of her friends had ever heard of it, but she watched it over and over again. It made her laugh, and, boy, did she need to laugh.

Caught up in the film, she lost track of time. So when the knock came on the door, it startled her and she tipped over her drink.

She gritted her teeth and cursed under her breath, then strode to the kitchen for a towel. Oddly, she was more concerned over the sticky spill than who happened to be knocking at the door. They could wait. The soda would wind up on her Persian rug if she didn't hurry.

Another knock.

"Traci? Is everything all right?"

In the middle of clean-up, she froze. Her heart leapt with joy.

Andrew ...

The balled-up wash rag stayed in the middle of the spill. She raced to the door and flung it open.

Even before he stepped inside, she wrapped her arms around him and held on tight. "I'm so glad it's you."

He laughed a timid laugh and moved her inside. Then, he shut the door. Donned in a long black frock coat and boots, he looked even better than the last time.

He must have come from Mobile during one of those winter scenes.

"Traci," he said, and took her hand. "Let's have a seat. I'm grateful you're pleased to see me, but we can't get carried away. Claire wouldn't understand."

Claire wouldn't understand? If they'd go to the bedroom and shut the door, she'd *become* Claire. Why be so uptight about affection from her?

No problem. She'd play along ... *again*.

"Can I get you something to drink?" She hovered as he took a seat.

"Coffee?"

"Sure. I'll make a pot." She headed for the kitchen. It seemed a bit late for caffeine, but she'd have a cup anyway. After all, the soda had already revved her up. And they might be up for quite a while.

The thought of what could be coming later made her stomach flutter. Andrew Fletcher. Better in the flesh than he'd ever been on paper, and countless women had fallen in love with him just by her written words.

If they could only see him like this.

No. She didn't want to share him.

When she returned to the living room, he'd removed his coat. His crisp, white cotton shirt and black pants were evidence of Claire's capable laundering skills. Or had she fallen into a scene before they were together again? It didn't matter. He looked great.

"The coffee will take a few minutes." Traci followed his gaze. His eyes were glued to the TV. "*American Dreamer.* It's a great movie. Have you ever seen it?"

Dumb question.

He pointed at the screen. "How is their image put in that frame?"

Explaining how a light bulb worked was hard enough. She'd never be able to give enough clarity to this to help him understand. So much now was taken for granted. She rarely gave any thought to all the intricacies of what made things tick.

"It's on a disc," she said, and his brows furrowed. So, she formed her hands into the shape of a circle. "Like a photograph that's burned into a piece of ... *plastic*. But, it moves. And it goes into this machine." She pointed to the DVD player.

I sound like an idiot.

"Amazing. They seem very real." He cocked his head, then gasped. "They kissed."

"Yes, they did. And if we were watching HBO they'd be doing much more."

His eyes popped wide. "Why would people want to display themselves this way?"

She scooted in beside him and grabbed the remote. "I'll turn it off. It's hard to explain."

With a simple push of a button the *offensive display* on the screen disappeared, followed by a heavy sigh from

Andrew. "I'd hate to see Claire that way on your moving frame."

"Don't worry. We never got a movie deal. Vivian's still trying to find someone who will do a mini-series."

"I don't understand."

"Never mind." She patted his hand. "Claire is for your eyes only. I know it was hard enough on you having her married to someone else before you." The moment she said it, his face fell. She should've learned these characters were sensitive about certain things and kept her mouth shut.

"Gerald." He spoke the name in a soft whisper.

"Yes. But she always loved you."

He stared at his hands. Why did she have to go and make him depressed?

"Andrew?" She waited until he looked at her. "I was married before Jack. It didn't last long. Did you know that?"

He shook his head. How could she expect him to know this? Only her closest friends knew, and she certainly never thought about her youthful mistake when she wrote her books. She'd done all she could to forget about it.

Then again, every feeling she ever had flowed through in her writing. Even her mistakes. If she'd been honest with herself, the mistakes in her life probably weighed heavier on her writing than anything else.

"I thought I was in love," she went on. "But I didn't understand true love until I met Jack. Love is so much more than good looks and hot kissing in the back seat of a car."

"What's a car?"

"A horseless carriage." Never in a million years did she think she'd use that terminology. She never wrote a time period where cars were a factor.

"Oh." He turned to face her. "And this man you married first, is he still living?"

"I don't know. I lost touch with him years ago. Honestly, I don't want to know where he is." She touched her cheek, recalling the sting of his hand.

Andrew pulled her hand away and held it in his. "He hurt you." It wasn't a question, rather a statement of fact.

She nodded. "It was a long time ago."

His thumb moved across her skin. Once again, his gentleness touched her heart.

"I think that's why I like to write *happily ever after* stories," she whispered. "I want women to know there are princes out there. They just have to find them. And if they happen to be in a bad relationship, maybe my books will show them something better is attainable, and they don't have to settle for ..." Dreaded tears returned to her eyes.

"Someone who hurts them?"

"Yes." She leaned into his shoulder, and he didn't stop her.

"Traci?"

"Yes?" At ease, she melted even further into him.

"I'm very glad you feel comfortable speaking to me about these things."

If only he knew how grateful she was to have him beside her. In so many ways, it felt like having Jack there. She could bare her soul to both of them.

A small light went on inside her brain. The first time they'd met, Andrew had said he'd come to help her. Strangely, he had, and continued to do so. She'd always miss Jack, but with Andrew beside her, her heart lifted.

She wiped away tears, yet kept her head resting on his shoulder. Then, when he smoothed her hair with his hand, she closed her eyes and sighed.

"Traci," he whispered. "Would you like me to take you to your room?"

Did he know what would happen, or was this the doctor in him coming out, knowing she needed sleep?

She lifted her head and locked eyes with him. "Yes, I would." She swallowed hard. Having no doubt in *her* mind what would happen, she chose not to second-guess his intentions.

He helped her to her feet, then they walked slowly down the hall. She stepped through the doorway. The lock clicked behind her.

* * *

The rush of anxious anticipation overwhelmed Traci. She'd become used to closing her eyes for a brief moment, and expected to find herself in Claire's room again when she opened them.

Nope. Somewhere completely different.

As if they'd taken their previous location on her sofa and whisked it through time, they sat side by side on a much smaller couch facing a fire. She scanned the large room; rustic logs, an enormous fireplace, and a loft overhead. Andrew and Claire's house in Mobile.

When she got a good look at Andrew, and the bits of gray in his black hair, she knew they were much older.

"Claire ..." He turned to face her. "You know it's the natural progression of things." He moved his fingers into her long hair. "Remember how it was for us?"

Think, Traci, think.

Her body wasn't quite so thin and her breasts not so perky. Yes, they were both older, but what did he mean by, *the natural progression of things*?

Silence in the house. No children. No Izzy. Maybe Izzy had already gone to bed—sound asleep in her bedroom down the hall.

Progression ...

Of course!

The scene after Michael's wedding. Their children were grown and gone, and it was the first time Claire and Andrew were virtually alone. So he wanted to be *adventurous*.

Time to let myself go.

"Of course I remember," she said. His hands in her hair sent tickling chills down her spine. "It's just hard to think about our children that way."

"So ... Izzy's asleep. We have the house to ourselves. Romance is in the air." He moved closer and brushed his lips over her cheek. "Do you know what I'm thinking?"

Yep. The same thing on her mind. However, recalling the plot, the time couldn't have been worse for them to have sex. But, they did anyway. Why change the story? It was in print. A good excuse not to mess with it.

"Claire, you didn't answer my question." His lips brushed her ear, and she trembled.

"I'm thinking it, too." She unbuttoned his shirt—the crisp white one—and drew a heart on his chest, their way of communicating a safe time to make love.

"I'm glad you did that," he said with a smile, and wasted no time working the buttons at the front of her dress.

Unlike the other *Claire* dress, this one had a more mature-looking style. But, it didn't matter. The gorgeous man removing her clothing seemed solely concerned with what lay beneath it. She didn't object. She enjoyed making love as Claire. With nothing about her body she wanted to hide, it was easy to let go with Andrew, her now-familiar lover.

"I take it you don't want to go to the bedroom." She said the line, although she already knew the answer.

"No. I want you here—*now*." He stood and removed his shirt. Older, but still toned and incredible.

I'll never get tired of looking at him.

She rapidly finished what he'd started and pushed her dress and underwear onto the floor.

He grinned at her as he dropped his pants, then lay atop her on the sofa. "I've always wanted to make love here—in front of the fire." He wasted no time.

It wasn't the most comfortable place to be doing this. Regardless, she wasn't about to dampen his enthusiasm. She grasped his back and savored his body. This felt right. As though she'd come home again to the man she belonged with. The man with Jack's heart.

Their lovemaking became more intense than ever. In a different way than it had been with Magnus. That had been *good,* but this ...

Indescribable.

They kissed deeply, and their bodies moved together like a graceful dance. When they finished, she held onto him as if her life depended on him. If only somehow she could stay here and be with him forever. Maybe as fictional characters, they'd never age. Death wouldn't be a factor.

She fought to keep her eyes open, certain that once she fell asleep, he'd be gone again.

Just like Jack.

Chapter 9

When Traci opened her eyes the next morning, tears readily fell. Why couldn't she keep him? Why did he have to fade away like everything else?

She stood from her bed and crossed to the large window that faced the atrium. Heat from the sun warmed her bare skin. She needed to tend her plants.

Maybe later.

When Jack had been alive she'd hired a gardener to keep it up along with the lawn and landscaping on the outside of the house. During the winter months, she believed she could take care of the atrium herself. Especially once Jack died and she'd been home all the time. It should've helped keep her busy and her mind off Jack, yet it only reminded her of how they'd enjoyed spending time in it together.

Would it have been easier to sell the house and move away? Staying might have been a mistake.

Her ringing cell brought her out of her thoughts.

She unlocked the bedroom door and rushed to the living room.

"Hello?"

"Hey, Mom."

"Jason—it's good to hear from you again."

She strolled through her house in the buff, not caring any longer. With the phone to her ear, she wandered into the kitchen and poured some remaining coffee into a cup. It wouldn't taste too bad heated up in the microwave.

"I have my flight times. I'm flying into Knoxville on Wednesday, the 26th, and I have to leave again on Saturday, the 29th. I know it's quick, but at least we'll have some time together. Oh ... and don't worry about picking me up. I'll rent a car. I also plan to stop on the way home and get some groceries. I'd like to cook for you."

He sounded cheerful and *eager*. "Are you sure? I don't mind coming to get you, and I certainly don't mind cooking. What about the turkey?"

"Okay, I'll let you help with the turkey. In fact, why don't you get one and have it thawed and ready to put in the oven Thursday morning?"

"I can do that." She'd done it for years. The easy things never gave her trouble.

"Great ..." His voice drifted away. Not so happy anymore.

"Are you okay, Jason?"

"Yeah. I just—well—how was Halloween?"

Now she understood. He must have been doing some reminiscing over his own Halloween memories. "It was fine. I ate popcorn and watched a movie."

"You didn't dress up, did you?"

"No. Not this year. Did you?"

"No. Amy and I were invited to a costume party. We turned it down. We weren't in the mood to celebrate. Maybe next year."

She wasn't about to ask. They probably wouldn't have turned down a party over his dad's death, not when it happened over a year ago. Something else must have happened. Possibly another disappointment? Another cycle that meant no baby in their future?

"Yeah," she said. "Maybe next year."

"So ..." He took a large breath. "I'll see you in a few weeks. I'll call you when I get to Knoxville. I love you, Mom."

"I love you too, Jason. And be sure to give Amy my love, too."

"I will. Bye."

"Bye."

They were blessed to be able to communicate over such a great distance, but it could also be painful. She couldn't hold him when she believed he needed a hug. There wasn't a lot she could do about it. But at least he had Amy. That made it *slightly* easier.

The microwave dinged and she fixed her cup of coffee. A little cream and sugar. First taste. Always the best. It would've been better if she'd made it fresh, but this would have to do. After all, the pot was full. She and Andrew hadn't had any last night. They'd become sidetracked and forgot to drink it. She smiled. What they'd shared had been better than any cup of java.

And it wasn't even so much about the great sex. He talked to her—*listened* to her. She'd believed her independence proved she could accomplish anything on her own. Jack's death showed her she needed someone. A successful life was worthless without someone to enjoy it with her.

Granted, Jason had always been proud of her. Even when he was too little to understand the content of her writing, he still encouraged her to do it. With him around, things had been easier. Now he had his own life to live. It wouldn't be right to glom onto him. Parents were responsible to rear up the kids to leave the nest, not be forced to come back home when the mama bird got lonely.

Being a hermit wasn't such a good idea, but how could she push herself out the door and face the world again? Without Jack's help, it wouldn't be easy. She'd just have to buck up and try.

She stared at the empty sofa, wishing she could relive last night. The dull pang of loneliness crept back in. If she didn't get busy, she'd slide into a deep depression and want to sleep for a week. Not healthy behavior at all.

Get your tail moving, Traci.

The balled-up rag lay on the coffee table. It'd take longer now to clean up the mess. Some of the soda had dried, and now she had a sticky residue on the glass.

First things first. Clothes. Even though she had an efficient furnace, it was cold outside, and her large, un-draped windows revealed some drifting snowflakes. When they built the house, they'd decided not to cover the beautiful panes of glass. There'd been no need. She loved that they framed the glory of her beloved mountains.

Looking down at herself, she let out a low chuckle. Even when Jack was alive she'd never run around the house naked.

Time to dress, make a fire, and start another day. And since she'd made it through a Friday night without any physical damage, she'd go to the grocery store and stock up for another week. A very good start.

What a life.

While pulling her sweater into place, she froze, then plopped down on the edge of her bed.

Jason will be here in a few weeks. Oh, God ... He'll be here on a Friday night!

How would she explain some half-naked man showing up at her door? Or, maybe not half-naked, but even if Andrew came, she'd never be able to explain him. She couldn't take the risk.

Somehow, she'd have to talk Jason into doing something on Friday night. Like, go into town to a movie. Or out to eat. If they didn't leave the house, she'd be a nervous wreck, and he'd know something was wrong. Something much worse than mourning his dad. But, would *Mr. Somebody* be at the door waiting for her when they returned home?

Because she still believed them to be illusions, most likely only *she* could see them. So, why worry? If luck was on her side, her visitors might stop coming long before Thanksgiving.

She gasped.

No ...

She burst into a fit of sobs that caught her completely off guard. A new kind of mourning. Her tears were shed over the idea of never seeing Andrew again—or any of the others. They'd become a welcome gift. A gift she didn't want to lose. She'd lost too much already.

"I can't take this!" She finished dressing, grabbed her coat and keys, and headed out the door.

* * *

Wrapped in a heavy wool coat with a scarf around her neck—for warmth this time—and heavy gloves, Traci sat on the bench at the cemetery. She rested for a brief moment to gather her thoughts before approaching Jack's grave.

Going to his grave angry wasn't a wise thing to do. This craziness wasn't his fault. Had it been up to Jack, he never would've died. Leaving her alone hadn't been his plan.

In a few weeks, she'd take time off from coming here. The holiday crowds would be in town, and for some reason they liked to *check out* the old cemetery. It wasn't far from the Parkway, where everyone went to shop. She couldn't deny them their curiosity. The cemetery held a lot of history. However, she didn't want anyone to recognize her in such a personal setting.

She shouldn't have come here empty-handed, but she rushed straight to White Oak Flats after a lengthy cry. The emptiness in her heart drew her to Jack, so she might as well face him and get off the bench.

Her breath puffed from her mouth in white bursts, and her nose ached, already icy cold. But, the frozen ground wasn't snow-covered. Not yet. Winter hadn't gotten into full swing.

She'd been smart enough to grab an old chair pad she kept in her SUV. She set it on the ground beside the tombstone. The cushion helped. Even though she wore her heaviest coat and thick jeans, the cold ground easily penetrated them.

"Hey, Jack." She patted the marker.

Closing her eyes, she pictured the way he'd looked when placed here. She'd dressed him in his favorite gray suit with a tie that Jason had given him on Father's Day. It had gray, red, and black swirls on it and gave an artsy flair to his solid-colored suit.

Jack loved that tie.

He'd lost most of his hair after he turned fifty. By sixty he might as well have shaved it all off. He just couldn't seem to part with the little tuft that hung around at the top. His face had grown round and plump, but when he smiled he lit up the room. And when he laughed ...

"God, I miss your laugh."

Knowing he lay six feet under her made her shudder. Though only his body and not his soul, her mind reeled with worry. *Is he cold?*

Alone in a box.

Her breath hitched. Tears stung her chilled eyes. She wiped her nose with her glove. Not very sanitary, but she didn't care.

"Jack—something strange has been happening to me." How would she say it? The best way would be to spit it out. She'd done it with Karla, so with Jack it should be simple. They'd always been able to talk about anything.

"Remember date night? Of course you do. Well, every Friday night since the anniversary of your death, I've had visitors. *Men.* And—the thing is—they're not real, but they feel real. I've ..." She took a huge breath of courage. "I've made love to them."

Okay, now he knew. She felt a sense of relief in telling him like this, even though he wasn't actually here any-more. With every part of her, she believed he'd gone someplace much better. In Heaven with all of their loved ones. He might even be with her mother. They'd gotten along *fairly* well, at least most of the time.

Maybe he could still hear her.

Somehow.

"Remember the first hero I wrote? Andrew? Well, he's come to me twice, and it's not just *sex*. The feelings I have when I'm with him are like ... *love*. But—it's only because it's like being with you. I'm at ease in his arms, and I feel safe. I know he doesn't look anything like you, but some-times the way he touches me reminds me of how you did. I don't know how or why this is happening, and I hope you can forgive me."

She pressed her forehead against the cold stone and embraced it as if it were Jack himself. "I miss you so much. All I know how to do is to take one day at a time. Somehow, let me know it's okay."

A gust of wind whipped against her skin and caused her to shiver. She raised her eyes to the sky. "Are you up there, Jack?"

Another blast of air moved the trees. Their naked branches swayed in the breeze. Traci stood and lifted her face into the cold wind. If Jack had just spoken to her, he must be telling her to go home before she froze to death.

"Okay, I'll go. I love you, Jack."

She put one foot in front of the other and headed for home.

Pulling onto the Parkway, her eyes caught sight of a sign she'd never noticed before. Lucky to spot an empty parking place on the upcoming side street, she flipped on her blinker and turned, taking the space. Aside from pouring out her tale to Karla, this had to be the stupidest thing she'd ever decided to do. Still, what could it hurt?

After promising herself she'd not mention her encounters to another soul, this decision made little sense. Regardless, she continued up the sidewalk and pushed the door open. Besides, she wouldn't be the one pouring out her thoughts if this person could do what she claimed.

Once inside the tiny building, she lifted her scarf from her neck and wrapped it around her mouth. Would it be possible to hide her identity? And then, when she got a whiff of a strange scent—probably incense—she moved the scarf up even further and covered her nose.

The room wasn't what she'd expected it to be. It looked more like the waiting area at Karla's office than a place where a psychic operated. No sign of a crystal ball, and what about all the colorful draperies and bead curtains these kinds of people were supposed to use?

In *Marked*, Traci's New Orleans seer lived in a cluttered home full of cats and scented candles. In the book, Madame Beaumont had been strange, yet oddly accurate. Pure fiction.

Traci chuckled. Why should she expect a real psychic to be anything like her character?

The sign over the door indicated she read palms and tarot cards. Traci never believed in those things, but there were other things she never believed could happen and she'd been proven wrong more than once. There could be something to this, but then again ...

Her stomach twisted.

I shouldn't have come here.

She was about to leave when someone walked up behind her. "May I help you?" The voice sounded female and ... *normal.*

But, with the vision of Madame Beaumont in her mind, Traci expected to see a gypsy woman wearing either a veil or a turban and decorated with bright-colored beads, large hoop earrings, and bracelets dangling from her bony wrists. She took a breath, then turned to face her.

This couldn't possibly be Cordelia Flowers ... *psychic.* This woman looked like a secretary with her gray wool skirt, white blouse, and eye-catching costume jewelry. She appeared to be in her forties. Her hair was a nice brunette, curled to frame her face, and she wore attractive modern glasses.

The psychic's assistant, maybe?

Why not? Lots of professional people had them.

"Help ... me?" Traci stammered. "Uh ... I don't know."

Boy did that come out well.

The woman smiled. "You don't feel you belong here." She said it like she knew it to be true. Maybe this well-dressed person actually was Cordelia, and there really could be something to her psychic ability.

No, she probably says that to everybody that comes in here.

"I've never believed in this sort of thing." Traci's scarf made her face sweat, and it wasn't helping her communicate.

The woman extended her hand. "I'm Cordelia. Why don't we go into the other room and have a seat?" She nodded toward another doorway.

"Okay."

So she didn't look the way Traci had imagined she would. Nevertheless, she followed her through the door. *This must be where she keeps her crystal ball.* Would there be a head inside it?

Traci took in her surroundings. No crystal ball. *Anywhere.* In fact, this room had a similarity to the one they'd just left. It looked like an office with a small round table and four wooden chairs. Cordelia gestured to the chair closest to Traci. Once she sat, Cordelia took a seat at the other side of the table and patted a stack of cards.

"No," Traci said. "I don't want a reading. Like I told you, I don't believe in those." She pointed to the cards. Truthfully, she believed them to be evil.

"You came for answers." Cordelia rested her hands on the table. "Will you allow me to look at your palm?"

"Shouldn't I know how much you charge first? I doubt you do this for free."

A mysterious smile covered Cordelia's face. "Money is not an issue with you. You have plenty. What I can offer you is invaluable."

Now how could she know that? She must have recognized her. "You know who I am?"

"I know many things. And I know I'm right."

"Yes, you're right. I'd still like to know how much this will cost."

Cordelia nodded. "For an hour, it will be two hundred dollars. But I promise it will be money well spent."

Traci clutched her purse. She never carried that much cash. "Plastic?"

Cordelia smiled, then followed it with another nod. It seemed their communication had just improved by leaps and bounds. "So now, let me have your hand."

Though hesitant, Traci extended her hand, palm up. Why hadn't she kept driving when she left the cemetery? If her priest had seen her go in here, she'd never hear the end of it.

"You don't look like a psychic," Traci said, but then the woman shook a finger at her.

"I need quiet." She studied Traci's palm, as if evaluating an intricate piece of artwork. With so many lines and wrinkles, it probably was.

Traci shifted in her chair. Although glad to be out of the cold air, she found the room to be stifling. Much too warm.

Cordelia raised her eyes. "You don't have to hide from me. You're safe here. I suggest you remove your scarf."

Good suggestion. She'd come close to hyperventilating. So, with her free hand, she lowered the scarf from her face, then loosened it around her neck.

Now that her features were revealed, Cordelia nodded with a satisfied grin. Oh yes, now she knew for sure she'd been right about Traci's financial status. Had she just guessed at her identity? No, *guess* probably wasn't used in her line of work.

Cordelia's attention returned to Traci's right hand. "You're very creative."

Really? Hmm ... How did she figure that one out?

Traci resisted rolling her eyes.

"Interesting ..." Cordelia's index finger moved back and forth along the lines of her hand. Traci couldn't help herself and jerked it away. It tickled.

"Sorry." She rubbed her hands together, then once again extended her right hand.

"As I was saying ..." Undaunted, Cordelia took hold of it. "I see something unusual and interesting in your palm. Have you been experiencing things you would consider uncommon?"

"You tell me." Traci couldn't be fooled. She'd heard about how these people could manipulate you into revealing things *they're* supposed to be telling you.

"You've experienced a great loss." Cordelia frowned. "I'm so sorry."

Everyone in Gatlinburg knew she'd lost her husband, so this wasn't any major revelation. "You know about Jack."

"Your husband. Yes, and you've had a difficult time letting go."

Traci breathed deeply. Even though this woman hadn't yet impressed her, maybe talking about it would help. "I don't *want* to let him go."

"You must. If you don't, he'll never cross over."

"Cross over? You mean … into the light?" She'd heard many stories about people who'd experienced dying and being brought back to life. They always talked about going into a light. She assumed Jack had gone there a long time ago. Why would he stick around?

"Yes." She released Traci's hand and sat back in her chair. "His aura is all around you." She waved her arms through the air, as if conducting an invisible orchestra. "Can't you feel it?"

"I feel him in here." Traci placed her hand on her heart. "I—I went to the cemetery and talked to him before I came here. Is that crazy?"

"No. But you don't have to go there to talk to him. Not when he's by your side."

"You see dead people?"

Cordelia laughed. "Not like you're thinking. There's a loving presence circling around you that's undeniable."

Traci had a hard time believing that Jack's spirit hung around her like a rainbow of colors only certain gifted people could see. A nice concept, but it didn't make sense. Jack had gone to Heaven. Besides, she didn't want to think he'd been anywhere near her these past weeks. He didn't need to see what she'd been doing.

"You're feeling guilty about something," Cordelia said. "You need to let it go. There's nothing to feel guilty about."

Traci stared at her, dumbfounded. Had she been listening at the grave? Creeping around the cemetery waiting for her next victim?

"I'm fine," Traci said. There were some things she wouldn't discuss with this stranger. "So, what do you see in my future?"

Cordelia cocked her head, then pursed her lips.

Traci held up her hand, and stopped her from speaking. "No, wait. I know what you're going to say. I'm going to meet a tall, dark stranger, right?"

"No." Cordelia shook her head. "You already have."

Traci froze. This hit a little too close to home. Did she know about Andrew?

"I see the confusion on your face," Cordelia went on. "Don't be ashamed of the encounter."

Encounter. The moment she said the word, Traci gasped, but then covered her mouth. She should never have let her guard down and revealed herself. "What do you know of my *encounter*?"

Cordelia lifted her chin. "All I see is light. Warmth. Nothing to fear or be ashamed of."

There she went and said it again. *Ashamed*. And though she kept emphasizing that Traci shouldn't feel that way, all that kept popping to mind was guilt. At least she'd told Jack everything.

"Let it go, Mrs. Oliver." Cordelia reached across the table and took her hands. "I assure you, you're doing nothing wrong."

Traci needed to leave. She believed this woman meant well, but something in the way she spoke confused her. How could she know anything by looking at her palm, or Jack's invisible aura?

She stood and pulled a credit card from her purse. "I've heard enough. I should never have come here." She held out the card.

Cordelia waved it away. "No. I don't want your money. Not today. You weren't here more than fifteen minutes."

"But, you need to be paid. At least take part of it. Maybe half?"

"Very well. If you insist." She took the card and walked away. Within a few moments, she returned with a white receipt and asked for Traci's signature. "Thank you," she said after Traci signed it and handed it back. "Oh, and I must tell you one more thing, Mrs. Oliver."

Did she want to hear it?

Cordelia rested her hand on Traci's arm and looked into her eyes. "All of your answers lie in the core of your encounters."

And exactly *what* did she mean by that? Even without understanding her, Traci shivered. What was in the core of her encounters?

Now more than ever, Traci wanted to flee. "I appreciate your time." She tightened the scarf around her neck, then covered her face.

"Someday," Cordelia said. "You'll know I spoke the truth."

Traci nodded, but said nothing and walked out the door.

Chapter 10

The psychic *encounter* had been odd and disturbing, but now that Traci had gone to the cemetery and told Jack what had happened, a weight lifted from her shoulders. Silly though the notion he heard her may be, she felt a sense of relief proving she wasn't trying to hide something from him. Still, she couldn't believe he roamed around beside her.

She'd never believed in ghosts or spirits that haunted a house they'd resided in when they were alive. Hopefully, any essence of Jack remained at the cemetery. Much safer that way. God help her if he'd been in their bedroom during her encounters with her men.

My men.

She'd created them, so in every sense of the word, they were hers. She owned their copyright. Actually, she and the publisher shared rights, yet she doubted they'd want a piece of them. They had their money from the deal, and plenty of it. What more could they want?

* * *

Traci woke on Monday morning with unexplained energy. After jumping from the bed, she immediately showered and dressed, then started a pot of coffee.

Grabbing her watering can, she headed for the atrium. A garden hose sat on the ground readily accessible, but there were a few spots it couldn't reach. Jack had wanted to put in a sprinkler system. Since they had such a small-scale atrium, she'd convinced him the old-fashioned way would work.

The place was brilliant. The glass-domed roof reflected sunlight into the garden below. A cobblestone pathway wound through it, and she even talked Jack into building a humpback bridge over the goldfish pond. Her fish were huge. They were safe here year-round with no risk of predatory birds scooping them from the water. There were five total—plenty for her pond, which stayed aerated by a large waterfall cascading into it.

Since the atrium had plenty of light, heat, and water, she managed to keep brightly colored tropical plants there. A bit of Hawaii in Tennessee. Not only did they *look* beautiful, the entire area held a sweet aroma. Though the tropicals were gorgeous, native orange honeysuckles were her favorite.

She set about watering and gave the fish some food, then returned to the kitchen and poured a cup of coffee. With it properly doctored, she cradled it in her hand and went back to the atrium, where she sat on a wrought iron bench that faced the waterfall.

"No, I could never sell this place. It's too beautiful." Too much a part of her.

If it turned out she'd have to go through the rest of her life entertaining on Friday nights, then so be it. She could try to have a little more fun with them when they came to her door. She hadn't exactly followed the scene with Gerald, so maybe it wouldn't hurt to shake things up a bit.

Not knowing who would come to the door next, she didn't know how much *shaking* she'd want to do. And with the exception of the Friday following Thanksgiving, she'd begun to look forward to whatever might happen. Besides, Cordelia Flowers had said she had nothing to be ashamed of. So why not let her hair down? Perhaps even figure out the mysterious *core*.

She leaned back and lifted her face into the sunlight, then closed her eyes. The perfect way to start each day. Exactly what she used to do before Jack's death, and it warmed her all the way to her soul to be doing it again. Perhaps a sense of normalcy had returned.

Normal? My life is far from normal.

At least she had a smile on her face. Friday night wasn't scary anymore. And until then, she'd wake every morning with a purpose. If only she could write that book. But, nothing had inspired her. Not yet anyway.

* * *

"Yes," Traci said, folding her hands in front of herself, "a table for one. Preferably a window seat by the water."

A major step for her. She'd parked the car, walked through the front door, and now she even managed to ask for a table.

This is so hard.

This place had been special to her and Jack.

"Of course, Mrs. Oliver." The hostess led her up the stairs to the second floor and motioned to a table facing the river. Traci's stomach rumbled. She'd not eaten much all day and congratulated herself for getting out of the house to have supper. Even prouder that she'd come *here*.

Her throat tightened as she took her seat. Memories of sitting at this table with Jack flashed through her brain. Not wanting the young girl to see the tears forming in her eyes, Traci looked away and focused on the rushing water.

Coming here might not have been a good idea, but she'd give it her best shot. She plastered a smile on her face and pushed away the tears as she placed her drink order. Just sweet tea tonight. She needed to keep her mind clear and remember the good times with Jack.

The Peddler had always been one of their favorite restaurants. Especially when they were in the mood for a great steak. One of the busiest restaurants in town, yet somehow Jack had always been able to get them right in *and* secure a waterside table.

Each night, as the sun set, lights from the building illuminated the water and gave their surroundings a serene atmosphere.

"Ma'am?"

Traci looked up at the waiter—a short, stocky, middle-aged man. "Yes?"

"I asked if you'd like more tea. You seemed to be lost in thought."

"Oh. I'm sorry. Yes, I'd love some."

He filled her glass and smiled. "Please help yourself to the salad bar whenever you're ready. The peddler will come by your table to take your order once you've gotten your salad."

Yes, she knew the drill. The waiter probably thought she was a little odd. When he'd first brought the tea, he'd already told her she could get salad. Most people jumped right up. Even so, getting her rump off the seat would take some effort.

She'd been enjoying the view and the memories. It had been *here* that she'd told Jack about her pregnancy. She closed her eyes, remembering the look on his face and the tears he'd shed the minute she said the words, *I'm pregnant.*

After a few more sips of tea, she set aside her napkin and went down the stairs to the salad bar. Deciding she'd rather fill up on steak, she put very few greens on her plate.

She managed to make eye contact with several people as she passed them. A weak smile was all she could offer them, and she received similar ones in return. Maybe they didn't recognize her. Probably for the best. Tonight she'd rather be left alone with her thoughts.

As promised, once she sat down and nibbled her salad, shortly thereafter, the peddler came to her table with his tray of raw meat. He lifted the black cloth that had been draped over it, and she selected the ribeye.

The first time Jack brought her here, she'd been amazed they'd bring the uncooked, uncut steak to the tables. Jack had chuckled at her reaction and assured her it was dead and wouldn't bite. In many ways, it seemed they were honoring the cow—what with the cloth draped over its remains. She certainly appreciated that it had given its life for her.

She valued the convenience of living in the modern world even more. Writing about how it *used to be done* made her glad she hadn't been born in the 1800s. Thank goodness she didn't have to butcher her own meat. She couldn't imagine having to chop off the head of a chicken or cut up a much larger animal. Staying in the make-believe world with Andrew might not be such a good idea. Being stuck doing Claire's chores, the fantasy would soon fade.

She lifted her glass of tea into the air in a silent salute to her favorite heroine.

You're quite the woman, Claire.

To reward her exceptional heroine, she'd put wonderful men in her life. They made up for the nastiness of her day-to-day work. Then again, Claire never complained. She worked her hands to the bone, never idle. *She* didn't mind living in the 1800s.

Traci chuckled. How could Claire mind? She didn't have a choice.

They all seemed so much more real to her now. Like they actually existed. With the way things were going, she imagined if she went to Mobile, Alabama, she'd probably find their tombstones.

It didn't take long, and her steak arrived accompanied by a baked potato. Cooked to perfection, she savored each bite. Eating had become a pleasant activity again. And the more she thought about it, the more she realized that somehow her encounters were helping.

It didn't matter that she didn't understand them. She'd take them for what they were, and as weird as Cordelia may have been, Traci made the decision to try to do what she'd been told and let her guilt go by the wayside.

And since guilt had taken a vacation, she ordered the Kahlua crème brulée and enjoyed every bit of it. It seemed she still belonged in the land of the living. It definitely tasted good.

* * *

So, maybe last night's meal had been a mistake. When Traci stepped on the bathroom scale, her eyes popped.

"I gained five pounds?" She stepped off, and then on again. Same result. It might be wise to lay off the desserts for a while. Right now the added weight was probably a healthy thing. If she kept it up, she'd be anything but that.

Her jeans fit comfortably, so the extra pounds didn't matter so much. Since she had her encounters in different bodies altogether, the men in her life wouldn't care. Tonight she'd leave on the jeans and a red sweater for her visitor. The bathrobe seemed too casual, and the cocktail dress went way over-the-top. Besides, the last time she wore a cocktail dress it got ruined. This outfit would be a happy medium.

She made a grilled cheese sandwich and tomato soup for dinner, then settled onto her sofa with a book. Not wanting to influence who might show up at her door, she chose a quick novella written by one of her friends instead of one of her own. Even though she wanted Andrew to come back again and again, a new face might be nice. With forty-nine books under her belt, there was a vast selection.

Six-thirty. Not long now.

How many times had she read the same page? She couldn't concentrate. Any second now, she'd know.

She giggled like a little girl—reminiscent of her childhood and waiting for Christmas morning. Then her giggling grew when she thought of something she'd heard many times: "Good things come in small packages."

Like Gerald Alexander.

"Okay, that was cruel." Especially since she'd been the one who'd written him that way.

She set the book on the coffee table, then twiddled her thumbs and watched the clock for the final minutes.

A single strand of yarn dangled from her wrist. It appeared her beautiful sweater had started to unravel. Too bad she didn't have Claire's abilities with needle and thread. Or knitting for that matter. Claire could do it all.

Knock. Knock-knock.

Hesitant.

Whoever stood on the other side of the door wasn't certain they wanted to be here. She took her time walking to the monitor.

What?

No. Things had gone completely out of whack. It never occurred to her that her visitor could be *female.*

Good thing I didn't wear something sexy.

Traci looked again. Yep. Not just any random female character, but the wife of the men she'd recently been in bed with.

Damn.

Claire stood on the other side of the door, nervously wringing her hands. Had Traci's thoughts only moments ago brought her?

Another timid knock.

I have no choice.

Traci opened the door and motioned her in. She stepped inside wearing that special scooped-neck dress and an old-fashioned sunbonnet. All the while, Claire scanned her as though measuring her up.

Claire. Young, perky, and beautiful.

"Welcome to my home," Traci said formally, staring at her. No wonder the men fell so hard. The woman was perfect.

Claire removed her bonnet. "Thank you, Miss Traci." Her southern accent sounded almost as heavy as Gerald's.

"Are you cold? You can warm yourself by the fire." Traci motioned into the living room, and Claire moved away from the door.

She walked with grace. Claire was a few inches shorter than her, but had that hourglass figure every heroine seemed to have. Almost. Traci had written a few that were *not* voluptuous.

When Claire reached the fire, she folded her hands in front of herself, then stared at the floor.

Something's wrong.

Traci followed her. A nervous twinge filled her belly. This situation gave *uncomfortable* a whole new meaning.

What am I supposed to do with her?

Traci cleared her throat. "Are you hungry? Thirsty? I— I can get you whatever you want. Wine, soda, water ..."

"Do you have sweet tea punch?" Claire finally raised her head and looked her in the eye.

"No, but I can try to make some. Not sure I'd get it just right. I never seem to put in enough sugar."

"Pay it no mind. Truthfully I'm not thirsty. I was simply tryin' to be polite."

"Okay." Traci looked around the room, nervous in her own home.

"Miss Traci?" Claire cocked her head to the side and wrung her hands. Her hardworking hands.

"Yes?"

"I'm concerned 'bout Andrew and Gerald. Ever since they met you, they've not been the same."

Okay. Too weird. How could what *she* did with them effect Claire? It didn't change the books, so how?

"I don't understand." Biggest understatement of the year.

"May I sit?" Claire pointed to the sofa.

"Of course." Traci *needed* to sit. This couldn't be good.

They sat on opposite ends of the sofa, each in their own segment of the L. Not knowing what to say, Traci kept silent, certain Claire would eventually break the ice. At least, she *hoped* she would.

Awkward. Awkward. Awkward.

Traci twiddled her thumbs, a habit her mother had tried to break her of years ago.

"You're an older woman," Claire finally said. "And please don't be offended by my words, but most women your age understand that young men have strong appetites and they make a point not to encourage them. Especially when they know those *particular* gentlemen are married."

Her implication set Traci's self-defense mechanism into motion. She sat upright and squared her jaw. "What are you saying?"

"I'm sayin' you took advantage of my poor Gerald and even Andrew."

"But ... I didn't. It wasn't me."

"Miss Traci." Odd. Claire sounded strangely like her mother had when she'd been about to read her the riot act. Next thing she knew Claire would be popping her on the hand to stop her from *twiddling*. "Please don't tell lies," Claire went on in her mother mode. "*I* don't, and you shouldn't either. I came here to talk to you woman to woman. My marriage is at stake."

At this point, Claire would still be married to Gerald. Even so, how could their encounter have had any bearing on their relationship?

"Claire ..." Traci leaned in to make a point. "I swear to you, I was never with them. They've not been with any-one but you."

"But I know they visited you, and when they came home they had enormous smiles on their faces. They looked like they'd been up to sumthin'. A woman knows these things." Claire's face contorted, undoubtedly about to cry.

Traci couldn't tolerate seeing her this way, so she stood and moved beside her. She then took her hand. "Claire, they love you. Truthfully, *I* love you. I'd never hurt you that way."

"So how did Andrew learn those *new* things? And Gerald has never been bolder."

"Andrew's a doctor. I'm sure he read about *things*. And Gerald has you to teach him. He's bound to be more confident the more you make love."

Claire's cheeks turned a brilliant shade of red. "You talk 'bout it so plainly. Did you talk 'bout it with them?"

"No." Traci's head shook back and forth. She racked her brain. What *had* they talked about? "Andrew fixed my knee. I cut myself on a piece of glass. And, we talked about Jack."

"Yes. Jack. I'm sorry you lost your husband. I don't know what I'd do if sumthin' happened to Gerald."

Traci pinched her lips tight. She'd learned her lesson. She patted Claire's hand in a gesture of reassurance, then looked away.

In many ways, she hated that she'd put Claire through so much pain. It was one thing she wished she could change. Nonetheless, Claire had to go through it to be with Andrew. Traci had to accept the fact that death was inevitable. For everyone.

Tears filled Claire's eyes. How could she make her understand?

"Claire?"

"Yes, Miss Traci?" She sniffled, then pulled a handkerchief from her dress pocket and dabbed at her eyes.

"I assure you, Gerald and Andrew both love you wholeheartedly. In their eyes, you're the only woman they'll ever see. They have no interest in anyone else. For me, Jack will always be my one true love. Even his death didn't change that. He's still in my heart."

Claire's chin quivered and she continued to sniffle. Talking wasn't going to work, so Traci decided to take drastic measures. "I'd like to show you something in my room."

Traci would be taking an enormous risk. Closing the door behind her and Claire would do one of two things. Maybe three. Most likely, Traci would become either Andrew or Gerald, and that would be more than strange. How would she ever know what to do with a man's body?

With a pounding heart, she led Claire down the hallway. "It's in there. In my closet." She pointed into the room, and Claire stepped through. Traci shut the door behind her and locked it.

* * *

Total darkness.

"What's goin' on?" Claire asked from across the room. "I can't see a thing."

Traci carefully felt the wall for the light switch. It wasn't there. They were *somewhere,* but where? "Try to find a lantern, or even a candle." *Hmm ...* Her voice came out female.

Whew, what a relief.

"Oh ..." Claire's voice brightened. "This is my home. I'll light the lantern."

After a few tense moments, a dim light filled the room. They were in Claire's bedroom in her house on Mobile Bay.

Traci glanced down at herself.

Claire's dress?

She stumbled backward and came down hard on the bed.

"What's goin' on here?" Claire pressed. Her voice shook, and the light from the lantern made her face grotesque. Her heavy breathing filled the otherwise-silent room.

Traci ran her fingers through her hair. Yep. Claire's hair. Perky boobs. How could they *both* be Claire?

"Claire," Traci spoke as calmly as she could. The last thing she wanted to happen would be for Claire to drop the lantern and set the place on fire. With her luck, it would burn down her precious log home. "Set the lantern on the dresser and come sit beside me."

Claire obeyed. Maybe out of fear, or possibly because the tone of Traci's voice commanded it.

"I don't understand." Claire licked her lips. "You look like me. How can that be possible?"

"Because in many ways, I *am* you. I created you, and you're a part of me. I know this is confusing." *And thank you God for not turning me into a man.* "When I was with Gerald and Andrew, I was you. Just like you see me here."

"You're me? Then, who am I?"

"You're you, too." A nervous giggle sputtered out of Traci.

Claire reached out and touched Traci's face. Then, with a pronounced sigh, her eyes rolled into her head, and she fell backward onto the bed.

Out cold.

Great. She fainted.

Traci shrugged, then got behind Claire and pulled her up onto a pillow. She'd probably have to sleep it off.

Excellent idea.

Traci lifted the blankets on the other side of the bed and climbed in. Tomorrow morning she'd wake up fully clothed and in her own bed. It wasn't the night she expected, but in some ways she was relieved.

The soft glow from the lantern light shadowed the real Claire's face. Truly beautiful inside and out.

Traci propped herself up on one elbow and watched her breathe. Easy to understand how Gerald and Andrew fell in love with her. Traci had created the perfect woman. A rare find.

"You would have loved her, too, Jack," she whispered. She stared upward into the darkness. Had she been a perfect enough woman for him? He'd said so many times, she'd just never believed him. No woman could be as perfect as Claire.

She smiled, suddenly covered in a peaceful calm. Yes, Jack loved her completely. Faults and all. No one could ever take that from her. She should start being grateful he'd died in her arms. At least he hadn't been alone when it happened.

Contented, she lay back against the pillows and closed her eyes. Claire's soft breathing sounded far different from any other noise she'd heard in her bed.

So ladylike.

She'd be able to sleep tonight, too. Claire would *never* snore.

Chapter 11

Traci lay calmly in bed and stared at the ceiling. The fan blades spun at a slow speed and nearly lulled her eyes closed again. After a good night's sleep—and no interruptions from Claire—she'd become well-rested and ready for a new day. Her fully illuminated room radiated a bright cheerfulness. She loved her king-sized bed, even though now it seemed enormous.

Jack had been a cuddler. She liked her space. So, they'd snuggle for a short time every night, then separate to fall asleep. A good compromise.

Andrew liked to cuddle, too. And for some reason, she'd let him hold her longer than she'd let Jack. Why? Because she'd been lonely for such a long time and needed reassurance? Or had she taken Jack too much for granted and pushed him away without a second thought?

It broke her heart seeing Claire so torn up. She'd never hurt a woman that way. Her encounters with Claire's men had seemed harmless, especially since at the time she'd been Claire in every respect. And *they'd* believed her to be Claire.

Andrew would've never made love to her as Traci. He'd made that very clear. As for Gerald, she'd written him to be so timid, that even making love to his *wife* had been a challenge.

One he decided he liked.

She'd get *Southern Secrets* off her mind, and maybe this coming Friday she'd have someone completely new.

She repeated her morning routine, then went to her bookcase. Could she *will* one of her heroes to come to her?

Her eyes shifted to the large poster above her desk. *Laird Gray ...*

That could be fun. What do you think, Jack? Would my Scottish lord be a good lover?

She smacked herself in the forehead. How had she gotten to this point? From fear, to guilt, to ... *lust*? Had she actually listened to the psychic and taken her assurance too far?

Even though Karla may have told her that fantasies were normal, and a *good thing* if they were helping her deal with the loss of Jack, how could it be right to *want* to have a fling with an Irish ... no, *Scottish* hunk?

Having Andrew come back again would be safer. She'd know what to expect. Besides, they were great together. However, now—after meeting Claire—she didn't know if it was such a good idea.

She ran her hands over the spines of each of her books. They were arranged by release date instead of alphabetical order like all her other books. Her last twenty-five years.

The late 1800s had always been her favorite time period for American historicals. She sometimes ventured into other countries, like she did with *Crimson Kilts.*

Big mistake!

There were a few medieval fantasies, but she had some freedom with those. The lovers of Scottish romance weren't so forgiving.

Her hand paused on *Beneath the Gladiator's Blade.*

No, I don't think I could take another night with Magnus.

She moved on quickly. After contemplating a number of possibilities, she decided to let fate decide. Until she got that knock at the door, she'd do all she could to keep a clear mind. Watch a few movies, maybe even some game shows.

* * *

Traci stoked the fire, so it burned hot and bright. She tried to ignore the ticking clock, but her eyes shifted to it like a magnet.

Opting for jeans and a sweater again, she paced.

How did the middle of November get here so fast?

Her weeks started out slow. Then, when she reached Wednesday, they sped by like a downhill skier. And now, any minute she'd meet her Friday night date.

Long ago, she'd gone on a blind date. In many ways, this was similar, but that *date* sure turned out poorly. She shuddered.

Almost as bad as Crimson Kilts.

Her eyes popped wide, and she covered her mouth as though she'd spoken a curse. Why did she have to think about that book right now? What if ...?

Knock. Knock.

Her heart raced. Dare she look in the monitor?

You better believe it.

With nerves that tingled across her skin like a bad rash, she looked.

Crap!

What had she done? Could this be the key? Thinking of a particular book?

Some of her thoughts had been put there for her—like the times *Deceptions* had appeared on her coffee table. Or the time Magnus appeared after she saw the postcard from Romè. Had it all been coincidence?

She looked at the monitor again.

Oh, God. Help me through this.

Laird Daniel Gray held a spot right up there with Andrew in the looks department. But Daniel was *different.* *This* guy looked exactly like the cover model. Barechested. *Begging to be touched.* Wavy black hair that brushed his shoulders, and a face almost too perfect to be real. Not to mention, that cute little red kilt made her insides flip.

"Traci?" Another knock. "Traci, are you gonna let me in, lass?"

She laughed aloud. His heavy *Irish* brogue had been one of the reasons the books were burned. She wrote him all wrong.

Yes, she'd let him in.

After primping her hair, she opened the door.

He stood taller than Andrew, but not as tall as Magnus. He fell right in between. As for age, probably early twenties. She'd give anything to be younger. Honestly, it didn't really matter. When he grinned at her, she felt like an awkward teenager. Besides, if she decided to take him to her room, she'd most likely become Marta, his one true love. Like Alexa, Marta had pale, white skin, but brilliant red hair. And of course, she was incredibly beautiful.

"Ah, Traci." He took her hand and kissed it. She swooned. "You're a fine lass."

"And you're not so bad either," she muttered and sputtered like a lovesick groupie.

He extended his arm and escorted her into the room. His bare skin felt unusually warm.

And there's so much of it.

Unlike Magnus, Daniel was gracious. He always tried to be a perfect gentleman, yet struggled with fitting into his life as a Scottish lord—or *laird* as they called it. No wonder. How could any Scottish man fit in with a noticeably Irish accent?

"Will you ever be able to forgive me?" The words came out of her mouth when she meant them to be a thought.

Damn.

He cocked his head. "Forgive you, lass? Whatever for?"

He sounds like the Lucky Charms guy. I deserved to have my books burned. Worse yet, focusing on his physique, she instantly had those lustful thoughts again.

"Why don't you have a seat?" She pointed to the sofa.

"Aye. I need to rest me bones." He plopped onto the couch, then lifted one foot and set it atop the coffee table.

Traci covered her eyes. *Why isn't he wearing underwear?*

Heat rose in her cheeks, and she had to turn around. She couldn't face him and his exposed man parts. Of course, she faulted herself. Inspired by watching *Braveheart* over and over again, no wonder the man came to her home bare-bottomed. Maybe men never wore underwear beneath kilts. More than likely, it simply allowed for *convenience.*

"Have I offended you, lass?"

She peered over her shoulder. "Nope," she squeaked.

Good, he put his leg down.

She sauntered over to him and sat down. "Forgive me for being a bit overwhelmed by you. You're better looking in person than I even dreamed you could be. I've stared at your poster for years." She gulped, once again feeling foolish.

"Poster?"

Might as well show him.

She took him by the hand and led him to her office. "There, above my desk."

Honestly, there'd been no need to point it out. It was by far the largest framed piece in the room. He walked across the floor until he stood face to face with himself. "I look fine."

"Yes, you do. Jack had the cover blown up and framed for me. I'm sure there are about ten thousand women with your image on their walls."

"Ten thousand?"

"Aye." She sighed, already getting into character.

"And you enjoy looking at me likeness?" He moved toward her and the air around them became thicker than the blarney in her book.

"Uh-huh," she rasped. His hand rested on her cheek. "In person is even better."

He eyed her up and down. "You're different than what I envisioned."

Not him, too.

"I am?"

"Aye. You may be old, yet you're fair."

"I am?" Did she really just flutter her lashes?

"Aye."

Yep. She assumed what would happen next. But how would they get there, and where would they be?

"Laird Gray?" She whimpered.

"Please, call me Daniel."

"Daniel ..." Already caught up in the dream, she floated on air. "Are you cold?"

"No."

Why didn't he say yes? It would've been a good excuse to go the bedroom. "Are you tired?"

He grinned. "No."

How could she accomplish this without being completely forward? Likely, it wasn't supposed to happen. "Would you like to go back to the other room by the fire?"

"Aye. I'm a wee bit thirsty. Do you have some wine?"

"Sure." Disappointed, she returned him to the living room, then went to the kitchen for wine.

To her dismay, when she handed him the glass, he propped his foot up on the coffee table again. This time she allowed herself a peek and pushed aside her embarrassment. Now more than ever, she was determined to get him in the bedroom.

"Your husband was a fine man," he said after taking a sip.

"Yes, he was."

Guilt, guilt, guilt.

"He loved you very much."

"And I loved him, too."

"'Tis a shame he had to die. But, you're young and full of life. I pray you don't throw it away pining over his memory."

"I'm *mourning* him. That's not throwing my life away."

"Aye. But don't mourn forever, lass. He would want you to be happy."

That's what everyone kept telling her. Even Jack. It wasn't so easy. Yet, lately her mind had been so full of other things, it didn't hurt quite so bad. Could she be starting to heal?

"I need to write another book," she said, and fidgeted with her wedding ring. It kept her from looking where she shouldn't.

"Aye. So what will you write this time?"

"I don't know." She chuckled. "It won't be a Scottish love story. I kind of blew it on yours."

He took her hand. "*I* was happy with it. You brought Marta and me together. She is the finest of lasses."

"And she loves you regardless of your accent." Again, she couldn't keep herself from laughing.

"Me accent? What's wrong with me accent?"

Traci, you still haven't learned ...

She closed her eyes and shook her head. She couldn't seem to keep herself from offending her characters. "Nothing's wrong with it. In fact, I like listening to you talk."

"Then we will talk until morning." He downed his wine and lifted the empty glass toward her, asking silently for more.

Talk until morning? TALK? Not what she had in mind. However, if nothing more was going to happen, she'd have to go along with it.

She took the glass from his hand and walked toward the kitchen. To her surprise, he followed her.

He touched her elbow. "Will you show me the rest of your fine home?"

Ah, now they were getting somewhere. "Sure thing. Follow me."

As they neared her bedroom door, her palms broke into a sweat. Should she feel ashamed for her aroused anticipation? She used to feel this way when she and Jack were first married—when she'd wait for him to come home from work to find her dressed in something seductive and enticing. It had been hard *then* to control the rate of her heart, just like now. Her mouth was dry, but she wasn't about to go back for wine.

She motioned him through the door, then quickly locked it.

* * *

Traci sputtered and coughed. Her arms flailed in the deep cold water.

"I'm drowning!" she yelled, and fought for her life.

Strong arms encircled her waist. "Put your feet down, Marta. You silly lass."

Daniel ...

She obeyed, and her feet landed firm on solid ground. Still, water came all the way up to her neck.

Where are we?

Now that her life wasn't in peril, she scanned the countryside. High mountain peaks framed the horizon, but they were near the shore of a lake. A very large lake. The sun had started to set, and the sky held incredibly beautiful purple and blue hues with wisps of white clouds. Thick green trees surrounded the shoreline. If she'd not begun to freeze, she'd probably be enjoying this.

Of course. Lough Leane.

"Hold me neck," Daniel said, with a grin.

She locked her hands behind his head. As he pulled her close, she realized they were both naked. It shouldn't have surprised her. Once again it all happened exactly as she'd written it.

By now, she should be used to these crazy scenarios. Even so, she'd never have thought they'd wind up in one of the Lakes of Killarney. Why not the scene later in the book, where they were in his castle? In a real bed. *Dry.*

Remember, Traci, you're supposed to be up to adventure. Let your hair down. Much easier to tell herself to let go than actually do it.

She took a huge breath and stopped thinking about it. Instead, she decided to focus on his firm body. Hers wasn't bad either. Like Claire, Marta had a lean and curvy body, with the skin tone of Alexa. Her long, wet, red hair stuck to her head. Then—because of its length—a great deal floated atop the water.

"Kiss me," Daniel said, but didn't wait for her to take action. He cupped one hand behind her head and kissed her with urgency.

Oh yeah, this one was a quickie, too.

A good thing. Otherwise she'd be so cold she probably wouldn't enjoy it. Her brain already seemed to be frozen. For the life of her, she couldn't remember what Marta said to him. So, she decided to wing it.

"Kiss me again, Daniel," she rasped, and then this time took the initiative. He tasted like lake water, but it didn't offend her. His need had become apparent, and hers had been there since he walked through her door, bouncing his crimson kilt with every step.

Making love in water felt a little odd. She and Jack had dabbled at it a few times. But this didn't come anywhere close to the times with Jack and seemed by far more difficult than the encounter with Magnus. Water didn't give the same resistance the stone wall had.

It didn't seem to bother Daniel.

She wrapped her legs around him and held on tight. He did the rest. Holding her tail with his hands, he got his balance and went to work.

Passion flooded from her like a bursting dam. She kissed him hard and deep and twisted her fingers into his thick curls. All the while, he moved with increased speed and force.

"Traci ..." he moaned. "I love you."

What? I'm not Traci, I'm Marta.

She started to say something, but his mouth covered hers again.

Forget it. It doesn't matter.

Whether numb to the bone or warm from their movement, she wasn't cold anymore. His hands pulsed in rhythm with the rest of his body as he squeezed and then relaxed his fingers over and over again, kneading her bottom like bread dough.

His mouth rarely strayed from hers. He'd come up for air, then cover her lips again with an accompanied, gasping moan.

And then, he closed his eyes, threw his head back, and cried out while holding her fast against him. His scream should've brought out all the lake residents, but they were nowhere to be found. Why? She wrote it that way. They had to have complete solitude or Marta would've never been able to do it outside. Neither would she.

"I love you, Marta," he said, opening his eyes. "You're more woman than I deserve."

Good, this time he got the name right. She'd worry about the mistake later.

"And you're quite the man, Laird Gray." She attempted to sound Scottish. He probably wouldn't know the difference.

"We best be gettin' out of the water and to the shore."

Where would they go? If she wandered too far, would she still wake up in her room?

"Are we beddin' down somewhere?" she asked. They needed to find a place to sleep, so her fantasy would end correctly.

"Aye. Though I must say, we don't need a bed." He winked, then jiggled his brows.

"To *sleep,* Daniel." She placed her hand against his wet skin. How could illusions be so alive? His heart beat heavily beneath her palm.

"Sleep? I suppose you're right. But we may have a go at it again, if you don't mind."

Mind? As long as she could be horizontal, it was fine by her.

They walked hand in hand from the water, and he led her to a log where their clothes were draped. He stared at her breasts and her cold, erect nipples.

"Can't let those go to waste," he said with a grin, then took one in his mouth. His gentle suction added goose bumps to her goose bumps.

Oh, mercy …

In no time at all, they were on the ground. Why bother getting dressed when they were *going at it* again?

They needed a soft bed of sand. Instead, they were on rocks. She flipped him onto his back and took the lead. No bruises for her this time.

He laughed, then pulled her down and kissed her. He then smacked his lips. "As I said, more woman than I deserve."

"You've not seen anything yet." Yes, she'd become bolder with every encounter. And there were no complaints from her Scottish laird.

I have nothing to feel guilty about.

Chapter 12

The bedding dripped with water. Not just damp. *Soaked.*

"This is ridiculous," Traci mumbled, while stripping the sheets. She then turned the ceiling fan on high, to help dry the pillow-top mattress.

A puddle of water also surrounded her crumpled jeans and sweater on the wood floor. It didn't seem quite right since Daniel and Marta's clothes were dry on the shoreline. She looked upward. "You got it wrong this time."

Who had she addressed? God? Had He orchestrated these trysts? Why would He do that? She doubted He would. More likely it had been Satan playing with her mind. Whatever or Whomever it had been, they messed up. A slight error in the manuscript.

Like Daniel calling me Traci.

And why did he? She hadn't looked like Traci or sounded like Traci—*well maybe a little*—but she'd definitely been Marta. Young, able, and willing. A gorgeous, feisty redhead any man would want.

The fact he'd followed the use of her name by saying, *I love you*, made it even harder to bear.

For the briefest moment, she'd been reminded of Jack. He'd always said the words when they made love. Totally appropriate, but they were never simply words. He loved her with every ounce of himself, and he'd have done anything for her.

She stuffed the sheets into the washer, then dropped to the floor. "I can't do this anymore."

Sure, it had been exciting, gratifying, and *fun*, but when Daniel spoke her name, it made it real. Thinking back on it, she should've stopped him right then.

Reading about two strangers falling in love and experiencing their story had been one thing. This was too much. She'd become a part of the book—body and soul —and therefore, it was no longer fiction.

Why did I listen to that stupid psychic?

She'd never been so angry with herself. Dressing quickly, she jumped into her car and headed toward town. She needed to get out of the house, no matter where she ended up.

November fifteenth, and the city had already been decorated for Christmas. Actually, the decorations had been up for about two weeks. She couldn't think about Christmas right now, Thanksgiving first.

The turkey!

It was still a week and a half away, but she needed to buy it now, stick it in the freezer, and then put it in the fridge next Sunday. She steered her car toward the grocery store.

The reality check helped. She couldn't wait to see Jason. A *real* person. And if she had any control at all over who came to her door, then she'd do her best to visualize every female character imaginable and forget the men. This Friday would be a test. If she could make it happen once, she could certainly make it happen again.

* * *

It became a mantra. A recitation of every female she'd ever written. From Claire and Alexa, to Marta and Olivia. And plenty more in between. It'd be a hoot if Madame Beaumont showed up. She might be able to help her make sense of Cordelia's words.

What a silly thought.

Traci had created Madame Beaumont, and if she didn't have a clue what Cordelia had been trying to tell her, how could Madame Beaumont know? They shared the same mind. Just like all her other characters.

Maybe that's the core Cordelia was talking about. The one thing they all had in common.

Traci shook her head and tried to dismiss thoughts of the psychic. They frustrated her, and she didn't need a headache. Still, she could be on to something.

Back to her mantra. She smiled thinking of sweet, naïve Cora. She'd love to have a talk with her. She could teach her a thing or two and save her some embarrassment.

Poor girl didn't have a mother to teach her a thing.

And so, when the knock came on her door, she assumed she'd open it to a woman. The last woman she'd thought about had been Cora from *Marked,* her first book in the River Romance series.

This knock was heavy-handed. Not a *Magnus* sort of knock, but far from girly.

His face filled the screen. Plump, with large jowls. Absolutely no doubt who he was. This time, a *real* Irishman with red sideburns and a body as big around as he was tall was about to walk through her door.

Captain William O'Brien.

She shook her head. "No. I can't do it. I won't play this part."

"Traci?" *Thump. Thump.* "Let me in, lass."

Again with the lass.

She paced in front of the door, mumbling all the while. "I wanted Cora, NOT him. And if it had to be a man, why not Douglas? A good-looking English gentleman. Not a gambling, *fat* Irishman."

"Traci?" *Thump.* "I'm freezing me tail off out here!"

How could she make him go away? She wasn't about to sleep with him. Perhaps she could drug him, or give him so much wine he'd think they'd done something and fall asleep. That sounded like a decent plan. Needless to say, with a body that large, it would take a lot of wine.

She had plenty.

Here goes nothing.

With a large smile plastered on her face, she opened the door. "Captain O'Brien? As I live and breathe!" Over the top? Maybe.

He chuckled and waddled into the room.

I shouldn't have made him so fat.

Though a gambler, William O'Brien had a kind heart. Unattractive, but nice. As captain of the *Bonny Lass*—a steamboat on the Mississippi River—he'd had his share of adventure. Traci was about to slap something new on him.

"How about some wine?" She took his arm and led him to the sofa. If all went well, he'd pass out here and never make it to her bedroom.

"I don't know that I should. After all, I assumed we'd want to spend some time together. Get acquainted. 'Tis not every day I meet me creator."

He flattered her.

Talk about guilt. "I'm pleased to meet you, sir. We can certainly talk, but a glass of wine couldn't hurt. I'm quite thirsty myself."

"Fine. I'll indulge. Make mine a wee glass." He showed a span of about two inches between his finger and thumb. Too *wee* for her liking. With his enormity, that amount of wine wouldn't even numb his tongue.

She bustled to the kitchen. Paying no mind to his request, she poured a generous portion into a tall drinking glass. Then, she poured one for herself. She'd need it.

"Here you are." She smiled like one of those overly friendly flight attendants. Offering him some peanuts might be a good idea. They could make him thirstier. *Nope.* She didn't have any.

Dang.

Already she felt like Cora.

And then, a plan popped into her head. A brilliant plan.

"That's a bit much," O'Brien said with a brogue that made Daniel's sound even more like a cartoon character. He hesitated taking it from her.

"You're a large man. I think you'll find it goes down easy." She pushed it toward him. Again she flashed a large, toothy grin.

"Very well then." He took it from her hand and drank a swallow. Then, after a satisfied grin, he downed the whole glass. "Aye. Very smooth."

"That's what I've always said." She followed suit. It warmed her through and through. "More?"

He chuckled. "Maybe a wee bit." He displayed his fingers again. This time they resembled a four-inch portion. A good sign. He liked it.

He pointed to the coffee table. "I see you've taken up poker."

Huh?

A deck of cards lay on the coffee table. Oddly, two hands had been dealt—face up—one of which was a full house.

"Did you put those there?" she asked him. It would be the only logical explanation.

"No, lass. They were there when I sat down. 'Tis a fine hand." He pointed to the full house, then leaned toward her. "I was never able to do so well without a little sleight of hands." He winked.

He didn't have to tell her that. She nodded, then shook her finger at him. "Just don't get caught."

"Aye." He chuckled, and she watched in amazement as his belly shook like that bowl full of jelly in the Christmas rhyme. William far outweighed any Santa Claus she'd ever seen.

My plan had better work.

"I'll get more wine," she said, and bustled off to the kitchen. She brought the bottle back with her. After filling his glass, she stopped. Needing to keep her head clear, she dared not touch another drop.

"So, Captain ..." She sat and placed her hands on her knees. "What would you like to talk about?"

"Francine."

Huh? The last thing she expected. "Francine?"

"Aye. The poor lass is troubled. Having difficulty with me new marriage."

"Uh-huh ..."

He tipped his glass and polished it off, then leaned it toward her, wanting more. She readily filled it.

"You need to help her," he said, with a very stern face. "She's achin' for a man."

"She's a prostitute."

"Aye. But even a woman in her position needs love. Can't you help her?"

He doesn't know about the sequel.

"Yes, I'll help her. I promise." If she told him, he might go back to *wherever* and tell her. And even though her books hadn't changed from any of the other experiences, Claire had noticed a difference in Gerald and Andrew. Traci couldn't risk having him mess things up with Francine.

"Thank you, lass." He stretched and yawned. "I suddenly feel a bit weary."

Good. Fall asleep. Right now. On the sofa.

"Well, you just make yourself comfortable. I don't mind at all. My home is your home." She handed him a decorative pillow, which strangely had blue swirls on it like the ones she'd described in his room on the boat.

He lay back and folded his hands over his belly. To add to his comfort, she covered him with the fleece throw. This had worked better than she'd planned. Within minutes, his lips vibrated and his nose twitched, as he snored heavily.

She tiptoed out of the room and went to her bedroom, then shut the door behind her.

Nothing happened.

With a sigh of relief, she climbed into bed. Tomorrow morning if all went well, he'd be gone, and maybe he'd take his mysterious deck of cards with him.

So, so tired ...

* * *

"What the?" Traci jerked upright. Someone had tugged on her leg.

"You're quite lovely, Cora. We'll make a handsome son."

Dang!

William O'Brien stood to the side of her bed, but it wasn't *her* bed. *How did he get in here?* Did she forget to lock the door?

Candlelight glimmered around them. She looked downward at a perfectly flat chest under a lightweight nightgown. Thin, tiny Cora.

She'd landed into the scene she'd feared. Their wedding night aboard the *Bonny Lass*.

Lord, no, I don't want to be Cora.

"So, Cora, is it your time? Are you bleeding?"

She could NOT go through with this. Not with this man. Sure, she'd made him as nice as nice could be, but dang! She didn't find him attractive in the least tiny bit. Cora had been naïve, yet didn't have a choice in the matter. Traci was anything *but* naïve. She'd been around the block more than once. *Recently.*

"Uh ... William?"

"Aye?"

She needed to sound like Cora and make it convincing. "I ain't bleedin'." *Just in case he decided to check.* "But, my pa lied to you."

Okay, so she wasn't following the plot. She had to do *something* to change the course of the night.

"I know. He cheated me."

"Yep. But more than that."

William crossed his arms. "What more?"

She swallowed hard. "I ain't unspoiled. I've been with a man before. Truth be told, more than one."

Breath puffed from his nostrils. "You mean to tell me you're not a virgin?"

Did they use that word back then? Oh, yeah. They used that way back in Jesus's time.

"Nope. Sorry." What more could she say?

"Do you know what this means?"

No, she didn't have a clue. They were going in an entirely new direction. She'd always been a good plotter, but now she had to fly by the seat of her pants. She shook her head.

His hands formed into fists. "I'll see to it your father is hung! He'll pay for this."

It wouldn't really happen. She knew from experience she could change the story and nothing bad would happen. She hoped so anyway.

"What 'bout me?" She scooted back against the bed frame.

"I may still take you."

Not the right answer.

Think fast.

"You wouldn't like it." *Dumb thing to say. What man didn't like it?* "I reckon you should know I got ..." *What disease would he know?* "I got a bad rash down there. You don't wanna see it. Trust me." Rashes of any sort were a turn-off to anyone. Man *or* woman.

Even in dim light, she could tell his face had turned the color of his sideburns. "I'm very disappointed, Cora. I believed we'd have something special between us." His anger subsided and turned to sorrow. Now she'd gone and hurt his feelings.

I'm a horrible, mean author.

"Dang, William. I'm sorry." She patted the spot next to her on the bed, and like a wounded child he lay down beside her. "Tell ya what. When the rash is gone, I'll let you have me. I'll still try to be a good wife." *Just please don't ever come back through my front door.*

He rolled over onto his side and faced her. "Thank you, lass. You know me first wife died with our child in her belly. All I've ever wanted is a son."

"I know." Compelled to touch him, she gently brushed the side of his face with her hand.

It would've helped both of them if she could've told him about Jack. Since she'd become Cora, if she mentioned losing her husband, it would confuse him even more. She couldn't do that to him. She'd hurt him enough already. "Go to sleep now, an' everythin' will be better in the mornin'."

"Aye," he said and closed his eyes. Was he truly tired, or had she hurt him so badly he no longer wanted to look at her?

She lay there for some time and watched his belly rise and fall with every deep breath. He wasn't a bad man. She probably should've gone through with it. Not every man in the world had a perfect body and beautiful face—not even Jack. But, they all needed love.

Oh, Jack. If only you were here, I wouldn't have to deal with all this.

After many minutes passed, his breathing slowed, and she had no doubt he'd fallen asleep. The gentle swaying of the steamboat soothed her. It rocked her just like a mother swaying with an infant in her arms. Her eyes were heavy, and soon, she, too, drifted off to sleep.

Chapter 13

"Jason!" Traci flung her arms around him and held him in a death grip. She never wanted to let go.

He laughed, then lifted her up off the ground and spun her around.

"Show off," she muttered. Her six-foot-three son had been able to lift her for years. She'd now become his *little* mom.

He set her down, then took a step back and looked at her. "I almost didn't recognize you. What with the ..." He circled his finger around his head and grinned.

"I know. Gray hair. I'm officially old." She pointed toward his rental car. "Do you need help bringing things in?"

"Nope. I traveled light. Do I still have my old room, or have you taken on boarders?"

"Ha! Funny." She rolled her eyes. *If he only knew.* "Bring in your things, and then we can talk."

He nodded and walked away. She hesitated for a brief moment before closing the door. If she told him how many people had come through it lately, he'd probably have her committed.

She couldn't help but smile. And not because she'd just thought of her other visitors. Her son always made her light up. At twenty-eight, Jason had grown even more handsome than the last time she'd seen him. Had it really been eight months? Much too long for a mother and son to be separated.

He looks more like Jack the older he gets. Jason was a few inches taller than Jack, but had the same dark hair and brown eyes. That is—the same hair from when Jack actually had hair.

Jack had been thirty-seven when they got married. A confirmed bachelor until she swept him off his feet.

She mulled around the room until Jason returned lugging a large suitcase.

"Down the hall and to the right," she said with a grin. "In case you forgot."

"Thanks, Mom. Oh ..." He tossed his head toward the door. "I think we're in for some snow. The clouds are kind of pink, and it sure smells like it." He passed by her and headed toward his room.

Snow?

No.

Returning to the front door, she flung it open and breathed in, wiggling her nose like a bunny. She was familiar with the smell. A hard thing to explain to anyone who didn't live here, and definitely not what they needed right now.

It would be just her luck to be snowed in on Friday night. But it would have to be a blizzard to keep her from leaving. At eight past seven on Friday night, she intended to be in a theater watching someone else's complicated life.

Jason grinned as he passed by her. He returned to his car and brought in two sacks of groceries. "C'mon, Mom. Why don't you shut the door and help me put these away?" He nodded toward the kitchen. "Like you always told me, you're heating the outside."

"Right." She shut the door and followed him. Trying to wish away a snowstorm wouldn't do any good.

"You got the turkey, didn't you?" He set the bags on the kitchen counter.

"Yep." To prove her point, she opened the refrigerator and pointed to the bird. "It's only a twelve-pounder. I figured that would be plenty for the two of us."

"Yeah, enough for tomorrow night's dinner, but most importantly—leftovers for sandwiches. Cranberry sauce and cream cheese?" He jiggled his brows and rubbed his hands together.

"Of course." Their favorite sandwich. She honestly preferred the leftovers to the dinner itself. "I thought tonight we'd have grilled cheese and tomato soup for old time's sake. Keep it simple since tomorrow will be such a big production. Is that okay?"

"Better than okay." He flashed one of his best smiles. "Perfect for this cold weather."

She couldn't help herself and hugged him again. "I'm so glad you're home."

"Me, too. Amy was sorry she couldn't be here." Something behind his eyes said more than his words, but now wasn't the time to ask questions. The time would come.

They walked arm in arm to the sofa. She sat, but he wandered to the window facing the atrium. "When I tell people about this house ..." He cast his eyes over his shoulder to look at her. "No one believes me about this garden. It really is amazing."

She joined him at the window. "C'mon, let's go out. You need to see how big the fish are."

Immediately greeted by the trickle of flowing water, they walked to the bench and sat. Jason leaned over and pointed into the pond. "They're *huge*."

"Yes, they are." She looked up toward the skylight. "I thought about getting some tropical birds and letting them live in here, but—"

He laughed. "You don't want to get pooped on, right?"

She playfully slapped his leg. "You know me well."

Man, she missed this. She never understood friends who had bad relationships with their kids. No child could by any means be perfect, but Jason came close. At least in her eyes. He was everything a mother could ask for.

He took hold of her hand, and they just sat there and silently watched the water.

"Do you remember when I wanted you to make the water chocolate?" Jason asked, while gazing at the waterfall.

"Yep. You watched *Willy Wonka* and thought it'd be a good idea. That was one time I had to tell you *no*."

He chuckled. "Yeah. You said the fish wouldn't like it."

"And do you remember how we appeased you?"

"Hmm …" He tapped his finger against his chin. "I believe it was a chocolate sundae, wasn't it?"

She nodded. "With a cherry on top and whipped cream."

"Good memories."

Silence again. If she could read his mind, he'd probably been thinking that all those memories included his dad. The sundae had been Jack's idea. Of course, Jack always looked for a good excuse to eat ice cream.

"Mom?" He shifted his body and faced her. His brow drew in and his smile vanished.

"What's wrong, Jason?"

"How do you do it? How do you stay here without Dad?"

She swallowed to moisten her dry throat. "It's hard. Still, every day it gets a little easier."

"Don't you get lonely? I mean, if I didn't have Amy, I'd go nuts. Not just for someone to talk to, but—well—you and Dad were always so affectionate. Whenever you were together, you were like two inseparable pieces of a puzzle. You'd either be holding hands, or Dad would have his arm around you. Don't you miss …" He huffed, then let out a sigh. "Oh, I don't know—just being held?"

The way Jason struggled with his words caused the pit of guilt in her stomach to feel like a lead weight. Yes, she missed Jack's affection, and she couldn't deny she'd been enjoying the physical aspect of her encounters. Humans were made to be physical.

Thoughts of her high school biology teacher, Mr. Sands, popped into her mind. His face had beamed red when he'd explained that humans and dolphins were the only species that had sexual relations for pleasure and not simply for reproduction. Then, the looks from the boys in the class confirmed they liked the lesson. Jiggling brows and stifled mumbles made every girl squirm in her chair. Mr. Sands affirmed what every high school boy thought about 24/7.

"Mom?" Jason patted her arm.

"Huh?"

"You were somewhere else right now."

"I'm sorry. I was just thinking."

"Are you wishing you would've moved?" His face fell, covered in pain.

"No." *You don't want to know my thoughts.* "Why would I give up all this?" She splayed her hands wide and shook her head. "Your father and I built this together. It means too much to me. Though it's hard, in some ways it makes it easier because I'm surrounded by our memories. Like the one you just shared about the chocolate water. If I got a new house it'd be like washing away the rest of him. I want to hold on to whatever I can."

He turned to face the water, then bent forward and put his head in his hands.

She rubbed his back, attempting to soothe away the suffering in his eyes. "You're the best thing he ever gave me."

Her words were supposed to please him, but his shoulders jerked and he burst into sobs. "I'm sorry, Mom. I just miss him so much." Even after a year, coming here must have reopened the wound. He'd cried at the funeral, but not like this.

There was no way to stop her own tears. No mother could endure watching her child in pain without feeling it herself. "I do, too," she whispered and closed her eyes.

He turned and clutched her, gripping her with the force of a man. Though fully grown, he ached like the hurt little boy she used to hold in her lap and cuddle close. His tears dampened her shoulders, and they stayed there oblivious to time. Long overdue. They needed this.

* * *

Traci slept better than she had in a long time. It might have been because she'd had a good cry and was worn out. Most likely, it was because her house wasn't empty. Best of all, the person in the room down the hall was real —someone she loved with all her heart.

Her automated blinds hadn't opened yet. Not quite eight o'clock. She swung her legs over the side of the bed anyway. The aroma coming from the kitchen made her smile, and it woke her up.

Sautéed onions.

Jason must have gotten an early start on the dressing. An old family recipe he loved and Jack's family hated. Even so, she made it every Thanksgiving regardless, just to keep Jason happy. Besides, she liked it, too.

Both sides of the family were small. She and Jack were *only* children, and because they were older than the norm when they got married, their parents were also quite old and died while Jason was little—except for her ornery mother whom Traci thought would outlive them all. It made family gatherings small, but very intimate.

Now, family consisted of her and Jason—and Amy, of course. The family line would end unless they had a miracle.

"That smells so good," Traci said, as she entered the kitchen. She tightened her bathrobe at the waist. "Need help?"

"Nope." He grinned. He'd found one of her old aprons and looked kind of cute wearing frills. "I got a handle on this. I had a good teacher."

He chopped up a few sticks of celery and added it to the simmering mix. Then he set about slicing up two loaves of bread. Once he added the poultry seasoning, it confirmed Thanksgiving had arrived.

Traci turned on the TV and found the Macy's Thanksgiving Day Parade. It had just started.

"It's not the way it used to be," she hollered toward the kitchen. "Why do they have to have all those snippets of Broadway shows? I'd rather just watch the parade."

He popped his head out of the kitchen. "Money. They're trying to get people to New York to fill the seats in the theaters."

"Oh."

She sat on the sofa and placed the remote on the coffee table. Touching Jack's little plastic *toy* seemed odd. But, over the last few weeks she'd watched more TV than she had all year. Maybe she'd taken some steps forward.

After bustling around in the kitchen for more than thirty minutes, Jason finally joined her. "It should be ready by about two o'clock. I have some time to relax for a while."

They stared at the TV.

"You see," she said, pointing at the screen. "Broadway musicals. They flipped from the floats to show the cast of *Mary Poppins* performing "Supercalifragilisticexpialidocious." I prefer the floats."

"You've never liked change, Mom." He took her hand and squeezed it.

She wouldn't argue that point. She hated change. Routine had always been one of her best friends. Perhaps she'd been a little angry with Jack for messing it up. Wasn't anger supposed to be another part of grieving? If so, she didn't want to be angry at him. Maybe at God, but not at Jack.

Once the parade ended, Jason set up a Scrabble game. She'd never let him win, even when he was little. Though he'd beaten her a time or two. He'd complained she had an unfair advantage, being that she surrounded herself with words every day of her life. However, a big part of the game was luck of the draw, so he still had a decent shot.

It seemed they were both trying to pretend everything was normal.

Not even close. The hole left by Jack's absence would never be filled. Not by anyone or anything. She should at least try to be honest with Jason. But she couldn't. Not about some things. If he knew what she'd been doing, he'd never look at her the same way again.

The baking turkey filled the house with a fantastic aroma. It got her mind on food and off her troubles. By the time they ate, her appetite had erupted. She stuffed herself fuller than the bird, and she couldn't pass up the pumpkin pie that Jason cheated on and bought at a local bakery.

They finished off the meal with a glass of wine. Mogen David. What else?

Jason grinned when she opened the bottle. "You've been drinking quite a lot of this lately, haven't you?"

How'd he know?

"Why do you say that?" She turned away from him as heat filled her face.

He chuckled. "I saw all the empty bottles in the recycle bin. I never thought my mom would become a Mogen David lush."

"Oh." She managed a nervous chuckle. She'd rather have him believe she was a lush than a harlot. "Yes, well, as you know, it has very little alcohol content. And, I like it. I promise you, I limit myself to only a glass or two a night."

He waved his hands at her. "You're a grown woman. And if it helps ..." He lifted his glass in the air as if to toast her, then gave her one of his best smiles and filled it full. He wandered over to the front window. "It's snowing, Mom."

What?

She hurried to his side and stared out the glass. Huge flakes fell from the sky and had already covered the driveway. Why now? It could've had the decency to wait a few days.

He placed an arm over her shoulder. "Good thing I got a rental with all-weather tires. It may be difficult getting to the airport Saturday. Then again, by then it might all be gone."

Yes, the unpredictable Tennessee weather. "I hope so. I'd hate for you to have to drive in this."

"At least we have plenty of food to get us through. No need to go anywhere until then."

"But ..." She looked outside again. How could she convince him to leave the house tomorrow night if this kept up? "I'd hoped we could go out to a movie or something."

"Why? You have plenty of DVDs, and there's always pay-per-view."

Because if we don't, you're more than likely going to meet a half-naked man who wants to have a fling with your mom.

"I thought you wouldn't want to stay here the whole time you're home."

He pulled her into a hug. "I love it here. I want to stop by Dad's grave on my way out of town. Otherwise, I'd prefer to stay home."

How could she argue with him?

God, I wish he was five, and I could just tell him we have to go out because I said so.

If the snow let up, she might be able to change his mind. If not, there was no sense going out. She'd have to pray very hard for nothing to happen. No visitors. Just a peaceful night at home with her son.

Chapter 14

Traci's prayers weren't answered. The snow fell throughout the night and at least four inches covered the ground in front of her house.

She could always pretend to be sick and go to bed early. If she was in bed, would they still come? She could lock her door. Maybe that was the key. Every time the lock clicked she'd been taken to another time and place. But, what would happen to Jason? Would he be sent to la-la land to join her? She had no idea what happened to things or people beyond her shut door.

Leaving would be out of the question. Even if it hadn't snowed so much, Jason made a point to remind her that the day after Thanksgiving boasted the biggest shopping day of the year. *Black Friday.* The restaurants would be jam-packed, and even the theaters would most likely be full. Most importantly, traffic would be a bear.

With the exception of Traci going to the window every five minutes to check on the snowfall, they went through the day as before, talking, eating, and watching TV.

She made a point *not* to bring up Amy's inability to conceive. They had enough pain in their lives without that. Their conversations were mainly *remember when's,* with a bit of architecture thrown in, and Traci's constant internal mutterings damning the snow.

And no matter what she did, the clock kept ticking, and the closer the moment of doom neared, the more she perspired.

"Are you okay, Mom?" Jason stopped her from pacing.

"Sure. Why?"

"You're wearing a hole in the floor."

"Oh." Nervous chuckle. "I'll sit down."

She sat, but tangled her fingers together into knots. And after her fingers wore out, she started twiddling her thumbs. Pacing had been easier. In two minutes, she might have to dig herself out of that hole in the floor.

"Mom ..." Jason grabbed her hands. "Tell me what's wrong."

His concern was genuine. Why wouldn't it be? His mother had been acting like a crazed woman.

Sweat dripped from her forehead. "Hot flashes." She forced a smile and tittered.

Tick. Tick. Tick.

She held her breath waiting for that inevitable knock.

She cocked her head toward the door.

No knock.

A long, drawn-out breath hissed from her lips, and she quickly covered her mouth. She considered doing a happy dance, but Jason would worry even more.

Had the divine universe given her a break?

Okay … that's weird.

"Mom, what's that scratching sound?" Jason stood and moved toward the front door.

Whoever was there decided to scratch instead of knock? Which one of her characters had incredibly long fingernails?

She jumped up and joined him before he turned the knob. The monitor showed no one.

God only knows what's out there. I'm so glad I'm not Stephen King right now.

Another scratch.

Jason twisted the knob and pulled the door open.

With a jump and a shake, a puppy raced inside and headed for the fireplace. He was black with a tiny patch of white on his chest, and enormous paws for such a little guy. He'd likely grow up to be a big dog.

"When did you get a puppy, Mom?" Jason shut the door and followed the dog.

"I—I didn't. He must be a stray." She thought long and hard and it hit her even harder.

Internally, she laughed, but hid her elation from Jason. "Sparky?"

The moment she spoke his name, he wiggled his tail, then bounded toward her.

"I thought you said he was a stray?" Jason bent down and patted him. "How do you know his name?"

"It took me a minute. He belongs to a neighbor. A—*new* neighbor. They just got him."

"He's a long way from home. There's no one else out here for miles." He scooped Sparky into his arms. "He sure is friendly." He was rewarded with a lick on the face.

"Yep. Likes the fire, too," she mumbled. Thus the name. Another visitor from the *Southern Secrets* saga. *What am I supposed to do with him?* "I hope he's housebroken."

"He's a puppy, Mom. It's unlikely."

Great. All she needed were puppy puddles all over her nice wood floors. But, she had to admit, she preferred this over having to explain Magnus or Daniel—or any other men from her books.

She looked upward and grinned.

Nice job. I can deal with this.

Sparky made himself at home and curled up in front of the fireplace.

Jason stood and headed to the kitchen, and in moments returned with a few scraps of left-over turkey in his hand. He knelt beside the dog and fed him, and Sparky showed his gratitude by licking his hand.

Then, as quickly as a light changes with the flip of a switch, Jason's mood darkened. The smile he'd previously had for Sparky faded, and he stepped away from him and sat on the sofa, instantly putting his head in his hands. The same pose he'd had before, when he'd grieved over his dad. Tonight it was something more.

Traci moved beside him. "Tell me what's wrong, Jason."

His body inflated as he took in air, then diminished as he slowly let it out. "Everything, Mom."

A tiny whimper came from Sparky, who left his spot at the fire and curled up at Jason's feet. As if the dog felt his pain.

Traci rubbed Jason's back in slow circles and waited for him to say more. She wouldn't push him.

His head turned slightly to face her. "I think I'm losing Amy."

"What?" It couldn't be. They loved each other. He had to be wrong.

"I love her so much, but all we ever do anymore is argue." His hands formed into fists and he gritted his teeth. "Everything would be fine if I could just get her pregnant."

Traci closed her eyes. *Of course.* She'd seen this coming. Optimism had turned to doubt, and now they'd started blaming each other. "Jason, you don't know that it's because of you. Your doctor said—"

"What else could it be?" After punching a fist into the sofa, he stood and moved toward the fire. Sparky stayed at his heels. "Amy's done everything she can. Her doctor said there's no reason why she shouldn't conceive, so *I* must be the problem. If I can't give her a baby, I know she'll find someone who can!"

Sparky sat on his rump and pawed at Jason's leg, whimpering all the while.

"Amy loves you." Traci quickly crossed the room to Jason, then grabbed his arms and made him look her in the eye. "Never give up hope."

She could tell he'd been fighting back tears, and she'd been doing her best to push hers aside. She had to stay strong for him. This was too important.

"It's hard not to, Mom." He looked down at the dog, then bent and scooped him up. Sparky nestled into his body. "Nothing makes sense anymore. Amy's not the same woman I married. I came home one night and found her in the corner of the room, trying to stand on her head. Someone told her it would help. All it did was give her a headache."

Traci led him back to the couch and they both sat. Sparky glued himself to Jason as if he belonged there.

"I think it's an old wives' tale," she said. "And, I think she was supposed to stand on her head *after* you made love, not before."

He covered his face with his hands. "I can't believe I'm talking to you about this. It's embarrassing. For all I know you've probably written something like this in one of your novels."

Embarrassed? Jason had never been embarrassed about anything they'd talked about. Starting with the time he'd come home from playing with the neighborhood kids and asked during dinner what *humping* was. That hadn't been a fun conversation. He was only six at the time. She'd let Jack handle that one.

"My books take place in the olden days. Fertility was a different kind of issue back then." She shook her head and waved her hands in the air. "But none of that matters! You can talk to me about anything. Bottom line is I know the two of you love each other, and you're going to get through this." She calmed and softened her voice. "I think you're trying too hard. The best thing you can do is to *stop* trying, and that's when it'll happen."

He ran his hands over the tiny puppy. It seemed to help calm him. "It hasn't even felt like making love anymore. And ..." He huffed out a breath. "The reason she went to see her parents without me, was because we had a huge fight." His face scrunched together, then he squared his jaw. "She's been talking about going to the sperm bank and getting someone else's. Just because I have a low count doesn't mean I want some other man's sperm to make our baby. I want it to be mine. Is that so wrong?"

She smoothed his hair. "No. It's not wrong." Her heart ached for him. She understood Amy's need to have a child, but not to the extent of ruining their marriage. Knowing what a difficult time Jason was having talking about this, she decided to tackle the issue head-on. "Do you wear boxers? I've heard it helps."

"Yes. I wear boxers, and I make certain to keep my cell phone away from my crotch." His tone sounded almost spiteful. She knew he didn't mean for it to be. He'd been deeply wounded, and struggled for answers. "I've heard it all, Mom. And I'm tired of it."

They both sat silently. How could she help him? Hurt covered his face like a dark mask. Almost too much to bear. There had to be an answer. Something neither of them had seen. Then, Sparky whimpered and broke the silence.

"Isn't it odd?" She patted the dog. "It's like he understands you. Like he's hurting for you, too."

Jason grunted. "I suggested to Amy that we get a dog. It didn't go over very well. She accused me of trying to fill the void she thinks about the minute she wakes up every day, with something other than a baby. And maybe I was." He cast a sad smile at Sparky, then ruffled his fur. "If he was a stray, I might consider taking him home. I just don't know how well he'd do on such a long flight."

Sparky wouldn't be around that long. She had no doubt. "Maybe this time apart from Amy will help both of you realize the most important thing is your relationship. The two of you. No matter whether or not anyone else comes into your lives." She placed her hand against his chest. "Your love is too important to let anything else get in the way. Don't let her slip out of your grasp. Be patient with her, and let her know you're not going to give up on the two of you no matter what happens."

His chin quivered, but then he firmed his jaw and lifted his face. "I won't give up. I've lost too much already. I know Dad would want me to fight for her. He liked her the minute he met her."

Sparky climbed up Jason's body and licked his face, causing him to break into a laugh. "The dog seems to agree."

Traci nodded. His laughter eased her worried heart. "He's a smart dog."

As if he knew what she said, Sparky crawled across Jason's lap and onto hers. He burrowed into her body.

"Traitor," Jason mumbled. At least now, he actually smiled. "Maybe *you* should get a dog, Mom."

"No. I don't think I'm ready for that responsibility. It'd be too hard for me when I travel."

He took her hand. "Will you ever travel again? I mean —*really* travel? You hardly get out of the house anymore."

He was right. The house had become her refuge, and the world was a very big place she used to enjoy. Without Jack, it was empty. "I'm doing better. I actually went out to dinner by myself a few times. I'll eventually travel again. I'm just not ready. Not yet."

He patted her hand, and then released it. "We're quite the pair, aren't we?"

"Yep. But remember, I'm here for you. And you can talk to me about anything. Even embarrassing things."

"Yes, my mom the romance writer." He chuckled. "You know kids used to tease me."

"I know."

"Then, when I got to high school, the guys came to me for all the answers to their questions about sex. I pretended I knew the answers."

"Did they know you never read any of my books?"

He shrugged. "It didn't matter. I winged it. What *did* matter is that I knew I had the smartest mom around. And still do." He pulled her into an embrace, then kissed her on the forehead. "Thanks for listening."

Her heart melted. "I'll always listen."

They held each other for a great length of time, drawing strength from simple, human contact. The true meaning of love. Being there for each other.

Sparky had kept his place wedged between them, as if he wanted to be a part of this, too.

A loud yawn from Jason indicated he needed sleep. "I'd better get to bed. Tomorrow's going to be a long day." This time he kissed her on the cheek, then stood from the sofa.

Sparky's ears perked up, and he hopped up on all fours, wagging his tail.

"Goodnight, Sparky," Jason said, and patted his head.

Sparky sat down again in Traci's lap, then snuggled into her body like he belonged there. Maybe she needed to take him to bed with her. Thank goodness she'd never written about a mate for him in her book. Becoming a dog could likely push her over the edge.

"I'll let him sleep in my room," she said, stroking his head. "No sense in putting him out in the cold to find his way back home tonight."

"If you tell me which house to go to, I can return him tomorrow when I leave."

She smiled and nodded, but didn't answer. There'd be no need. Sparky would take care of himself.

Jason walked down the hallway to his room and shut the door. She stood and held Sparky over her shoulder like an infant. If only he was that grandchild she longed for, but more than anything, Jason and Amy needed.

"Jack, I wish you were here to help." Sparky squirmed, then licked her face. She took a deep breath, then walked through her door and shut it tight.

Chapter 15

Sure enough, when Traci woke up, Sparky had disappeared. He'd spent the night in the crook of her arm, but vanished sometime before the rising of the sun. How would she explain it to Jason?

Keep it simple.

"It's a shame he ran off," Jason said.

"Yep. He was scratching on the door like he needed to go out. I never dreamed he'd run away." She hated lying to him, yet couldn't avoid it. This was easier to explain than the truth—especially when she didn't have a grasp on it herself.

Jason's flight would be leaving at one, so they ate a quick breakfast and started their goodbyes. The hardest part of all. At least she knew she'd see him again, and it offered a little comfort.

He stood beside her in her office, looking from picture to picture. "Mom, did Dad ever get jealous of all these guys on your wall?"

"No." She leaned into his shoulder and savored the last minutes with him. "Remember, it was your dad who had them framed. He was proud of what I did, and though you might find it hard to believe, he inspired every one of them."

"How?" He looked sideways at her. "Dad was nothing like these men."

"Yes, he was."

She strolled over to the poster of Laird Gray. "He was adventurous and fun, but also warm and loving." Her eyes shifted to the cover of *Beneath the Gladiator's Blade.* "And he was strong and daring."

"I hope we're talking about the same man. He wasn't like them." Jason waved his hand around the room. "Dad was just ... *Dad.* A normal, everyday architect like me."

She placed her hand against his cheek. "I know. That's what I loved about him. I appreciated the comfort of the ordinary everyday life with him, but there were sides of him you never saw. Parts of himself he reserved for me alone."

He held up his hand. "I don't need to know *those* things."

She grinned. "No, you don't." She touched the framed book cover from *Deceptions*, smiling at Andrew's image. "What you *need* to know is that I loved him for his heart more than anything. He had a never-ending amount of love to give. Your dad was *my* prince, but he shared his love with you, too."

When she turned to face Jason again, she expected him to roll his eyes or shake his head at her mushy words. Instead, he wiped away a tear. "So why don't you have a picture of *him* hanging in here?" He sniffled, then took a deep breath. "After all, your love story is the best one I've ever known—aside from me and Amy, of course. I just hope *we'll* have a happy ending."

The best love story ever. A happy ending ...

A strange daze messed with her brain. "You and Amy will be fine. I'm sure of it," she mumbled. "But—what was that you said about me and your dad?"

"You and Dad had a great love story."

Oh, God ...

She wavered and clutched his arm. Without intending to, she'd put panic in his eyes.

"Mom?" He grabbed her and led her to a chair. "You're as white as a sheet. What's wrong?"

Every bit of air left her body. As if a large fist had pounded into her belly, or an enormous hand had slapped her upside the head. The answer had been staring her in the face. Why hadn't she seen it sooner?

She clutched her chest and tried to breathe.

Jason knelt beside her. "I can change my flight. I'm not going to leave you like this."

She flung her arms around him, and buried her head into his neck. "Thank you."

"For saying I'll stay?"

"No, I don't want you to stay. No—no that's not what I mean. God knows I'd love for you to stay with me forever, but you need to get back to Amy." She lifted her head and held his face in her hands. "Jason, you solved my problem. You just told me who I'm going to write about."

"Who you're going to write about?" He looked at her as though she'd gone nuts. "You mean ... *Dad*?"

"Yes. Your dad. The most wonderful man I've ever known. And the love of my life."

"He's not exactly a *poster boy*."

"No. But he's *my* poster boy. Vivian may not like it, but I don't care." She laughed aloud. "I don't care."

She jumped to her feet, then took him by the arm and dragged him to the living room. "If you don't go now, you won't have time to go by your dad's grave. That's important."

Tempted to say he should tell his father she'd see him soon, she decided against it. Jason would take it horribly wrong. But her insides were bursting with renewed hope and excitement. She wanted to scream it at the top of her lungs.

Instead, she walked with him to the car, traipsing across packed snow. The weather had turned, but there was still snow on the ground—just not falling from the sky.

He hugged her a final time, then climbed inside. "Are you sure you'll be all right?"

"I'm better than all right! I can't explain everything now, but one day I will."

He gave her a sideways look, then shook his head. "Wish me luck with Amy."

"You don't need luck, Jason. You have love. It's all that matters."

"I love *you*, Mom."

"I love you, too." She tapped the top of his car and stepped back.

She waited until he'd gone out of sight, then dashed into the house and grabbed her laptop.

* * *

"Hey, Vivian?" Traci took the initiative this time and called her. She finally had good news.

"Traci?" *Groggy—not good.*

Crap. "Did I wake you up?"

"What time is it?"

"Nine."

"Traci—that means it's six here. And—it's Sunday. Did you forget the time difference?"

"Sorry. I just wanted to tell you I'm writing again. Now, go back to sleep. We'll talk more later." She hung up the phone before Vivian could reply.

That'll give her something to think about.

She felt almost giddy. After Jason left, she'd started typing and hadn't stopped since. Well, she slept for maybe four hours, then got at it again. She wanted this book done by Christmas. If all went as she'd planned, Jack would be her Christmas present.

When a plot whirled around in her mind, she could easily type a thousand words an hour. So, for a decent-sized book, she could get it done in a week—possibly two. At the rate she'd been going, it'd probably hit the one week mark. After all, the story had already been written. She simply had to transfer it onto the blank pages.

Naming the book had been easy. Being it was her *golden* book, and written about the most precious life she'd ever known, she titled it *A Golden Life*.

Her light heart danced as she typed away. An ever-present box of tissues came in handy. Writing Jack's story was the therapeutic medicine she needed. All of her cherished memories would be immortalized in written word.

It might have been a good idea to ask Jason's permission to tell some of these things, especially since no names were changed. Still, she kept on going. He'd surely understand. Their lives were here in black and white for everyone to read and know.

Her fans would see her through different eyes. For some reason, she didn't care. It was possible they'd find her boring. But, it had been her life, and the one she'd shared with the greatest hero on the face of the earth. He didn't fight dragons or battle evil demons, but he knew how to love. The most important part of any story.

I'm a romance novelist and this is the greatest love story I'll ever tell.

Boring or not, she'd lay it out there.

When Friday came, she kept on typing. Nothing would stop her from getting it done. No man, no hero, nobody.

She sat on her sofa feeling like she used to. *Incredible.* Creating gave her the biggest high she could ever wish for.

Okay, I don't need this now.

These quirky things were getting old. Out of nowhere, the envelope holding her most recent contract appeared on the corner of the coffee table. She knew without a doubt she hadn't placed it there. The last time she'd seen it, it had been tucked away in her desk drawer.

There'd been no need to go over it. In her early years she'd hired a contract attorney, but as many books as she had under her belt now, she knew the ins and outs of the contracts well. An attorney had become unnecessary.

She chose to ignore the manila envelope and kept on typing. The mystical forces would have to deal with it. Why of all things did they choose to put her contract there? What did it have to do with any of her heroes? Then again, Claire wasn't a hero. Neither was Sparky. She could be in for a real surprise.

Forget about it.

The knock on the door interrupted her and borderline pissed her off. She waved her hand at the annoyance and kept on typing.

Another knock.

Another dismissal.

The next knock grew substantially louder.

Persistent bastard.

Okay. Not so nice. But, she honestly didn't want to have to entertain anyone right now. She'd finally started doing something important.

Knock. Knock. Knock.

"Okay! I'm coming!"

Before turning the knob, she glanced in the monitor. *Bastard* fit.

On the other side of the door—with an egotistical smile—stood one of the most hated men in all her creations. Another flashback from the *Southern Secrets* series. John Martin. Attorney at law.

She looked upward. "Nice one. I get it now."

In the looks department, he was a cross between a forty-something Brad Pitt and Robert Redford, and she'd always thought the two of them looked like they could be father and son. John Martin was gorgeous. Tall, fit, mature, and a ladies man. He'd bed anyone he could get his hands on, and his hands had traveled farther than Gulliver.

She flung the door open. "Come in, John."

He tipped his top hat and strode through the door as arrogant as ever. He had the right to be proud. He was well-dressed, dashing, and by all accounts, a great lover. However, she wasn't about to find out for herself.

"Traci," he whispered, and then lifted her hand to his lips and kissed it. "I've looked forward to meeting you."

"I wish I could say the same for you, John." Was that rude?

He smirked. "You're being coy."

"No, *truthful*. I know you well."

He blinked slowly, with an air of sophistication that oozed with conceited pride. "Shall we sit? Warm ourselves by the fire?"

She didn't want to waste any of her time with him. If she didn't get her manuscript to Vivian soon, there wouldn't be enough time to get the book into print by Christmas. They'd be pushing it regardless. It would take an enormous miracle.

Without a response from her, he made himself comfortable on the sofa. With his art of seduction, she could be in for a lot of trouble. But, there were more important things to do.

"Traci ..." He patted the spot next to him. "Come sit."

Her laptop lay there on the coffee table begging her to touch it. She sat beside him, but wished he'd go away.

"You're quite beautiful," he said and caressed her cheek.

She backed away. "Uh-uh. Don't get any ideas."

"Ideas?" He touched his hand to his chest. "Me?"

"Yes, you. You're the king of ideas."

"You made me that way." He wiggled his stupid brows, then leaned back against the sofa. "And why did you?"

Why did she? She'd never given it much thought. Every book needed a villain, and he happened to fit the bill. But, she'd also made him desirable, sexy, and charming. A detriment for every unsuspecting female between her pages.

"It—just—worked out that way." She fiddled with the bottom of her sweater. "Did it make you unhappy?"

"Unhappy?" He laughed heartily. "God, no. You created Victoria to satisfy my needs and then added all the others. How can a man be unhappy with so many women readily available?"

"You have a point. But ..." Should she clue him in on Victoria? *No. Let him find out for himself.* "Be sure you treat her well. Victoria, that is."

"Oh, I do. Believe me." He sat up straight. "Do you happen to have any wine?"

"Yes, though I doubt you'll like it. I know you're particular about wines and want only the finest." And most expensive.

"I'll try anything once." He winked, and she jumped from the sofa. The more distance she could put between them, the better off she'd be.

For John Martin, a fancy, crystal goblet would be appropriate. She poured some for herself in a similar glass and returned to her guest. Somehow, she had to keep him out of her bedroom. But then how would he go away?

First things first. She sat down and handed him the glass.

He took a sip. "Mmm ... expensive, isn't it?"

"*Very.*" *This is actually kind of fun.* She'd play around with him for a while, then lock herself in her room. She'd come to the conclusion that the only way William O'Brien had gotten in had been because she'd forgotten to lock the door. She wouldn't make that mistake twice.

He sat back, looking more comfortable in her home than he should. After loosening his collar, he took another sip and gave her the once-over—for the second time. "You don't happen to need some legal counsel, do you?"

"Me?" Why would he think that? "No."

He pointed to the manila envelope. "Contract negotiations? Or perhaps final details regarding your husband's demise?"

"Demise?" She considered slapping him. "I'd appreciate some respect concerning Jack. And to answer your question—though I don't know why I'm even talking to you about it—everything has been taken care of. *Legally* I'm in great shape." Her mind and heart were the troubled areas.

He sighed, then took a larger swig from his glass. Arrogance seeped from every corner of his being. "Yes, from where I'm sitting, you're in excellent shape." He leaned toward her and shifted his eyes up and down her body, until they came to rest on her boobs.

Not so much to see there.

She put her hand under his chin and forced him to look her in the eye. "You truly are disgusting."

Her comment didn't faze him. In fact, he grinned as if her words were a welcomed part of the game he'd been playing. She'd written him to view every woman as a challenge, but she never dreamed she'd be the one he'd pursue one day. His author. The ultimate conquest.

"So ..." He stroked the back of the couch like a lover. "Tell me, Traci. What do you love most about writing?"

Oh. That was unexpected. Did he really care? Or was this his way to get her talking and into bed? She'd answer his question, proceeding with caution.

"I love writing about relationships. *Genuine* love." She stared at him without blinking. Had she made her point?

"I see. And why is that?"

"Because ..." She took a breath. "Because people need to believe it exists. And it does." Like she'd told Andrew about writing happily ever afters. Still, no relationship would be happy without *real* love. After her horrible first marriage, Jack showed her the difference between good and bad men. He'd filled her heart with love. If it hadn't been there, she couldn't have written about it.

"*I* believe ..." He scooted closer, massaging the leather cushion with one hand while steadying his wineglass with the other. "I *truly* believe that deep inside of you, you love *me*." With his final words, he rested his hand on her leg.

194 · JEANNE HARDT

"Ha!" She nearly showered him with a mouthful of wine. "Love *you*?" She shoved his hand away. This game had gone too far.

Her action prompted an unconvincing pout. "Oh, Traci. You're breaking my heart. I know you feel something for me. You enjoyed writing my chapters. Didn't you?"

"Yes." Truthfully, it had been a lot of fun. What girl wasn't attracted for some strange, unknown reason to a bad boy? She'd written John as the baddest of bad.

"Well then, perhaps deep down inside that beautiful body of yours, you long to have me." He licked his lips, then raised his chin with that damn John Martin air of confidence.

She folded her hands together. "John, may I be perfectly honest with you?"

"Of course."

She nodded toward his lower extremities. "I wouldn't touch *that* with a ten-foot pole. I know where it's been."

He smirked. "You put it there." He was smug, and got that sly little grin she'd also created.

"Ugh!" She raised her fists in the air. Why did he have to be right?

"Traci—let's get this over with. You want me, and I'm *willing* to have you. Besides, I promise you a night you won't soon forget. I *assure* you, Jack won't mind."

He inched toward her.

Okay, enough is enough!

She jumped to her feet and faced him squarely. "I'll have you know …" She clinched her fists and made a conscious effort not to deck him. "You're the last man

Jack would ever want me to take to my bed! Jack always wanted the best for me, and that doesn't include having a fling with a notorious playboy!"

"Ah, Traci." He tilted his head and grinned. "You really should calm down." Then, he had the nerve to splay his hands and look at her with puppy eyes, as if it would help.

"Don't tell me to calm down! It's not all about sex, John! It's about love. *Real* love. Don't you get it?" Her breaths came out in heavy puffs. She'd better calm down or her blood pressure would shoot through the roof.

"If the sex doesn't matter so much, then why write about it, hmm?" He crossed one leg over the other, leaned back, and sipped his wine.

Damn his arrogance.

She shouldn't have to explain herself, but she wasn't about to let him win this argument.

"Because ... Because it's part of it. A beautiful part of love you somehow always manage to corrupt and make ugly." She shook her finger in his face. "Don't you *ever* throw Jack's name out again, like he's someone I could dismiss as easily as you toss away every woman in your life!"

Ready to bawl, she scooped up her laptop and made a dash for her bedroom. She had to get away from him. She locked the door, then backed up onto the bed and waited. If this didn't work she wasn't sure what she'd do.

"Traci?" John rapped at the door. "I'm sorry I upset you. Please, let me in."

"No. You can sleep on the sofa."

"I don't want to sleep. On the sofa, or *anywhere* for that matter. I promise to behave myself. Come out and we'll talk. I won't mention your husband again."

"You could learn a lot from Jack!"

Silence.

She crept to the door and pressed her ear to it. His heavy breathing proved he'd not left. What was he waiting for? He couldn't actually believe she'd open the door.

"Traci?" He lightly tapped on the wood. "Please forgive me. You know I can't help myself. You made me what I am. You should understand me better than anyone."

Ugh.

He hit her where it hurt the most. She'd created a monster, so why should she expect more from him? She should've let him freeze to death outside and never let him in in the first place.

Her other encounters were gentle—*caring*. They showed compassion over her loss. John didn't seem to care at all. He only wanted to get her between the sheets. And like she'd told him, it wasn't just about sex. She needed love. Something John didn't know how to give.

"Go away, John." She couldn't talk to him. He'd never understand. He'd not been created to comprehend women, only to use them.

Persistent as ever, he knocked again.

Deciding it best to ignore him, she worked on her manuscript.

A sense of accomplishment made her type even faster. She'd stood up to John Martin. She'd accomplished quite a feat. Getting angry, honestly felt kind of good.

But that's weird. Her emotional roller coaster ride twisted and turned with surprises.

After an hour went by, it seemed he'd finally given up. No more knocking. So she set the computer aside, then went to the door once again and pressed her ear to it. Nothing. However, she didn't dare go out to see if he was still in the house. She'd wait until morning, then hopefully he'd be gone.

* * *

Traci had typed nonstop until after 3:00 a.m. She woke with her laptop tucked in bed beside her and in desperate need of recharging.

Bright light filled the room from the open windows. Did she dare go into the living room?

Hopefully, he'd be gone. If not, she might be stuck with him for good. That would ruin everything. John Martin was the last man she wanted to spend eternity with.

Her hand shook, as she turned the knob and pulled the door open.

"John?" She tiptoed down the hallway.

Any moment, she expected to see him, yet there wasn't a trace of him.

Atop the coffee table in the spot where the manila envelope had been, *Incivilities, Southern Secrets, Book Four,* lay wide open.

Did John put it there?

Maybe he'd gone through the books in her office and found it. She scanned the page. It had been opened to a spot near the end. The top right-hand corner had been turned down and creased.

Crap, now he knows.

Would his knowledge of his own fate harm the book? How could it? It'd already been published, and nothing else that happened in her house had ever affected anyone. He'd vanished back into the literary world, probably in Victoria's arms now, being nicer than ever. His discovery might have been a good thing.

With renewed calm, Traci returned to her bedroom to retrieve the laptop. She couldn't waste any time today. If all went well, she'd have her book finished by late afternoon.

A note pinned to her door caught her eye. Aside from physical marks, no evidence of a nighttime visitor had ever been left behind. She flipped it open.

Traci,
Forgive my rudeness.
I am forever indebted to you for my creation.
With Sincerity,
John Martin

She gripped the note in her palm. Should she burn it? She held physical evidence. Proof of her sanity. Even so, how could she ever explain it to anyone?

At least he realized he'd been rude. There might be an ounce of decency in his body.

Still, some things needed to be kept hidden—including this note. She placed it in the secret compartment of her jewelry box. If ever found, it would prompt a mystery. No problem. She'd be long gone by then.

Her thoughts returned to Jack. She plugged in her laptop and got to work.

Chapter 16

"You finished it?"

The surprise in Vivian's voice made Traci laugh. "Yes, I did. I just sent it to you in an email attachment."

At least this time, Vivian was wide awake. And more alive than ever, now that Traci shared the news of her completed manuscript. Still, that could all change when Vivian opened the attachment and read it.

"So, tell me ..." Vivian almost tripped over her words. "What's it about this time? Is it medieval, or American history?"

"Neither."

"Oh. Want me to keep guessing?"

Sure. Go ahead. You'll never guess in a million years.

Traci held her breath. She needed to break this in a gentle way, but with a firm hand. This would be the first time ever that she required an immediate release. No time for a deep revision or heavy editing. It had to go into print as soon as possible. The publisher would have a fit. This sort of thing just wasn't done.

"Viv ..." *Just say it.* "It's different from my other books."

"That can be a good thing. Your readers will love whatever you've done. Especially if we get a good cover model." Even without seeing her, Traci knew Vivian had winked.

"We don't need a cover model. I attached a photo I want you to use."

"A photo? I don't understand."

"Tell you what, why don't you go to your computer and pull up what I sent. Then call me back after you've looked at it. It'll be easier to explain then."

"Would you rather stay on the line? I can pull it up while we talk."

"No. I'll hang up."

"Okay. But you're starting to scare me."

"I've been a little scared, too, Viv. Writing this book helped. I'll wait for your call."

Traci ended the call, then fixed herself a cup of coffee. No wine right now. She needed to keep her head clear for the upcoming conversation. Hopefully, Vivian's husband had been home to pick her up off the floor after she read the first few lines of the manuscript.

Silence hung in the air. So much so, that Traci began to pace. The perfect way to pass the time. But in her nervousness she spilled a bit of coffee and had to clean it up.

What's taking her so long?

She decided to sit and leisurely sip her drink. The ring of the cell jerked her out of her leisure. Luckily, she had a strong grip on her coffee cup.

"Hey, Viv!" Might as well sound cheerful.

"Traci, you're not serious about this, are you?"

"Of course I am. How much did you read?"

"I got to the chapter where you threw up after you rode the carnival ride."

Traci giggled. The disgust in Vivian's voice accentuated the event. "Yep. Not a fun time."

Vivian cleared her throat. "This isn't fiction, Traci. This is an autobiography. Granted, your readers *might* find it interesting, but it's not what they're expecting. You're not Dolly Parton. Your life hasn't been that exciting."

"I know. But, it's mine and Jack's life—together. Jason gave me the idea. He said we had a great love story."

"Yes, but this photo of you and Jack that you want on the cover? Why not use an old one? One from when you were first dating?"

"Because I want to show us the way we were right before he died. He was the man I continued to love after all those years. To me, he was still handsome. My Prince Charming."

Silence. For the first time in their history as partners, Vivian wasn't happy about Traci's *project*. A phone line didn't keep disappointment from coming through loud and clear.

"I'll have to run it by the publisher," Vivian finally said, with a sigh.

"They *have* to print it."

"Traci, it's not what they asked for. We may need to go a different direction."

"I don't care how it gets done, I want it in print. And I want it out before Christmas." She wasn't about to take no for an answer. She wanted Jack home for the holiday. *Forever* if she could somehow make it work.

"Christmas? We're contracted for a late January release. You know they can't get a book out that fast."

"They can if they really want to."

Silence again.

"Vivian, if I have to, I'll self-publish. I know a lot of authors are doing it. I can figure it out."

"No." Vivian held her ground, just as firm. "I'll see what I can do."

"Thank you." Traci's heart rested.

She didn't want to have to make an attempt to format something for any of the self-publishing venues. It wasn't her forte. But, she'd do whatever she had to in order to accomplish her goal. The only man she'd ever wanted in her life—not to mention in her *bed*—had always been Jack. If she had to overcome her fear of formatting a manuscript, then so be it.

Vivian ended the call with another pronounced sigh.

Was my life so dull and boring it won't sell books?

It could be that Vivian feared the unknown. She could be horrified they'd have another *Crimson Kilts*. This book wouldn't even have the same eye appeal. There'd be no bare-chested man in a kilt on the cover, only an over-weight old man in a gray suit with brown eyes that sparkled when he laughed, who'd been captured in a photo with her at his retirement party.

Nothing sexy, just ... *Jack.*

Far-fetched? Maybe so. Since nothing in her life lately seemed real, why not tamper with the unknown and shoot for the moon? And even if she could only have him one Friday night at a time, she'd take him that way. Simply to be held in his arms again. That's all she wanted.

Vivian had less than three weeks to read through the manuscript and take it to the publisher to plead their case. This time of year was hectic in the industry to begin with. Putting pressure like this on anyone almost guaranteed negative results. Still, it could be done. It *had* to be done. Jason and Amy would be in Europe for Christmas, and Traci didn't want to be alone.

She wasn't about to ask Jason to fly home again to see her. He needed to stay with Amy now more than ever. Hopefully, Christmas joy would overshadow their baby frustrations.

My plan has to work.

With the manuscript finished, Traci was restless. She peered out the window. With no snow falling, she decided to head downtown.

I really am crazy.

The Christmas rush would be in full force and the streets bursting with shoppers. The bumper-to-bumper traffic she hated was inevitable, but she didn't want to stay at home and pace. In a weird way, she'd be taking a step in the right direction.

She dressed warm, and took along a scarf so she could wrap her face when she walked down the street. If luck happened to be on her side, no one would recognize her.

She parked in the lot behind Calhoun's and passed by her favorite jewelry shop, Angelic Whispers. She'd make a point to swing in there on her way out. Something always caught her eye there.

Being a weekday, it wasn't as bad as she feared. Lots of people, but nowhere close to how many would be there over the weekend.

The Parkway bustled with holiday shoppers. The main street lay on the rise of a hill, so depending on which way she'd go, she could get quite a workout. In no time at all, she was winded. The price she paid for sitting at home on her rear for hours on end.

I need to start taking better care of myself.

A waft of sweet-smelling enticement drifted by, and she had to follow her stomach to the funnel cake vendor. Not the healthiest choice, but too delicious to deny. The more powdered sugar, the better.

She took a seat on a bench and enjoyed the warm, delicious treat. So much like a doughnut, yet ten times tastier.

Another weight had been lifted from her shoulders. She'd finished the book, resulting in a pleasant sense of peace. Something she didn't quite understand, but accepted without question.

I'm happy.

She broke off a bite of her pastry and stared at it. A smile warmed her even more than the dough. People passed by her with smiles of their own. The holiday spirit filled the air. A magical time of year that made even the grumpiest of scrooges plaster grins on their faces. She didn't feel this way last year. It had all been too fresh. She'd come a long way.

Tipping her head upward, she looked toward the mountains. Snowcapped peaks stood high above the tree lines. The infamous *smoke* that hovered over them lay heavy. The low-lying clouds made the mountains appear ominous—as if hidden secrets lay below their wispy masses.

Her home happened to be one of those secrets. Maybe the mountains held magic. *Maybe ...*

A tiny bell rang when she pushed open the door of Angelic Whispers. Everything in the store had been handmade by the owner. Rows and rows of earrings in every color imaginable lined the walls. In addition, there were sets with matching necklaces. Everything was reasonably priced and lasted forever.

Usually when Traci came here, she searched for a particular color to match something she already had. Today she just wanted to look.

She lowered her scarf. Having only seen one other customer in the store, she decided to take the risk.

"Are you looking for anything special?" the owner asked. She sat perched on a stool, working on a new item. Traci had never seen her idle, or without a smile on her face.

"No. Just looking."

"It's nice to see you again, Mrs. Oliver," the woman said, with her constant smile.

"Thank you." Traci approached the counter. "You're always so kind and know me by name. I'm afraid I don't know yours."

"I'm Kasey." She grinned. "Of course, everyone in Gatlinburg knows *you*."

"Even with my gray hair?" Traci shook her head. What should it matter? "Don't answer that." She didn't want to put the poor woman on the spot. "And please, call me Traci. As much jewelry as I've bought here, I feel like we're old friends."

Kasey brightened. "I appreciate your business—and your books, for that matter. I think I've read most all of them."

"Well then, it seems we've helped support each other. We *should* be on a first-name basis."

"I'm proud to be." Kasey sat a little taller on her stool. "Let me know if you need help finding something."

Traci smiled and nodded. The other customer had approached the sales counter, so she meandered through the small shop and scanned the numerous items. A feeling of tranquility surrounded her that was hard to explain. No pressure to buy, just women shopping for something to decorate themselves with. No expensive diamonds or rubies, rather colorful bobbles carefully crafted by hand. Nothing elaborate. Simple, but beautiful.

The bell jingled as the customer exited, leaving her and Kasey alone.

"Kasey?" Traci paused and admired an old mirror that hung on the wall. "I'm curious, what made you name your shop, *Angelic Whispers*?"

Kasey stood from her stool. "After my parents passed away, I thought it'd be a way to honor their memory." She pointed toward the mirror. "All of the decorations you see were from them, as well as others in my life that passed away. They're reminders of people I've lost."

"Where did the mirror come from?"

"My grandfather. It used to hang in what we would now call a mud room. He called it a parlor." She laughed softly. "Whenever I went there, he'd tell me to go and look for the angel in the mirror."

"And that angel was you, wasn't it?"

Kasey nodded with a bright smile. What a wonderful memory to hold onto. No wonder this shop felt so tranquil. The walls held a lot of love within them.

"So, you're surrounded by memories that whisper to you with the voices of angels?" Traci's heart fluttered.

"Yes. In many ways." The woman laughed. "I don't actually hear voices. The memories speak to me."

She didn't have to explain *that* to Traci. Memories of Jack kept her going.

"But, there *is* something else." She moved from behind the counter and led Traci to a beautiful angel doll with long blond curls and gold wings. The wings moved in a lulling fashion, and the doll held an illuminated star. "Her name is Miss Ginny. My boys bought her for me after my mom died. Mom's name was Virginia, so that's how we came up with the name for the doll." She placed her hand on Traci's arm. "Sometimes Ginny can be mischievous. She surprises us all from time to time when she makes little noises."

"So, your angels *do* speak?"

"Maybe. Ginny's very special. She's the first thing I turn on in the morning, and the last thing I turn off at night."

"She's gorgeous." Traci fingered the doll's white wispy dress. "Do you believe in *real* angels?"

"Yes, I do." Kasey looked her in the eye. "I think they're all around us."

Traci smiled, then returned her attention to Ginny, mesmerized by her pulsing wings.

"A while back," Kasey went on, "I had a house fire and lost everything. You can't imagine how grateful I was to have so many treasures here in my shop. It makes these mementos even more valuable to me."

"I'm so sorry." Traci didn't know what she'd do if her precious home went up in flames.

"Thank you. But even if I'd lost everything, I'd still have the memories." Kasey returned to her seat and picked up her project.

Traci stood facing Ginny a little longer. A chill crept down her back and made her shudder. Yes, something special resided in this shop.

After thanking Kasey for taking the time to share her stories, Traci left with a promise to return soon and a headful of thoughts about angels.

* * *

"Jason? I hope I didn't wake you up." Traci never knew a good time to call.

"No, Mom. Amy and I were just getting ready for bed."

The tone of his voice almost always gave him away. He sounded pretty good. Much better than when he left Gatlinburg. "Is everything going well?"

His voice was muffled, and she couldn't make out his words. "Jason? Are you still there?"

"I'm here. Sorry about that. I just told Amy I'd be right there."

"Oh. Did I interrupt something?" She cleared her throat. Could she have been any more obvious?

He chuckled. "We're fine, Mom. I should've called you sooner. I didn't want you to worry about us."

"Good. I'm glad. But that worry thing—it won't ever go away. It comes with being a mom."

"We're going to Paris for Christmas. Wanna come?"

Paris. She loved Paris. Tempting, but she had other things to do. People to see. A husband to bring back from the dead for the reunion of a lifetime. Paris paled in comparison.

"I'm not ready to fly." Seemed like a good excuse. Easier than telling him the truth. "However, I appreciate the offer."

"Are you sure?"

"Yep. I just called to check on you. I'm glad you're okay. Now, get back to Amy. And please give her my love."

"I will, Mom. We'll call again soon."

After saying *I love you,* they ended the call.

That night when she put her head on the pillows, a real smile warmed her face. Somehow she knew Jason and Amy would be all right. Maybe they had a *Miss Ginny* watching over them. Peace covered her along with her down comforter. Sweet dreams awaited her.

Soon, Jack. Soon.

Chapter 17

Traci clapped her hands and laughed, ready for another Friday night. Now that she knew it was unnecessary to stick to the script, or even take them to her room to get them to disappear, she could deal with anyone who came through her door.

If John Martin returned, she'd give him a real piece of her mind this time, and try to teach him a thing or two about how to properly treat a woman. She doubted the sincerity of his apology note. The man always had underlying motives.

She might as well teach something to all of her characters. After all, she'd done wonders for Gerald Alexander.

She planned to enjoy the adventure, but wouldn't sleep with any of them ever again. Not even Andrew. She'd save herself for Jack, and only him.

With all her binge eating, she'd packed on another five pounds since Thanksgiving. Time to buy healthier food. Otherwise, she'd have to invest in a new wardrobe. At least she felt good. As happy as she'd been getting her appetite back, the chocolate cravings would have to be dealt with.

Vivian had called to let her know she was still working on the publisher. They hadn't been happy. They'd expected the world's greatest romance novel, not an autobiography with a photo of a slightly chubby man on the cover. Even so, Vivian sounded hopeful. If she could talk them into it, the book *might* hit the shelves Christmas week.

Traci assumed they'd be chomping at the bit to get it out before Christmas. It would be an opportunity to rake in some extra holiday cash. After all, money mattered to them. For her, it was much, much more.

Boxes filled with family heirloom Christmas decorations lined her living room wall. One box held the artificial tree, and she was determined to get it up tonight.

Her visitor could help decorate. She chuckled at the thought, then went to her sound system and selected a Christmas CD. This one had an assortment of Christmas favorites by a number of different artists. Bing Crosby's *White Christmas* was one of the best.

After dragging an end table from the living room into the guest bedroom, she cleared the spot for the tree. It would sit to the left of the fireplace—where it had always been in years past. Then, she opened the box and pulled out the instructions. No matter how many times she put this thing together, she still had to read them.

She fluffed each branch and poked it into its proper place, and when the tree was done, she stood back to admire her work. Yes, she could afford a pre-lit tree, but she liked this one. Jason had picked it out, and it had endured the last fifteen years. It was perfectly formed for hanging their many ornaments—those little pieces of Christmases past.

At the top of one of the ornament boxes lay an extra special memory—a castle given to her when she released her first medieval, *Island in the Forest*. She cradled it in her palm.

Nope. Lights first.

While stringing the lights, the knock came.

With a cheerful spring in her step, she opened the door without bothering to look in the monitor. Nothing or nobody would dampen her Christmas spirit.

"Lady Traci?"

She clasped her hands together. They were in for a fun night. He started it by calling her *lady* and his bouncing blond curls made her grin.

"Jonah?" Who else could he be? He looked exactly the way she wrote him. Around five feet seven inches and dressed in tights and a cloak. Of course, the blond curls were a dead giveaway. She'd just held the ornament, and now—here he was. The defender of the castle and servant to Prince Sebastian.

"Yes, m'lady." He bowed low, then took her hand and kissed it.

Such a gentleman.

"I'm surprised it's you and not Sebastian." Sebastian had been the hero in that book. Jonah was his sidekick and one of her favorite characters.

He frowned. "Are you disappointed?"

"No. Not at all. Please, come in and have some eggnog."

"Eggnog?" His lip curled.

"It's very good. It's sweet, and if you'd like, I can give it a little *kick*." She punched her fist in the air to make her point.

"A kick?"

"Never mind. Go have a seat on the sofa. I'll be right there."

She had to remind herself that these characters didn't understand present-day quips. She'd need to speak in Old English for the remainder of the evening if she wanted to have a decent conversation.

Eggnog wasn't on her diet. Then again, neither was she. She hated dieting. Any word that started with *die* was meant to be troublesome. She'd concentrate on her figure *after* the holidays.

She handed him a ceramic mug shaped like Santa's head, and he eyed it quizzically.

"Santa Claus," she said, pointing to the cup. "He's a symbol of Christmas nowadays."

"Oh."

"Try it."

He tipped the cup, then drank it down. A large smile covered his previously cautious face. He licked his lips. "It is good."

She stood and got him some more. "Would you like to help me decorate the tree? I was just getting started."

"Very well. Tell me what to do."

So polite ...

She'd written Jonah as a complainer, so his demeanor surprised her. Possibly, he had the Christmas spirit like everyone else in Gatlinburg. Once she'd gotten him hanging ornaments, he seemed to be thoroughly enjoying himself.

From the corner of her eye he looked somewhat like a Christmas elf in his forest green tights. She had to keep herself from laughing.

"You appear very joyful," Jonah said, while looping an angel ornament over a bough.

"I am. I've always loved this time of year. And ..." She beamed, unable to control herself. "I have something to look forward to."

"A gift?"

"You could say that." She didn't want to say aloud what she hoped would happen. Somehow she feared it would ruin it.

He pointed at the castle she hung on the tree. "It reminds me of home. It is very finely made."

"Vivian gave it to me when *Island in the Forest* was released. She knew I love castles."

"My book?"

"Yes, your book." Funny he should ask that question. She still couldn't quite grasp that her characters knew they came from her books, and that she'd created them. "Jonah, are you happy in Basilia?"

He nodded rapidly. "Very happy. But—Lady Traci ..." He stepped away from the tree. "May we sit and talk for a moment?"

"Of course." The tree was nearly finished and talking had been exactly what she'd had in mind.

She was at ease with him, with no burning desire to whisk him away. It could have something to do with the elf suit. But more than that, she'd made up her mind to wait patiently for Jack.

They settled on the sofa with another mug of eggnog and watched the crackling fire.

"I could live here forever," he said, looking around the room. "It is warm and very comfortable."

"Yes, it is. That's one reason I didn't want to leave here after Jack died."

"And your memories are the other reasons." He nodded to her with a silent salute.

"Yes. You know about my memories?"

"Only what you have shown me. I know you loved your husband very much. That thought was forefront in your mind when you penned our story. Your thoughts also revealed other things when you wrote about me, but ..." He held the Santa mug in his lap. "Lady Traci, what I truthfully wish to speak of is my concern about Allana."

Where did that come from? "Why?"

"As I said, I only know what you put in my mind. I have no idea what I'm going to do with Allana when I'm alone with her—once we're married, of course."

This had to be a joke. Jonah had been notorious for his activities with women. He didn't rank up there on the *nasty* scale with John Martin, but he'd had his share of romps in the hay. "Jonah, you can't be serious."

"But, I am."

"All the stories you told Sebastian—"

"Now, wait." He held up his hand. "Every story I *began* to tell Sebastian. If you remember correctly, every time you wrote one of our conversations, you stopped me before I could give any details. Therefore, I do not know *what* I did with any of those women. You never elaborated."

She drew back. He had a good point. "I couldn't. If I had, the book would've become borderline erotica—not my sub-genre. I had to leave things to my reader's imaginations."

"Don't you see? Since you were vague, I haven't a clue as to what I need to do."

Wow. She never thought about it like that. "Jonah, you won't have any trouble. It's natural. Trust me."

"Natural? I'm supposed to be experienced. I'm as much a maid as Allana."

Traci couldn't help herself and let out a chuckle. "I'm sorry. I don't mean to laugh, but you of all people—you have a reputation."

"One which *you* created. It's no laughing matter. When Allana and I finally wed, she'll expect me to know things. I know nothing. What will I do?"

His persistence pained her. The sad look in his eyes reminded her of Sparky when he'd curled up with Jason, trying to comfort him. Then, she had an idea. Jonah could read, so why not let him read a proper love scene? Maybe even *several*.

"Follow me." She waved him toward her office.

After grabbing *Deceptions* from its place, she flipped through it until she found Claire and Andrew's first love scene. Perfectly pure and tender—the way he needed to treat Allana. She'd do all she could to steer him far away from the scenes between John Martin and Victoria.

Not so pure.

"Have a seat and read," she said, and handed him the book. "And when you're done with this one, I'll find the appropriate chapters in the others. You should get some good ideas from these."

He sat in her leather office chair, and she flipped on the desk lamp.

"Magic surrounds me," he said, eyeing the lamp. "Instant fire without heat, and music that surrounds us without an instrument in sight. You are not only my creator, you're a wizard."

"Nope. That's J.K. Rowling's territory, not mine. I just write love stories."

"May I have more eggnog while I read?"

"Sure." She left him to retrieve his Santa mug from the coffee table.

She couldn't erase the smile from her face.

Am I more like Alice in Wonderland *or Dorothy from* The Wizard of Oz? Somehow she'd been caught up in her own magical fairytale, but unlike them, already home.

Home? Is it a place or Jack himself? Clicking her heels together wouldn't bring him here. Hopefully, getting his book in print might. She had more hope than ever.

She took Jonah his eggnog, but he hardly noticed her. His eyes remained glued to the page. So, she left him alone and went to finish putting the remaining ornaments on the tree.

"Angels We Have Heard on High" played, as she added tinsel to the decorated boughs. She smiled, thinking about Miss Ginny and Kasey's beautiful little shop.

Could Jonah be an angel? Maybe they all were. Still, why would angels want to make love to her? It didn't seem *Biblical.*

She hadn't been to confession in years, and she wasn't about to start again now. Though priests were sworn to secrecy, and she believed were acting on God's behalf, she wouldn't want to give hers a heart attack. Confessing to fornication with characters from books would probably be one he'd never heard before.

He definitely won't hear it from ME.

She intended to go to Mass on Christmas Eve. She was overdue. Besides, a few added prayers said properly at the altar couldn't hurt.

"Lady Traci?" Jonah crept into the room with a book in hand. "Can you please explain this to me?"

"What?"

He cleared his throat. *"And then it happened. A strange, but intoxicating sensation swept over her, beginning at the point of their union and bursting out all the way to the tips of her fingers and toes."* He wiped his brow with the back of his hand. "Are you saying women feel something *special* from the act?"

She looked at the spine. *Marked.* He'd helped himself to another book and found the love scene. Not too difficult since they were in every novel. "Yes. Sometimes. If it's good." Her cheeks heated. This situation proved to be more uncomfortable than anything she'd written.

"Oh. And, making it *good* is up to me?"

"Yes. Well—that is—the man is a very important part of it. It takes *both* people to make it exceptional." She waved him back to the office. "Go and read some more. Then, if you still have questions, I'll try to answer."

This time she wasn't Mrs. Robinson—*thank goodness* —more like Dr. Ruth.

Whatever happened to her?

She poured herself another mug of eggnog, then plugged in the tree lights and sat on the sofa to admire them. *Memories.* Barring some unforeseen medical condition that robbed her of them, they couldn't be taken from her. Each ornament held at least one: The tiny baby booties from Jason's first Christmas, the crystal heart Vivian gave her the year she got her first contract, the crocheted candy canes that old Mrs. Thornton from St. Mary's made, and that cute framed photo of Jason from Kindergarten. And so many more.

Hmm ... maybe I can get Jonah's nose out of those books and have him watch It's a Wonderful Life *with me.*

It felt like the right thing to do. She'd finally stopped feeling sorry for herself and realized what a blessing her life had been. She didn't die with Jack, and as long as she held tight to his memories, he wasn't dead either.

"Hey, Jonah!" She giggled. "Want to see some *real* magic?"

He popped his head out from the office. "More magic?"

"Yes. And a nice love story, too. Don't worry, you can read more later."

He set down the book in his hand and joined her in the living room.

"Get comfortable on the sofa," she said over her shoulder. "I'm going to make some popcorn. It's pretty magical, too."

"Yes, m'lady."

The aroma of freshly popped corn filled the room after she nuked a few bags and astonished him even more. Then she put the DVD in the player and settled down beside him. His eyes popped wide at the sight of the magical frame. She doubted he'd be offended by the kissing—especially after reading her books.

"You truly are a wizard," he said, munching on popcorn. "I can't wait to tell Sebastian about my adventure here."

"Better than going to Black Wood?"

He shuddered. "Far better. I am forever indebted to you, m'lady."

No, she was indebted to him. This would be a night to remember. She was making a happy memory with a good friend.

Chapter 18

What a fun night.

Traci and Jonah stayed up well past midnight. She finally told him goodnight and tucked the fleece throw around him on the sofa. He made no objections. There had never been expectations of something more coming from their night together. She suspected he might return to her office for more reading once she'd gone to her room.

Though she hated waking to an empty house, she jumped right up. Even before making coffee, she plugged in the Christmas tree.

The tree was missing something.

Presents.

Why would there be any? Until she got a package from Jason ...

Damn!

Only two weeks until Christmas, and she hadn't purchased their gifts.

What was I thinking? They'll never make it overseas in time.

She'd always frowned on the idea, but decided to do a bit of online shopping. It would be the only way to get the gifts to them by Christmas. After going from site to site, she finally ended up ordering matching sweaters, assorted chocolates, and an automated angel—much like Miss Ginny at Angelic Whispers. She'd also wire money. Sending money alone never felt right. She liked receiving something tangible, and she assumed they did, too.

Her Christmas spirit wasn't at all dampened; in fact she was bursting at the seams. Once again, she was a child waiting for that special present on Christmas morning.

God, I hope I'm not disappointed.

She looked at the clock. Too early to call Vivian to check on her progress with the publisher. As far as she knew, they hadn't said, *no,* so she still had hope.

Feeling hungry, she went to the kitchen to scramble some eggs. With a small amount of cream cheese left over from Thanksgiving, she made herself an omelet.

She hummed as she flipped the fluffy eggs over. Filled with a sense of accomplishment, she pushed her masterpiece onto a plate, then carried it into the living room and flopped down on the sofa.

The throw lay in a heap on the floor. It had served its purpose for Jonah, and now, merely a reminder of what, or *who,* had once been here. It would be interesting to see how these illusions disappeared.

One night she'd have to stay awake long enough to witness it. Would they be like a mist that kept growing thinner until they were gone from sight, or would they be *beamed up* like the crew on *Star Trek?*

"Mmm ... this is good." She savored the omelet. She couldn't remember the last time she'd fixed one like this.

After polishing off her breakfast, she went to the atrium to water the plants, then after milling around and pacing, she decided it would be safe to call Vivian.

"Hello?"

"Hey, Viv! It's Traci."

"You sure sound chipper."

"I didn't wake you up, did I?"

"Not this time. What's up?"

Why did she even ask? Of course, there had to be only one reason for her to call. It was probably just her way of being polite.

Traci had learned from Vivian not to beat around the bush, so she got right to it. "Well, how are things coming along with the publisher?"

"You mean, with the book?"

What a dumb question. "Of course with the book. There's not a problem is there?"

The silence that followed made Traci's stomach ache.

"Well ..." The tremor in Vivian's voice made matters worse.

"Tell me."

"Does it *have* to be out by Christmas?"

Traci wanted to jump up and down, and scream and yell, *of course it does,* but instead, she kept her cool. "I'd like it to be."

"You're asking a lot."

"I know. It's just that ... having it come out *now* makes more sense than January."

"Traci, can I be honest with you?"

Her heart pounded. The book *had* to be published now. "Go ahead."

"They like the book and have agreed to publish it, but want more time to promote it. They think they can get greater sales with a huge buildup to the release. They'd like to get you on some talk shows and news broadcasts to hype it up. With the rush you're asking for, it's not possible."

How could she make her understand? It wasn't about money or hype—or talk shows. She didn't care how many books sold, she simply wanted it out there. *Anywhere.*

"What about a limited release?" Traci asked. "Say— only to a few local stores in Gatlinburg? Anything in print would do."

"That makes no sense, Traci. I don't understand why you have to have it *now,* when a few months ago you had nothing written and didn't seem to be concerned about it."

Traci stared mindlessly across the room. Her bright spirit had been doused. Did it matter whether Jack came for Christmas, or New Year's, or even next Halloween as long as he came?

Yes, it did. She stomped her right foot and gripped the phone tighter. He *had* to be home for Christmas. Her heart counted on it.

"Traci? Are you still there?" Vivian's voice sounded timid.

"I'm here. So in a nutshell—even though you said you got them to agree to publish it—they want to do it in their own time. Not mine. Right?"

"Yes. I'm sorry, Traci. But you know the industry better than anyone."

"Yes, I do. Still—can't you try? Get it out for Christmas, and we can hype up an after-Christmas sale. Please?"

"I'll talk to them."

"Thank you. I appreciate anything you can do."

"Traci, you aren't going to be alone for the holidays, are you?"

Not if I can help it.

"No. I'm going to Mass on Christmas Eve, and Karla Peterson invited me for Christmas dinner. Don't worry about me. I'll be fine."

"Sure you don't want to fly to L.A.?"

"No. Thank you anyway. You're the best, Vivian, and I can't thank you enough for all you do. Even so, I want to stay here."

They ended their conversation with a promise to catch up again next week. Traci would cross her fingers and pray the publishers would grant her Christmas wish and push the publication forward. If she listened to sensibility, it wouldn't be possible. The industry just didn't work like that.

Definitely a longshot, but my prayers have been answered before.

* * *

Talk about memories ...

Traci hadn't made shaped sugar cookies since Jason attended elementary school. Since she expected a guest tonight, it seemed like a good idea. She even frosted them and decorated them with colored sprinkles.

As the clock clicked closer to eight past seven, she heated milk for hot cocoa.

Not the proper food for a romantic evening, but she wasn't expecting one. She hoped for another night like last Friday with Jonah. With a vast selection of Christmas DVDs, she could easily entertain her guest.

The house smelled fantastic. She floated about with a smile on her face, breathing in the scent of freshly baked cookies, topped off with aromatic hot cocoa. Hopefully, whoever came for a visit would appreciate her efforts and share her fondness for sweets.

When the knock came on the door, she answered it with a sing-song, "Just a minute."

Decked out in a green Christmas sweater and blue jeans, with jingle bell earrings, she didn't really care who'd knocked. She only hoped it would be one of her nice, happy, easy-to-get-along-with characters. Someone willing to have a good time.

She swung the door wide.

"Hello, Traci." Andrew smiled and nodded.

After her visit with Claire, she didn't think Andrew would come back again. She gaped for a brief moment, then recovered her surprise and returned his gracious smile. She'd never be unhappy to see him.

"Merry Christmas, Andrew." She took him by the arm and led him inside.

He gestured toward the tree. "Your tree is lovely. Claire and I just erected ours."

Don't go there, Traci.

She had to keep her mind going in the right direction. "So, it's Christmas in Mobile now, too?"

"Yes, it is." He brushed snow from his shoulders. "But we don't have the snow that you do."

She wanted to hug him. He was so familiar to her now, he might as well be Jack walking through the door—the husband she longed for.

Nope. She wasn't about to cause problems between him and Claire. Claire was too sweet to hurt again. Besides, she'd made a promise to herself she intended to keep. Touching him in any fashion wouldn't be wise.

"Would you like some cocoa? Or how about a sugar cookie?"

He tipped his head. "Thank you. I would very much."

He took a seat in front of the fire and appeared as comfortable in her home as she was with him. She made a tray of goodies, then carried it out and set it on the coffee table.

"I'm surprised you came back," she said, and handed him a mug. Not one with Santa on it this time. These were a set of Christmas mugs with *Ho, Ho, Ho* printed on the sides.

"Why? I enjoy our visits."

"So do I. But Claire ..."

"Claire has been troubled since she came to see you. So, I reassured her that you and I are strictly friends. Nothing more." He took a bite out of one of the cookies and then grinned. "I love sweets."

"Me, too."

And you're one of the sweetest men I've ever encountered.

Regardless of the fact she'd created him, having him sit here before her made him a real man. The hero with Jack's heart—the part of him she cherished the most. Unfortunately, it also happened to be the part that gave out and ended his life.

In many ways, Jack stared her in the face. Maybe Andrew didn't have Jack's eyes, or anything that resembled him, but he was Jack where it mattered most. And though she'd promised herself she wouldn't sleep with any of her visitors, Andrew tugged at her core.

My core …

Was that what Cordelia meant as the core of her encounters? That longing she felt when she wanted to be near a man?

After spinning it around her brain, she disregarded it. Bottom line, it didn't make sense. She had to fight the need to take him to her bedroom, which would likely lead to sex and ruin the promise she'd made to herself and Jack. If she broke it, she'd have something huge to feel guilty about and be ashamed of. No matter what Cordelia had said.

She wished it wasn't so, but the ongoing debate in her mind had two sides. The little devil had come back again, battling the angel on the other shoulder. Would it hurt to allow herself to get lost in Andrew's arms one more time? She had no guarantee her plan with Jack would work, and Andrew seemed more like him than any of her other visitors. Maybe he was supposed to be Jack's replacement.

No. No one can replace Jack.

She stared at Andrew's defined cheekbones and the formation of his lips. Their lovemaking lingered in her memory, more wonderful than she dared to recall.

Don't think about it!

"How are you faring?" He rested back against the cushions and looked even more gorgeous.

Why does he have to make it so difficult?

"I'm doing better. Each day gets a little easier." True, and it would've been even more so if Jonah had come back instead of Andrew.

"That's good. You have a great deal of life remaining."

His comment took her aback. "Do you know that for certain? I mean—do you have some sort of connection with God or something?"

He laughed in a sophisticated way. Not stuffy, but refined and educated. "No. I'm speaking as a doctor. You're quite healthy. And ... you have more color in your cheeks than the last time I saw you."

She'd probably been flushing a brilliant red. With him around, heat remained in her cheeks. He warmed her to the tips of her toes. She sipped her cocoa and tried to ignore the needful ache that had been pulling her toward the bedroom.

I have to wait for Jack.

"What do you like best about being a doctor?" she asked. Good idea. Change the course of the conversation.

He sat up straight. "I like helping people. You know my history, and what happened to my mother."

"Yes, I do."

"It feels good in here," he said, and touched his hand

to his chest, "when I help take the pain away. I don't care to see anyone suffer."

"And that's why you came to me. That first night you said you were here to help me. I'm right, aren't I?"

He nodded. "And, please tell me. Have I helped?"

"Yes, you all have. Somewhere along the way I stopped feeling sorry for myself. Don't get me wrong—I still miss Jack. But, it's easier now."

"I'm glad."

She swallowed the lump in her throat. Time to ask the question she'd been dying to ask. "Andrew? Are you an angel?"

He stood from the sofa and moved in front of the tree. *A perfect picture.*

Before he could answer, she rushed to her office for her camera. Why hadn't she thought of it before? A picture would prove he was real.

He questioned her with his eyes.

"No. Don't move. Just smile." She centered him in the frame and pushed the button. "There." Yep, as real as anything.

"So ..." She set the camera aside. "Are you? An angel, that is?"

"Why do you think so?"

She moved beside him. "It's the only explanation. You can't be real." Being this close to him wasn't a good idea. Her pulse quickened, and she wanted to touch him.

"I'm as real as you believe me to be." He placed his hand against her cheek, the way he had that very first night—exactly the way Jack used to. "Have you had enough cocoa?"

His eyes penetrated hers, and she had to look away.

It would've been easy leading him down the hall. Instead, she backed away. "I think I'll have another cup." She scurried to the kitchen and braced herself against the counter.

The way Andrew had touched her ripped her in two. He behaved more like Jack than she ever realized, but no matter how similar they might be, he wasn't Jack. That horrible feeling returned. Her throat dried, and her stomach knotted. Her eyes puddled full of tears. What if Jack never came back? What if none of them did?

Wanting to run into Andrew's arms, she tightened her grip on the counter.

Just breathe ...

The ache in her heart grew, but she wouldn't allow her tears to fall. She simply had to pour another cup of cocoa and return to Andrew for a night filled with nothing more than conversation. It was wrong to want more. Regardless of whether or not she'd become Claire if they walked into her bedroom, she was still Traci. She might look like Claire, but *Traci* felt every touch, every caress— every kiss from his delicious mouth.

She banged her head against the cupboard, yet couldn't beat out the memory of his lips.

She shouldn't have made sugar cookies and cocoa. It would've been a better idea to serve him garlic bread—or pizza with anchovies. Then it would've been easier to keep her distance.

Why hadn't he been a horrible kisser with bad breath and too much saliva?

Because you wrote him really well, dummy.

Her first hero. She poured her heart and soul into Andrew and made him her perfect man. Perfect looks, perfect kisses, perfect body parts. *Complete FICTION.*

Jack had been real. Not so perfect, but still the best thing that ever happened in her life. He was worth waiting for. Come hell or high water, she would *not* take Andrew to bed.

She plastered a smile on her face and returned to him. He'd taken a seat again on the sofa and appeared at ease.

"These cookies are truly delicious," he said, and took another bite.

"I'm glad you like them. I can pass on the recipe to Claire if you want."

He nodded. "Claire is a remarkable cook. I have you to thank for that, don't I?"

"I guess you do. I wrote her that way."

Traci could take credit for everything they were. Warmth filled her belly and replaced that awful ache that lay there only moments ago.

She'd always marveled at how her friends and fans would talk about her characters as though they existed. One fan had told her that when she read her books, she added a whole new addition to her list of friends. And she especially loved the series books because she could share in the continued lives of her *friends.*

What an incredible gift. How many times had she taken for granted the fact that she'd made women smile? And some men, too. Of course, she believed the men smiled for different reasons. They weren't as prone to making *friends* from reading romance.

She'd never forget the man who asked her to dog-ear

the corners of the love scenes. After abiding by his request, she'd signed his book: *Get a life ... I'm serious ... Traci Oliver.*

When he read it, he'd laughed out loud and strode away. Every fan had been different but had one thing in common. The love of a good story. Or a good love scene if they were anything like Mr. *Get a Life.*

"Andrew?" She propped her feet up on the coffee table. "If I could change your story at all, would you want me to?"

He cradled his cup of cocoa, then stared into the fire. "Selfishly, yes."

"Because of Gerald?"

He nodded. "And I understand why you wrote it the way you did." When he shifted his body to face her, tears glistened in his eyes. "Gerald needed Claire as much as I did. But I'm grateful she came back to me."

Traci's own tears bubbled up again and spilled over onto her cheeks. Would Jack come back to her? And what if he'd never come into her life at all? She doubted she'd ever have known real love.

"Andrew. I know now why I love you."

"You love me?"

"Yes." Gingerly, she touched his chest. "Jack is in there. From the minute you stepped into my house, a part of Jack returned. The part I love and miss the most."

He took her hand and held it. Nothing sensual. He held it like a friend. "You know you'll see him again."

"In Heaven?"

"Of course." A playful smile turned the corners of his lips. He obviously held something back, but she didn't want to push him. She wouldn't reveal her plan to him for fear of spoiling it.

"I considered taking you to my room, Andrew. But I changed my mind. No matter how much I love you, you'll never be Jack."

"And you aren't Claire. So your decision was best for both of us." He raised her hand to his lips and gave it a tender kiss.

Somehow, everything felt right now. They stared at one another for what seemed like a long time, then he released her hand, and she pulled it to herself. Their tears had dried.

Her heart lifted. Now she wanted to do something fun. Since their feelings were out in the open, they could be friends.

She suggested they watch the moving frame, and chose something without kissing. At least not the kind he'd seen before.

"Yes, it's the work of Charles Dickens," she said as she inserted the DVD. "In a way you should find entertaining."

He claimed familiarity with *A Christmas Carol,* but had no concept of Mr. Magoo. She explained that it happened to be her favorite version of the classic story. Most of all, she liked the music, and as it turned out, so did Andrew.

They remained on the sofa, until she fell asleep with her head on his shoulder. Her last memory of their night together was when he kissed the top of her head and said, "Sleep well, Traci." Oddly, she could've sworn he sounded just like Jack.

Chapter 19

Traci startled when the buzzer for the front gate went off. At least it was midday and not a Friday. She shouldn't be scared of an alarm—especially from the entrance gate. Her visitors always came to the front door.

She pushed the intercom button. "May I help you?"

"UPS, ma'am. I have a delivery for Traci Oliver."

"Thank you." She keyed in the automated entry to open the front gate. Since she hadn't ordered anything lately, she assumed it must be a package from Jason and Amy.

Then, her heart began to race. Could it be her book?

She checked the monitor before opening the front door. The young man wore a proper brown UPS suit, so she opened it.

He was handsome, with deep dimples that deepened when he smiled. "Mrs. Oliver?"

"Yes?"

"You're that author, aren't you?"

"Yes, I am."

He nodded and his grin didn't diminish. "My girl-friend reads your books. She says they're good."

"Thank you."

He handed her an electronic signature device, then when she signed and returned it, he gave her a medium-sized package. *Heavy.* It could very well be a book.

"Mrs. Oliver?" He tucked the device under his arm.

"Yes?"

"I could get in a lot of trouble for asking for this ..." He glanced around the driveway, then returned his attention to her. "Could I get your autograph?"

She chuckled. He'd shown his professional side, now a more charming man emerged. "I thought I just gave it to you."

"Well—you did—but ..."

"I'm teasing. What would you like me to sign?"

He scratched his head and looked over his shoulder toward his van. "How about a sticky note?"

"I have a better idea. What's your girlfriend's name?"

"Alicia." His eyes grew wide, filled with hope.

"Wait here." She left him in the cold for a few short minutes. She figured his girlfriend would be much happier with a signed book than a sticky note. "Here." She handed him a copy of *Marked.* "I made it out to her. Maybe it's one she hasn't read yet."

He beamed. "Even if she has, this'll be the best Christmas present I could ever give her."

"Women also like jewelry." She leaned toward him and winked.

Until a few years ago, jewelry had definitely been a favorite of *hers*. But now, the gift she hoped for was priceless. No Christmas present could come close to matching it.

He dipped his head. "Thank you so much, Mrs. Oliver. And I want you to know, your home is incredible. I don't think I've ever seen another one like it. I can't wait to tell Alicia I met you, *and* I know where you live."

She playfully shook her finger at him. "Don't be telling all my secrets."

Again, he flashed his adorable, dimpled smile.

Lucky girl.

"I don't want to lose my job, ma'am. Your secret is safe with me."

Once he'd taken a seat in his van, she closed the door. She watched the exterior monitors until he'd gone safely out the gate, then she sealed it again.

She grabbed a pair of scissors and carefully opened the package. Though disappointed when it wasn't her book, she was pleased to find a wrapped gift from Jason and Amy. Tempted to open it, she forced herself to place it under the tree. Once there, it actually looked a bit pitiful all by itself. Still, it was better than none at all.

She cocked her head, staring at the parcel. It couldn't hurt to open the card on top of it.

She pulled it out from under the candy-striped ribbon, tightly tied around the package. It gave it that festive touch that had to have been Amy's doing. Jason's artistic penmanship spelled out *Mom* on the face of the white envelope.

The Christmas card she pulled out pictured a Santa placing gifts beneath a tree. The tree stood beside a large window, and the lights from the Eiffel Tower showed through the pane of glass, twinkling in the distant background.

Must be specially made in Paris.

She flipped it over. Nope. *Made in China* had been printed on the back.

Oh well, it's the thought that counts.

The center of the card held a folded letter, so she got comfortable on the sofa and opened it.

Mom,

Thank you for Thanksgiving and being there for me as you always have been. Even though I already knew it, having you tell me to hold onto Amy no matter what happened was something I needed to hear. It seems that so many people give up too easily on their relationships and throw in the towel without giving it all they have to give. I didn't want to be like everyone else. You were right. This is too important.

Amy told me she couldn't stop crying when she went home to see her parents. I told her she wasn't the only one. Where Amy's concerned, I'll never be ashamed to say I cried. We've decided to stop blaming each other and are making plans to look into the option of adoption. There are so many kids on this side of the ocean who need parents. Maybe that's what's been meant for us all along.

We both feel that a weight has been lifted from our shoulders. Going a different direction is obviously the right thing to do. The most important thing about it is that we're going together. No matter where our lives take us, we'll go there hand in hand.

We wish you were with us for Christmas, but understand your reasons for staying home. Hopefully, next year we'll all be together again. Well—all of us except Dad. I still miss him so much, and yet, when I was home it felt like he was there with us. Probably because he'll always be in my heart, and his memories are ever-present in that house.

When I was growing up—and old enough to understand things—I knew I wanted what you and Dad had. I found that with Amy and don't ever want to lose it. I don't even want to imagine my life without her.

You told me to tell her every day that I love her, and I do. Just like I love you, Mom.

Call me if you ever need to talk, or even if you only want to say, "Hello." I'm here for you. Oh—and I'm curious to know if you've seen Sparky again. He was a pretty cool dog.

Merry Christmas,

Jason

P.S. Amy said to tell you thank you, too. She sends her love.

Traci held the letter to her chest and sighed, then followed it with a chuckle.

Sparky. If he only knew.

She read the letter a second time, then lay back against the stuffed cushions. No matter what the box under the tree held, this was the best part of the gift. No inanimate object was better than knowing her son was loved by a good woman. Amy was exactly that. Traci had loved her from the first time Jason brought her home to meet them. Jack had loved her, too.

She waved the letter in the air. "They're going to be fine, Jack." Calm blanketed her, and she sat still, absently staring at the sparkling tree.

As for gifts—Vivian's was already in use. Every year she sent a basket of Christmas confections and a bottle of expensive wine. For some reason she thought she had to break Traci's Mogen David habit. Traci planned to take the wine with her to dinner at Karla's.

She pondered the lonely gift under the artificial branches. From out of nowhere, emptiness set in. Her heart sunk. Had she been setting her hopes too high? How could she ever believe she had the capability to create a miracle?

Her cell rang and brought her out of her brief slump. She stood and retrieved it from the kitchen counter.

"Hello?"

"Traci?"

Who else? It was Vivian, but the sound of her voice brought back her poor mood.

"What's wrong, Viv?"

"Traci—I tried. You know this business. Publishers do things on their time, not ours. I hope you understand. They aren't going to release your book until spring. They want time to do a thorough edit as well as the promotions I mentioned before."

Traci's knees buckled, and she dropped to the floor. She clutched the phone in her hand, unable to speak. The heartache that consumed her took her voice.

"Traci?" Vivian's words seemed distant. As distant as Vivian herself. "Traci!"

She shook her head, trying to clear it, then returned the phone to her ear. "Spring?"

"Yes. Please don't be upset. They have wonderful plans for it. Honestly, they *love* it. They think your fans will like it, too."

"I—I understand. I'm disappointed, that's all."

"Traci, you sound awful. If I have to, I'll fly there tonight. Please, tell me you'll be all right."

"I'll be fine." She took large breaths and tried to ease her heart. She'd always been terrible at lying.

"I love you, Traci. I mean that. Say the word, and I'll be there in a heartbeat."

She managed to smile. Vivian would stick to her word. But, she wasn't about to have her fly to Gatlinburg in the middle of winter. She'd worry too much about the flight. Besides, she could get through this. She'd gotten this far, and a few more months couldn't be too bad.

Keep telling yourself that.

"I love you too, Viv. Now, don't worry about me. Really, I'll be fine." Maybe saying it would make it so. "Karla is bound to cheer me up. I won't be alone."

"That's right. You're having dinner with your doctor. I guess I have no need to worry then."

"Yes, I'll be in very good hands. You go on and have a merry Christmas with Jim."

"Okay, but will you promise to call me if you need me?"

"I promise."

Vivian sighed. She sounded hesitant about ending the call, and Traci felt the need to appease her somehow. "Vivian, you did your best. I understand."

"Thank you," Vivian said, after a drawn-out moment of silence. "Merry Christmas, Traci."

"Merry Christmas."

They hung up, and Traci stayed on the floor digesting the news.

Spring ...

Tears returned. Her Christmas tree glittered with shimmering lights, contorted by the water in her eyes. How could she ever have thought they could push her book through so fast? Sure, she might be Traci Oliver, but she wasn't the queen. She had to abide by industry standards.

She probably should've self-published. Though, she doubted she'd have done it right. What kind of tribute would that have been to Jack? Not a very good one.

After wallowing in self-pity for a short time, she stood and squared her jaw. Jack was worth waiting for. No matter how long it took.

The biggest problem she faced would be how to handle her Friday night visitors.

If this continued for months on end, would she be able to resist the comfort of their arms?

I resisted Andrew. I can resist anyone.

She looked upward and sighed. "Do me a favor. Send Jonah back again and keep Andrew under lock and key. Okay?"

It couldn't hurt to ask.

* * *

Traci hadn't put on a dress since that black cocktail dress so many Fridays ago. But it didn't seem right going to Mass in anything but. So she wore an appropriate Christmas-red dress, more conservative than the black one. She slipped on her knee-high leather boots and covered up with a dark, wool coat.

The service started at five o'clock. Still, she arrived plenty early. Modest in size, the church had a tendency to fill up quickly with tourists. She took a seat in a back pew, hoping to remain invisible.

Her eyes were drawn to a painting at the front of the sanctuary. A dove with its wings spread, looking as if it floated on white clouds. Truly beautiful.

Jack's service had been held here, and she'd always imagined him floating up to Heaven like the dove. One day she'd join him. How many times over the last year had she wished she already had?

People packed in like sardines, and the room warmed around her. She loved to listen to the singing of Christmas songs and managed to squeak out a few notes of her own. The woman sitting beside her didn't appear to know her. A good thing. Tonight anonymity suited her.

As the priest began to pray, Traci's mind wandered. It might not have been polite not focusing on the words he said, but she had her own prayer. God could hear a multitude of prayers, so it shouldn't matter that hers would be different from that of the priest.

Help me to be at peace, Lord. Help me accept Jack's absence and understand the unusual things I've been experiencing. And if you see fit to bring Jack to me as the others have come, then please, Lord, let him come soon.

Spring wasn't *that* far away. Nevertheless, there were too many Friday nights between now and then.

"Ma'am, are you okay?"

Traci opened her eyes and turned to face the woman beside her. The prayer had ended, but Traci hadn't noticed, and her head had remained bowed. "Yes, I'm fine. Thank you."

The blond woman looked to be about Jason's age. She smiled with a warm, *Christmassy* smile, then patted Traci's arm. "He'll answer your prayers."

Lifting her chin high in the air, Traci sighed. "I hope so." She pivoted her head to address the woman again. In her place stood a much older woman with hair grayer than Traci's. Her eyes widened, and she looked at Traci as though she'd just talked to thin air.

Maybe I did.

Had she not experienced so many strange things over the past few months, this incident would've disturbed her, but she brushed it off as another unexplained apparition.

I'm like the little boy from that movie who saw dead people, but my people aren't dead, just fictitious.

The one exception was Jack. How could she expect her plan to work, when he didn't fit the mold? *A Golden Life* wasn't fiction. Her chances of having Jack walk through her front door were slim to none.

"Miss?" The little old lady nudged her. "Are you going to light your candle?"

"Oh. Yes." Traci dipped her candle toward the woman's lit one. "Sorry." Being the last one in her row, she had no one to pass the flame to. Once all the candles were lit, the church lights would be dimmed, then they'd sing "Silent Night." It had been a tradition she loved, though as a young mother she'd worried about Jason burning himself.

I hope Jason and Amy are having a good Christmas.

The beautiful hymn filled the building. Traci sang every word, only kept her voice mostly to herself.

"Sleep in heavenly peace. Sleep in heavenly peace."

Calm covered her. It started at the top of her head and worked down her body until it filled her boots. A strange sensation—like she'd been covered by a warm blanket—wrapped around her body and folded itself across her back. Her eyes shifted to the painting of the dove. Were the wings moving? They looked as animated as Miss Ginny.

After shaking her head a few times, they stopped.

Insanity or paranormal activity? Which would be considered worse? Whichever, she wasn't afraid. Her heart was at peace, and her spirit lifted.

Row by row, the congregation made their way out into the cold night. As they left the church, they extinguished their candles and placed them in a collection basket. A light snow fell, and soft flakes alighted on Traci's warm skin, melting instantly.

It was still early; so many people would head for the handful of restaurants that remained open on Christmas Eve as well as Christmas Day. It seemed a shame that anyone would have to work on these days, but being a tourist town, they wanted to accommodate everyone. Traci wasn't hungry. She just wanted to go home and wait.

Waiting for what? Not Jack. Not now. And yet, home beckoned her.

She'd find a movie to watch, drink her fill of eggnog, then go to bed. In the morning she'd open her gift and relax until it was time to head to Karla's for an early dinner. Things could be much worse. She could be homeless and completely alone.

I will NOT feel sorry for myself.

She smiled at every person she passed on the way to her car. Wishes of "Merry Christmas" rang out around her. The birth of a baby long ago brought joy and hope to all these happy faces, and she felt it, too.

Would the feeling fade when the season ended?

If only Christmas cheer would carry on through the rest of the year.

She shrugged, took a deep breath of crisp December air and climbed into her car. For now, she'd enjoy the feeling and not worry about what lay ahead. Why worry? Life would be life, and she had little control.

Roll with the punches, right Jack?

And in her mind he said, "*That's my girl.*"

Chapter 20

Apparently, the theme for Christmas this year had been angels. Jason and Amy had sent an intricately carved, wooden one. A note inside the box indicated it had been crafted in Venice. It had a new home now atop the mantel. It stood a full eighteen inches tall and had a wing span of almost a foot. Its head lifted upward—as if in prayer—but its arms were open wide. Completely natural wood and polished to a smooth finish. Absolutely gorgeous.

"Yes, I do believe I'm surrounded by angels," Traci muttered, as she pulled her door shut and headed for her car.

She hoped Karla wouldn't bring up her office visit. That was the last thing she wanted to think about on Christmas Day.

Karla lived in a two-story white house that looked like something from *Gone with the Wind*. She and her husband, Bill, had restored it and completely remodeled the inside. The outside retained its four-column front and widow's walk on the second floor. Walking up to it made her feel like she'd stepped back into the 1800s. It would've made more sense if she'd had her encounters with Andrew here. Hopefully he wouldn't be a dinner guest tonight.

It wouldn't surprise me if he was.

Karla opened the door and waved Traci in. A mixture of sweet cinnamon and roasted turkey floated around her and made her stomach rumble. She'd hardly eaten a thing the past few days and couldn't wait for a Christmas feast.

"You brought wine?" Karla asked, and nodded to the bottle tucked under her arm.

"Yes. Merry Christmas." She handed it to her. Was it wrong to re-gift it? Maybe not, as long as she had a glass of it with dinner.

Bill came out of the galley-style kitchen wearing an apron. Karla had been blessed with a husband who loved to cook. Attorney by day, master chef by night. He raised his brows at the bottle of wine, then gave Traci a kiss on the cheek. He had to bend *way* down. Bill stood at least six-six, with blond hair and blue eyes. Karla had always said his towering height gave him an advantage in the courtroom.

"Merry Christmas, Traci." He smiled at her, then excused himself to the kitchen. She didn't even have time to return the greeting.

"He takes the meal very seriously," Karla said. She motioned to their living room. "We can have a seat while he puts on the final touches. Trust me. Supper will look like a masterpiece when he's finished."

Traci had no doubts about that one. Bill had been known to post photos of some of his creations on Facebook and, of course, Pinterest.

In the center of their living room, they, too, had an enormous stone fireplace. They were popular here, and came in handy when the snow caused power outages.

Unlike Traci, Karla had put up a real tree. Traci buried her nose in it. "I love the smell. I just don't like to clean up after them."

"Me, too. At least it's only once a year." Karla stood beside her. "I even used fresh boughs on the mantel."

"Your house looks beautiful." Traci sensed Karla had something more on her mind. Small talk was leading up to something.

"Traci?"

Here it comes ...

"Yes?" Sure enough, Karla's brows were doing the *concerned doctor* weave.

"Let's sit down." Karla rested a hand on Traci's arm and gestured toward the sofa.

"Is something wrong?"

With a shake of her head, Karla took a seat, then Traci sat beside her. Though Traci didn't like to lie, she didn't want to have to answer questions about her visitors. She wished she'd never brought them up with Karla to begin with.

"I'm glad you're here, Traci." She took hold of her hands. "Vivian called me. She's been worried about you."

Now it made sense. Vivian had somehow been involved. "I'm fine."

"She told me how disappointed you were about the book release—the fact it's been delayed."

Traci nodded. She could handle *this* subject.

"I know how important it is for you to share things about your life with Jack," Karla went on. "And, I think it's wonderful you've written about him. I can tell you're healing."

"It's getting easier. Although times like this make me miss him more than ordinary days of the week."

"Yes, holidays are hard."

As if on cue, Bill began to hum from the kitchen. It sounded a bit like "Jolly Old Saint Nicholas" but with a dash of "Jingle Bells" thrown in. Karla chuckled, and Traci joined her. The mood in the house had become exactly what she needed. Warm, friendly, and fun. The way holidays should be.

"I'm glad you invited me to dinner," she said.

"Oh—I nearly forgot." Karla stood, then reached under the tree and pulled out a package.

I hope that's not for me.

Re-gifting the bottle of wine made her feel even worse now. "Karla, you didn't need to get me anything. Dinner is more than enough."

"It's not from me." The playful grin on Karla's face said volumes. "It came by special delivery yesterday."

"I don't understand."

Karla returned to her seat and handed the brown paper-wrapped package to Traci. "Vivian."

Vivian?

Why the special delivery? She'd already given her a gift. Traci held the package in her lap and ran her hands over the paper. It was the size and shape of a book.

"Aren't you going to open it?" Karla asked.

"I guess I should since she went to so much trouble." Probably some sort of *coping with grief*, self-help book. Maybe she thought Karla needed to be close by to coach her through it. Vivian meant well, but sometimes her methods weren't the best.

Inside the brown paper was Christmas wrap. Another layer to undo. And Vivian never skimped on tape.

"Like breaking into Fort Knox," Traci mumbled.

She tore through the wrap decorated with angels. The theme continued.

Traci gasped, then clutched her chest. "Oh, God ..."

"What's wrong?" Karla reached for her hand, which happened to be shaking out of control.

"It's—my book. *Jack's* book." Tears flooded her eyes. *How?* She sniffled and wiped them away with the back of her trembling hand.

"I thought they were delaying the release."

"So did I." Traci's labored breath caused her throat to dry. Could her Christmas wish come true?

"There's a card," Karla said, and pointed to an envelope that had fallen on the floor at Traci's feet.

Traci's fingers barely functioned. As if her body had gone on a leave of absence, and her brain had tried to tell invisible body parts to do things they were incapable of. Luckily, Karla remained beside her, because she very well might be going into shock. A doctor could come in handy.

Sweat beaded on her forehead as she tried to control her feelings. With great effort, she scooped up the envelope, then once again smoothed away tears. The tiny envelope had her name on the front followed by a red heart, and the words, *sent with love*.

Pulling the note from that envelope had to be one of the hardest things she'd ever done. Her heart thumped.

Traci, this isn't the finished product, but I know how much it meant to you to see what it will eventually look like. Use this as your advanced reader's copy to read through and make notes in. I know how much you prefer having a book in your hands than on your computer. The photo looks great. Don't you agree?

Merry Christmas.

With love, Vivian

Traci sucked in a roomful of air. Yes, the photo looked perfect. "Look, Karla. My hair was dark. That seems like a lifetime ago, and yet it was taken only three years ago." She touched Jack's face with her fingertip.

"It's a great photo of you two." Karla eyed the picture. "*A Golden Life*? It's a good title. That fits Jack."

A flood of emotions washed over her, and she couldn't hold back. She burst into sobs and pressed the book to her heart. These were tears of hope, not pain. She blubbered like an out-of-control baby, and Karla sat silently beside her and gently rubbed her back.

Bill walked in and extended a wineglass. "Here. This might help."

With a sniffle, Traci took it. "Thank you." After a small sip, she managed to catch her breath. The wine wasn't half bad and soothed her dry throat.

The concern on her friends' faces troubled her. She didn't want to spoil their Christmas cheer. Especially when she'd been overjoyed by Vivian's gift. Her tears had given them the wrong impression.

"Please," Traci said, "don't look so worried. Believe it or not, I'm crying because I'm happy." She took a huge breath, then let it out in one puff. "I'm starved, too." She grinned at Bill. "How long till we eat?"

Good, his expression changed, and he started to laugh. "We can eat now if you'd like."

Perfect.

No more tears.

Before they dug in, Bill took a photo of the fabulous spread on the table. Yes, a masterpiece that led to happy taste buds and warm conversation. By morning, it'd be the envy of every one of their online friends.

The rest of the evening continued to be light. Cheerful. Fun. Exactly what Traci needed.

Karla and Bill filled her in on their daughters' lives and their three grandchildren. One family lived in Nebraska, and the other in Arizona. It was hard for them to get everyone together for a holiday. Skype helped.

"Jason called earlier today to wish me a merry Christmas," Traci said. "He and Amy sound happy—which is good. They've had it rough these past few years. I think I told you they've been trying to have a baby. It seems it's not meant to happen."

"Are they seeing a specialist?" Karla asked.

"They've seen several. But now, they're also looking into adoption."

Bill nodded. "That's wonderful. There are a lot of children who need good homes."

He was right. Still, she understood Amy's desire to conceive. She'd never forget telling Jack when she'd found out she was pregnant with Jason. It had been one of the best days of both of their lives. Chapter four in the book.

Traci leaned back in her chair and patted her full belly. "Bill, that was wonderful. And your cornbread dressing was incredible. I'd ask for the recipe, but Jason wouldn't be happy if I switched up."

"Then you'll have to come back for it again. I'm glad you enjoyed the meal."

"I did. Very much. Thank you."

They left the table and returned to the living room. After letting their meal digest for a short time, Karla brought out dessert and coffee. Pecan pie with a scoop of vanilla bean ice cream. Another five pounds destined to appear the next time Traci stepped on her scale. New jeans were in her future.

She left them with a round of hugs and generous thank-yous. As Traci walked to her car, large snowflakes cascaded through the air. These were the kind that would accumulate quickly, so she needed to get home as fast as she could.

Tomorrow would be date night, and one she'd prepare for. Now, she'd just hope and pray. She'd done everything else possible.

Chapter 21

Friday, December 26th.

Traci stared at the calendar. Date night. She felt a little like a zombie, unable to move and feeling the need to moan. Last night had been torture. Had she even slept a wink?

A Golden Life rested on the coffee table. Thinking back over every Friday night encounter, they all seemed to have a common thread. Prior to the arrival of her visitor, she'd had something pop into mind about that character. Sometimes it had been put there for her through a linking item—like the mysterious appearance of *Deceptions,* which ultimately brought Andrew to her.

The postcard of the Colosseum had brought Magnus.

Claire was a bit of a puzzle. Her guilt might have caused that one. Regardless of how they'd come to be, she'd been thinking about them before they arrived.

With that in mind, she intended to read *A Golden Life* all day long from cover to cover. If she finished it, she'd start again. She planned to make notes in the margins for Vivian's benefit, but honestly none of this had anything to do with business. Today she'd focus solely on Jack and no one else. No other hero. Just Jack. Her one and only.

Then, at page 105, her thoughts wandered. Like a slow motion movie reel, her mind began to play back every encounter she'd had since Andrew first knocked on her door.

Andrew—the man with Jack's heart. The incredible, gentle lover who grabbed hold of *her* heart and never let go. The man she'd had such a hard time resisting the last time he'd come to her door.

And then ... Gerald. Gerald had that sweet innocence Jack displayed whenever he met her friends for the first time. Not to mention the fact that Jack had been inexperienced in the bedroom. He'd never been with anyone else. If only *she* hadn't. If she could erase her first marriage from her memories, she'd do it in a heartbeat.

And though she didn't mind teaching Jack a few things about lovemaking, he taught her much more. Lovemaking went far beyond the physical act. Gerald had that special something with Claire.

Magnus. Another story entirely. Nothing sweet about him. He'd been bold and daring. She chuckled. He'd behaved just like Jack after he'd learned a trick or two in the bedroom.

The scene she'd written about Magnus having his way with Alexa against the stone wall had been inspired by a night with Jack. He'd tried to take her against their bedroom wall, but their night hadn't been so successful. They'd ended up falling on the floor and laughing so

hard that it changed the mood entirely. Fictitious encounters could be extremely more acrobatic. Fake people
were more pliable and had perfect balance.

*Real people fall on their butts and get bruises and abra-
sions.*

She shook her head, recalling the deep scratches Magnus had given her. She didn't regret the experience. Exciting, but heart-wrenching. She'd never look at the
Colosseum the same way again.

And what about Laird Daniel Gray? The man who had
such a hard time fitting in.

Thanks to my ignorance.

Maybe he held a part of Jack, too. Jack had never
known what to say at her book signings. He'd always felt
out of place, but went anyway. He couldn't speak their
language. The writer/reader circle had its own way of
communicating.

On the other hand, if they were put in a room full of
architects, then *she'd* been the one who'd felt like a for-
eigner. Jack did all he could to make her feel comfortable
in those situations. Had she given him the same courtesy?
She racked her brain trying to remember all those events.
For the life of her, she couldn't envision even one right
now.

Why does there have to be so much regret?

Okay. She had to change her line of thinking, or she'd
mire herself down into a pity pit again. If Jack was coming, he definitely wouldn't want to see her like this. She
had to stay upbeat—with a dash of Pollyanna happy
thoughts thrown in.

She moved on to her other encounters. There'd probably been a bit of Jack in her minor male characters as well. Even the notorious John Martin. Jack would never have cheated on her, but he'd been a very suave lover. His confidence in their relationship prompted him to give her an occasional pat on the rear end when they were in public. Of course, he'd tried to do it discreetly. No doubt they'd been caught a time or two.

As for Jonah ... He and Jack had many similarities. Though Jonah hadn't displayed his impatience when he'd visited, it had been one of his most prominent characteristic in *Island in the Forest*. Jack had been known to be impatient.

His biggest frustration would come to light in restaurants, when a server took too long bringing their check. When Jack had finished his meal, he'd be ready to leave and would start to fidget. He'd complain to Traci, but never to the server. However, the tip scale declined the longer it took the bill to get to their table. She'd learned quickly to make an excuse to linger behind and add to it.

And—like Jonah—Jack had been fun to be around. Just to sit with and watch movies, or drink coffee on the front porch. They knew how to laugh, and they'd done it often.

William O'Brien. Jack had never come close to the man's size, and had been much better looking. Still, something in William's mannerism resembled Jack. William had been written as the older *father figure* who'd treated Cora with kindness and gave her everything she needed. All he'd asked for in return was a son. Just as Jack never denied *her* anything, and when Traci gave *him* a son, he'd been the happiest man alive.

Jason is such a blessing. We did good, Jack.

She took a great length of time thinking about each visit in turn, then rolled them over in her mind again. Sparky made no sense whatsoever. She wrote him off as a nice gesture on the part of whoever had been calling the shots.

Once believing them to be apparitions, she now accepted that they were much more. Physically *and* emotionally. Truthfully, she appreciated each one. They'd taught her things about herself *and* about Jack. It boggled her mind that she hadn't realized it when he'd been alive. It had to be the reason why writing was so difficult now. Without him, she'd become the often referred to *glass half empty.*

Now she needed to focus on what really mattered. *Jack's return.*

Gluing her eyes to the manuscript, she found numerous typos. Since she'd typed it so fast, they were understandable. She noted them and would pass on the page numbers and errors to the editor. Even though they'd most likely found them, too.

The day ticked by at a snail's pace. By three o'clock in the afternoon, she'd already read the book all the way through two times. Her eyes were beginning to dry out and ache, so she took a break. After applying eye drops, she went to the kitchen and fixed a sandwich with some leftover turkey Karla had sent home with her.

She strolled through the atrium and inhaled the floral aroma. The trickling water soothed her, tempting her to take a nap. If eating turkey truly made people sleepy, she shouldn't have eaten the sandwich. She'd already been tired, even before she devoured it. It seemed to make matters worse, and it could be a long night. But, she didn't want to risk sleeping through his arrival. If only she could've slept last night, it would've helped.

When the thought of Andrew showing up again popped in her mind, she scolded herself. She had to forget about him.

Jack, Jack, Jack ...

She started to recite the nursery rhyme, *Jack Be Nimble, Jack Be Quick,* to ensure she'd concentrate on his name.

So close. Five-thirty.

The house looked good. Clean and orderly. It should be just as Jack remembered it. But, to make sure, she went through every room and confirmed everything was in its proper place. She had enough time, so she got out the duster and did another round of cleaning. Then, believing she'd gotten dirty, she changed her clothes.

What if she'd put on the wrong dress? She'd already changed twice.

I can't keep doing this. This one will have to do.

She ended up in the royal blue dress she wore to his retirement party. He loved the color on her. But, he'd never seen her fully gray.

She ran to the bathroom and looked in the mirror.

What if he doesn't recognize me?

That had to be the stupidest thought she'd ever had. He'd wanted her to let her hair go gray for years. He'd said he thought she'd look pretty with silvery-gray hair.

Stop doing this to yourself. If he comes, he won't care what color your dress is and he probably wouldn't even notice if you were shaved bald.

If...

That one word put a rock in the depths of her stomach. She didn't want to think about what she might do if he didn't show up.

Perk yourself up, Traci.

She remembered a fun game she used to play with her mother. She needed fun. They'd choose a word, then see how many songs they could come up with that had it in their title. Then, they'd sing a few bars.

How many songs could she think of with *Jack* in their title?

She found herself dancing around the living room to her own rendition of "Jumpin' Jack Flash." When she followed it with "Hit the Road, Jack," she quickly stopped when she realized the words she'd been singing. She wanted him to come back, and the song said just the opposite.

"Enough singing."

She'd reached the countdown to the final minutes, so it was time to pace. She slipped off her high heels. Why be uncomfortable?

The chimes rang out on the clock. Seven dongs. Eight more minutes.

She rubbed her neck, which was damp with sweat. A quick glance in the monitor, and then she moved to the window.

The snow fell even harder and reflected off the light coming from the lamppost at the corner of the driveway.

262 · JEANNE HARDT

No one would be out driving in this mess. But, she shouldn't be concerned about the roads. None of her other visitors drove a car.

One more minute. She swallowed hard. Her nerves had dried her throat.

I'm a wreck.

She braced herself in front of the door. Eight minutes after seven. Her knees quivered.

Silence.

As she scanned the monitor, her heart thumped.

Empty.

Why?

No Jack. Nobody.

What did she do wrong? Had she tempted fate and pissed it off? As each second passed, her heart sped up.

Maybe the clock was wrong. She shifted her eyes to the mantel. Before she could look at the clock, the angel caught her eye. The beautiful gift from her son with its hands lifted in reverence.

Please, God ...

Another minute ticked by, and the monitor remained empty.

No, I won't cry. I'm done crying.

As much as she tried to convince herself, it didn't work. Tears bubbled out of her as hard and fast as the water that fell from the waterfall in the atrium. *It's not fair.* What more could she have done to make it happen?

She squeezed her eyes tight in silent prayer.

What do you want from me?

"Traci?"

Her breath hitched.

Her heart raced faster and faster.

She had to have imagined his voice, wishing for an answer to her prayers.

Then, a hand rested on her shoulder, and she froze. Her staggered breath made her knees weak. Slowly—almost afraid to look—she glanced at the fingers that hadn't moved from where they'd come to rest. Dotted with age spots, plump, and slightly wrinkled.

Her hand flew to her mouth.

Jack.

The realization didn't stop her tears. Instead, they streamed even harder.

As if she'd been made from fine porcelain, he gently turned her toward him. "Why would I knock when I live here?"

Swallowing the lump in her throat, she silently touched his face. His eyes glistened with their own fresh tears, and she beheld the miracle of him. Exactly as she remembered. His mouth curled into that smile she loved, and after he pushed his wire-rimmed glasses up on the bridge of his nose, a warm chuckle came from deep within his belly.

He smoothed her hair with his hand, then ever-so-slowly pulled her to him and pressed his lips to hers.

No kiss had ever been so warm, so loving, or so real. He breathed renewed life into her, and her heart slowed to a steady, strong pace.

"Jack ... How?" She clutched onto him, feeling the body she knew from head to toe. She breathed in his Old Spice cologne, then buried her head into the crook of his neck. Maybe if she held him tight forever, he wouldn't disappear. Then, maybe—just *maybe*—she could keep him.

"You brought me here," he whispered.

His body had always radiated heat, but now there was something greater. He felt more alive than before his death. But how could that be? She burrowed into him, nesting into the loving arms that had always sustained her—gave her something to live for.

"The book I wrote about you. That's how I brought you, isn't it?"

He nodded. "But more than that. Your love has kept me alive." He cupped her cheek with his hand—the same way Andrew had. "Traci, you're more beautiful than ever."

She broke into a heavy bawl.

He pulled her close and held her like a vice with one arm, while he stroked her hair with his other hand. "I don't want you to cry for me. You've cried so much already."

"Of course, I've cried. I've missed you." She held him even tighter. "You left me too soon."

"I know. I never wanted to leave you." His voice wavered. With two fingers he lifted her chin and made her look at him. "Tonight, let's forget the pain and enjoy what time we have."

"How much time is there?" *Please don't tell me you'll be gone in the morning.*

"Does it matter?"

She shook her head. She'd been given a miracle. Why question anything?

She couldn't stop looking at him—touching him. "What do you want to do?"

His lips formed into the smile she'd never forgotten. "Hold you."

She took a deep breath and nodded. Then, without a word, they walked clutching onto one another, and made their way to the bedroom.

How many times had they come here out of routine, each doing their own thing and hardly noticing the other? Why hadn't she appreciated him more? Was this her second chance?

He locked the door behind them.

Chapter 22

Jack scooped Traci into his arms.

"Are you ready for this, Mrs. Oliver?"

The room was brighter than normal, and Jack appeared younger than ever. He had a full head of dark hair and looked thin and sharp in a black tuxedo.

She glanced down at herself, dressed in silky white. Her wedding gown. They were in a hotel room at the Opryland Hotel.

Our wedding night.

He flung her onto the bed, then laughed and flopped down beside her.

I'm young, too. Talk about second chances!

Her long brown hair twisted into a French braid that fell to the middle of her back. Her pre-baby body didn't look half bad, though nothing like Claire's. After all, Traci was real. Not a Barbie doll cut-out.

"You're being awfully quiet," Jack said, and cupped her cheek. "Are you okay?"

No, I'm not.

She burst with joy. "I'm better than okay. I'm Mrs. Jack Oliver, and I'm the happiest woman alive." She grabbed him by the neck and kissed him long and deep. Love consumed her. This outdid Andrew, Gerald, Magnus, Daniel, and all the rest rolled into one. Jack was everything to her.

Within moments they were frantically freeing themselves of every trace of clothing, and in no time were making love like savage beasts.

She'd forgotten their wedding night had been like this. Or maybe it wasn't. She could possibly still have a trace of all her heroines inside her. She had the energy of a twenty-eight-year-old, and she wasn't about to let it go to waste.

After they caught their breath and downed some chilled champagne, she pushed him onto the bed and climbed atop him, ready for more.

"I love you, Jack Oliver." She bent down and kissed him, then sat up and moved like a sleek, lithe acrobat running on high-powered batteries. She didn't have a tired bone in her body.

"I love *you*, Traci Oliver. And I'll love you forever." His eyes widened as she moved in a new way, swiveling her hips. "And if you keep doing *that*, I'll have you bronzed."

She laughed aloud and kept going until he screamed her name in utter ecstasy. Then, before he pulled from her, she managed her own gratification. Being fully satiated, she took a breath and rested by laying down flat upon him.

His strong hands ran up and down her back. She closed her eyes and enjoyed the incredible sensation his able fingers always brought her. A good back rub was almost as good as sex itself, and Jack knew how to give them. Chills cascaded down her spine.

When their breathing returned to a normal rate, he flipped her over onto her back and moved his hand along her damp skin, until it came to rest on her breast. They both breathed hard and heavy.

"We'll have to sleep sometime tonight," he said. "Otherwise, you might kill me."

"I won't kill you. We have a lot more years to come." She moistened her lips, waiting for another kiss.

"I'm counting on it." He leaned up on his elbow and stared at her. "You're beautiful. And I'm the luckiest man on Earth."

"You're my angel, Jack."

She closed her eyes and prepared for his kiss. The moment his lips touched hers, a breeze blew across her shoulders, and she was no longer lying down.

Radiant sunlight pierced her eyes.

They were still naked, but in the back seat of his old blue Dodge. She sat fully upright and looked out the window.

Hot, dry air surrounded them, and yet she shivered.

The dirt road in the middle of nowhere.

Tumbleweeds drifted past them. No trees in sight, just an empty road that stretched on for miles. They'd returned to that crazy road trip they'd taken, when they wanted to see America and got lost in the middle of Texas after deciding to take a shortcut.

Jack turned her head to face him. "This is kind of fun, don't you think? Lost and naked. It might be a good title for one of those books you want to write." He flashed a sexy grin.

She'd been blessed with another second chance. She knew they'd not be found, so it didn't matter what they did. They could run around outside in the buff, and it wouldn't hurt a thing.

He wiggled his brows. "So, my dear. What now?"

The first time they'd been here, she reluctantly laid back and let him have his way. Then, she had a wrench in her left hip for the remainder of the trip. Not to mention a headache from worrying herself sick. She wouldn't make that mistake again.

"I'll show you what now." She shot him a naughty grin, then straddled his lap. Much easier this way in the back seat of a car.

The windows were rolled down, and even though the breeze coming through felt warm, it kept them from getting completely overheated. Her long hair blew around her face, but she paid no attention to it. She focused on their bodies, joined as one. Moving together like a perfectly orchestrated symphony. Mozart or Bach at their finest. Real love. The kind of love she wished for every woman, and the reason she wrote about it.

"I'm going to write those books, Jack. And you'll be my hero in every one of them."

His hands moved up and down her back in tender caresses. "I don't look like the men on those romance novel covers."

"Maybe not. I might have to hire models. But, I swear to you. You'll be a part of every man I ever write. You'll make them real."

She kissed him, slowly this time, memorizing every curve of his mouth and the softness of his lips.

"And will every woman have a part of you?" His mouth searched her breasts and caused her to tremble.

"Yes," she rasped.

"Good. Otherwise, the men wouldn't have the best woman possible to love."

"Oh, Jack. I love you so much."

"I love you more."

They made love until the sun began to set. Odd how they'd experienced two sunsets in one night. And when they stepped out of the car to return to the front seat, they were back in their bedroom in Gatlinburg, facing one another.

Jack wasn't so young anymore. He lay on his back with one arm raised over his head. "I don't want you to be scared for me, Traci."

His words shot an instant jolt of pain through her heart. The concern on his face brought back horrible memories.

Why did they have to be *here*? Why had this time in their past been chosen? She *never* wanted to relive this. It was too painful.

She ran her hand along the fresh, bright, reddish-purple scar on his chest. His triple bypass had been successful, but left its mark. After swallowing hard to dampen her dry throat, she thought about what to say.

When she'd lived this moment, she feared every second. Worried any exertion would cause another heart attack, she went easy on him. Regardless of the fact the doctor had assured them it would be all right, she wasn't convinced—mostly because they'd made love only thirty minutes before his heart attack. She'd never stopped blaming herself.

But, they'd made love anyway back then, and he survived it. He went on to live for another ten years. Maybe that's why she had to go through it again. This was her chance to love him fearlessly, and know she shouldn't have blamed herself. For any of it.

"I'm scared, Jack, but I'm willing to go slow." She placed her hand flat against his chest. The steady beat of a fully repaired heart pulsed into her palm. Rising up, she bent down and kissed him along the scar line. "I love you, Jack."

His hands raked into her hair, and he gently pulled her head up and kissed her lips. "Six months has been a long time. Still, I think I can remember how." He grinned and rolled her over.

It probably would've been easier on him had she been on top, but it seemed he wanted to do this to prove he could. How could she not let him?

Maybe he felt a little scared, too. She could've sworn his body shook. "Love me, Jack," she whispered in his ear. "I know it'll be fine."

He moved into her as though he feared she'd break, but honestly he feared his own body. His hesitance made it obvious. She wouldn't push him. It was likely why he'd wanted to take the lead—to do things in *his* time.

She couldn't love him more than she loved him at this very moment. They were no longer young and energetic, but they could still make love. Even if they hadn't had sex. Every touch, caress, and gentle kiss was lovemaking. Their hearts were joined. The only parts of their bodies necessary for real love.

Because he wanted to please her, he was doing his best. Nothing could've been more beautiful. Eventually, his movement quickened, but ended shortly thereafter. It had been such a long time that gratification came easily for him. Though *she* could've gone on longer, it didn't matter. They'd accomplished something wonderful.

He rolled off of her and sighed. "I'm sorry, Traci. I know you didn't get much out of that."

Tears blurred her vision. "You don't have to tell me you're sorry. I think we did great for a first time. It'll get easier."

"I wish I was younger."

She kissed his cheek. "I wish I was, too. But it doesn't matter. All that matters is we're together. I'm happy simply to be able to hold you."

"Are you sure?"

She squeezed him, then laid her head on his chest. "Of course, I'm sure."

And so, they held each other. Breathed together. Loved
...

Chapter 23

The night seemed to last forever. A hundred memories or more squeezed into what should've been an eight-hour period. Time didn't exist.

Contented, Traci lay peacefully beside Jack. This time, when she closed her eyes and opened them again, they hadn't moved but had returned to the present day.

He'd grown old again—looking the age he'd been the day he'd died. In her eyes, he was as handsome as ever.

He let out a long sigh. "You know I can't do anything anymore." He ran his hand along the scar that went vertically down the middle of his chest.

"I know." By the time he'd died, he had so much medication in his body that even if he'd wanted to, he wouldn't have been able to make love to her. "Just keep holding me."

She rolled onto her side and faced away from him. It was best this way. He couldn't see the puddle of tears in her eyes.

His body pressed against hers, exactly how she remembered it. No, he wasn't lean and trim. His belly fit into the curve of her back. Yet, she loved this man more than all of her book heroes put together. Her prince. Her knight in shining armor. The man who rescued her from the pancake house, saved her from being haunted by horrible memories with an unsuitable man, and gave her a loving and fulfilling life. Most importantly, they created a son. A lasting sign of their love.

His fingers weaved along her arm. "Traci ..." He spoke her name as if he was about to recite poetry. Love flowed from his lips. "Did you enjoy the others?" A soft kiss on her shoulder followed his question.

What?

Her heart fell. She scooted her body and lay on her back so she could look up at him, needing to see into his eyes. "How did you know?"

He showed no evidence of pain. No sign of betrayal. "Because ... I was with you."

"You watched?"

"No." Warmth covered his face. "I was them. Or, maybe I should say they were me."

"You?" Her heart raced. Her mind spun in circles. *How?* "All of them? Andrew. And Daniel. And—"

"Yes, all of them. I wanted to help you, and I know how much each of them held a part of your heart."

"But ..." She wanted to scream. "Why not come as *you* the whole time. You're the only one I really wanted."

"Because you needed to be able to let go of me." He caressed her cheek and looked deeply into her eyes. "I also had to find some way to get you to write again. Writing is as much a part of you as I am. I hoped that by guiding you, I could help you heal."

She laid there and silently took in what he said. Had this been some sort of test? She didn't want to let go of him. *Ever.* And why do it in the arms of other men—regardless of whether or not they were actually him. She didn't know it at the time, and guilt had plagued her worse than the nasty rash she'd pretended to have with William O'Brien.

Cordelia Flowers popped into her mind and made her heart pound even harder. Could that have been why she told her she had nothing to be ashamed of? Did she know all along that all of her encounters had been with Jack?

The core of my encounters ... Jack.

There could be something to psychic ability after all. If she'd stuck around a little longer, Cordelia might have told her everything. Seems she needed to find out for herself. Just like Dorothy had to find her way home in *The Wizard of Oz.* The journey taught a valuable lesson.

Jack traced invisible patterns on her skin. "You're thinking too hard, Traci. It's actually quite simple. You and I were given a gift. And there's so much more in store for us. Things that I'll be waiting to show you."

"In Heaven?"

He nodded.

"Wait a minute." This was almost too much to grasp. "What about Claire? Why did you come as a woman?"

He cleared his throat and licked his lips. "Oh, yes. Claire. I nearly forgot about that one. It wasn't me."

She rose up on her elbows. "Then, who was it?"

"Claire was your mother's idea. It was her. And, by the way, she asked me to tell you hello and give you her love."

Traci flopped back against the pillow. Even in death her mother acted obnoxious. "Did she know how badly it tore me up thinking I'd hurt Claire's feelings?"

"She just wanted to give you something to think about. It took your mind off of feeling sorry for yourself, didn't it?"

"Yes." She hated to admit it. Her mother always had unusual ways of teaching her lessons.

"Well, there you are." He cuddled closer and rested his head against her breasts. She looped her fingers into the tiny tuft of hair that remained atop his head.

"Was she also the dog?"

He bellowed with laughter. "No, that was me." He sighed. "I can't tell you how wonderful it was to see Jason—to be held by him. And, for the first time in many years, I could kiss him without making him feel awkward."

"A puppy's kiss?"

"It was better than none at all." His laughter subsided. "It was hard for me to see him hurting."

She nestled even closer to him. They'd always shared Jason's troubles. "It makes sense now. Sparky—*you*—whimpered. You felt his pain. You heard everything he said."

Jack let out a long breath. "Yes, I did. You guided him well—said all the right things. I'm just glad you let me sleep in *your* arms. I needed to be near you." He kissed the top of her head, then continued his soft caresses. For the first time in a year, she felt as if she was truly home.

"You know, Traci," he said, after moments of silence. "You might want to consider getting a dog. He'd keep you warm at night."

She couldn't respond. Her mind spun out of control on overload. Had other people experienced this sort of thing? Or was it a weird phenomenon reserved solely for romance writers? Whatever the case might be, she was grateful. She could get through the rest of her life being able to have Jack in her bed every Friday night, no matter what form he chose to take. But, she'd prefer him as himself.

His mouth brushed her ear. "I know what you're thinking."

"You read minds now?"

"It's another afterlife gift."

Scary. There were some thoughts she didn't want him to read. However, since he knew her better than anyone, what could it hurt?

"So," she teased. "What was I thinking?"

He didn't answer right away, and his smile turned to a frown. Her stomach knotted. Why did she believe he was about to reveal something terrible?

"I won't be coming back again."

"What?" Her body tensed. *No!* She couldn't imagine anything worse. She finally got him here, and now she'd never have him again? Andrew had come back multiple times, so why not Jack?

"The others won't be coming back either."

He really *could* read her mind. She couldn't utter a sound. It felt as if he'd just died all over again, and she grew angrier by the minute. Why was *everything* being taken from her?

"You don't need us anymore. It's time for me to go home. As I said, we were given a gift, but one that wasn't meant to last forever here on Earth."

"But ..." She grasped him with every ounce of strength she could muster. Was he about to go off into that mysterious light Cordelia spoke of? "Take me with you. I don't want to stay here alone for the rest of my life. And suggesting a dog as a companion won't do!" Now she knew exactly how Amy felt when Jason suggested a dog might take the place of a child.

"It's not your time."

"Don't say that! Time doesn't matter. You've proved that to me!" She flung the covers back and jumped out of bed. Furious, she clenched her fists and turned her back on him.

A mean, cruel trick had been played on her. Why had she been given such a wonderful gift, if all along they planned to take it from her again? Who could she complain to? *No one.* It wouldn't do any good. They were dealing with something bigger than anything on Earth.

Jack crept up behind her and encircled her with his arms. His lips brushed across her shoulder. "Traci, I understand why you're angry. But I promise you won't be alone. And I'm not referring to the dog."

She whipped around to face him. "But you said—"

"Honey ..." He looked straight at her with his gorgeous brown eyes and stroked her face. How could she stay mad at him? "You're going to be a grandmother."

"A what?" She couldn't have heard him correctly, but his eyes remained affixed to hers, and he nodded.

Okay, now she couldn't breathe. Her knees shook out of control. She'd never intended to buy a ticket for this roller coaster ride. She couldn't take much more.

He led her back to the bed and helped her sit on the edge. "Jason and Amy are going to have a son. He's already been conceived. You can expect a call in a day or two."

She covered her mouth with her hand and fought back tears. Her entire body shook.

Jack lifted a blanket from the bed and draped it across her shoulders, then laid his hand on her knee and soothed her with a gentle stroke. "Our grandson will need you. I expect you to tell him all about his grandpa. You'll have to tell him for both of us, but I promise I'll be out there watching him become a man."

With complete devotion, she managed to move her trembling arms and took his face in her hands and kissed him. She fought back tears and wanted to shout for joy. Her ride had plummeted, then rose to an even higher height than she'd ever thought possible. How could she stay angry when her heart replaced it with hope and love for an unborn child? "But, I wish you could be beside me."

"I will be. You just won't see me."

"Oh, Jack!" Fear of losing him gripped her again, and she blubbered into tears. He helped her under the covers, then comforted her in his arms, shushing her with butterfly-soft kisses. She nestled into his shoulder. "Can't we stay awake forever? I don't want this night to end."

"It has to, Traci. For now. One day, time truly won't matter any longer." He framed her face with his soft hands, and then kissed the tip of her nose. "You have to promise me you'll be happy. Know that I'm waiting for you, and we won't be apart for long. Life here is like the blink of an eye compared to eternity. Besides, you owe it to our grandson to be happy. He doesn't need a cranky, dour old grandma." He gave her that *Jack* look. Scolding her in a way only he could.

"Grandma. That sounds really good."

He drew her in closer. "We still have more time *tonight.*"

"How much?"

"You asked me that before. Haven't I shown you that time doesn't matter?"

She sighed. To him it didn't, but to her it was everything. She'd do all she could to make it last as long as possible.

He glided his finger down the bridge of her nose, then tapped the tip. "So, who would you like to spend your final hours with? I know you're fond of Andrew. But I can be whoever you want me to be."

She didn't have to think about it. Not for one second.

"Be Jack. Just as you are now, and hold me until morning." Expecting him to appreciate what she'd said, his glum expression caused her to draw back.

Does he look disappointed?

Definitely. He pouted like he used to do when he didn't get his way. Or, when she insisted they go visit her mother. Of all the *Jack* faces, she knew this one better than any of them.

And then it hit her upside the head. "Oh, I know what's wrong. You were hoping I'd say Andrew, so I'd be Claire again." She pointed her finger in his face. "I got your number, Mr. Oliver."

"Well, you have to admit, you wrote Claire very well."

"And you were always a breast man." She giggled. "Fine. But only for an hour, and then I want *you* back again."

"I like that idea." His broad grin returned and stretched nearly to his ears. "And don't think you've got me fooled, Traci. I know you like Andrew's attributes."

"Is that what they call it in Heaven?"

"No. But it's one of the ways you referred to it in your books. We might as well keep your terminologies."

They laughed together, then nuzzled down under the covers. Her mind started whirling again. She thought back on all of their encounters as other people. It was different now that she knew it had been him playing the parts.

"You asked me if I enjoyed the others." She cascaded her hand across his chest. "You know I did, and thinking back on all of them, you did, too. We really were given a wonderful gift, weren't we?"

"Yes, we were." He chuckled and tickled her under the chin. "When you told me you had a rash—I nearly lost it right then."

"But ..." Now she really felt bad about refusing William O'Brien. "I just didn't want to do it with him."

"I understand. It wasn't the most romantic situation. But I thought it would be good for you to feel something different. To help you understand your characters a little bit more."

"I do. And I didn't like hurting his feelings. Everyone needs love."

He smiled, then kissed her with a soft, inviting kiss. "And you've given me a lifetime of it." Another kiss, enticingly more fervent. "Are you ready?"

She held up her hand. "Before we—*change*—I want to know something. Why did you come to me so many times as characters from *Southern Secrets* when there were all those others to choose from in my later books?"

"You began your career as a writer with those books. Yes, you poured your heart into everything you wrote, but there was something special about that first one. Andrew and Claire were your firstborn in many ways. They held a vast amount of love. I wanted you to experience them as you wrote them, and as many people have read them. Besides, I admit I've always had a horrible crush on Claire."

She giggled. "I knew it. I should've made you a poster."

"Never mind the poster. This is much better." His smile turned enormous, and in the blink of an eye they changed for a final time.

Lightning struck around them and rain beat hard against the rooftop. Their bed transformed into the bed in the old house on Mobile Bay. Their bodies were young and energetic, filled with desire and heated passion.

And though they made love to each other as Andrew and Claire, it was more powerful. Because without a doubt, she was making love to Jack. It lasted longer than any hour, and when they were fully satisfied, they fell asleep clinging to one another as Jack and Traci.

Chapter 24

Traci would never be able to tell a soul about the Christmas gift she'd been given. Even if she did, no one would believe her—except for Cordelia Flowers, of course. But, she didn't plan to tell even her. Oh, maybe on her deathbed, she'd tell Jason. Or perhaps she'd write a book about it. She could hide it away with the note from John Martin.

The warmth of the shower didn't compare to the feel of Jack's arms. She hugged herself remembering the promise he'd made. He'd be waiting for her.

Up until now, she'd told people she believed in life after death, but there had always been traces of uncertainty in the shadows of her thoughts. Not any longer. Something even better waited for her. It was hard to imagine *anything* better than their love, or what they'd shared together over the last few months.

She scolded herself for forgetting to turn on the exhaust fan, and the steam from the shower filled the bathroom and fogged up the mirror. Then, her heart leapt at the sight before her. A final reminder of her night with Jack.

He used to do this when they were first married—especially in hotel rooms. The words *I'll love you forever* were on the mirror. Made by his angelic finger. She pressed her forehead against the glass.

I love you too, Jack.

She hummed as she made her way around their beautiful home. Once she made coffee, she went to the atrium and watered the plants. She caught herself talking aloud to Jack. After all, he said he'd be by her side. Though it confused her as to how he could both *go home into the light* and still remain with her, she accepted it without question. At peace, her heart rested.

It probably wouldn't be wise to carry on conversations with Jack in public, but at home she'd talk up a storm.

Her cell rang, and she ran for it. Light as air.

"Hello?"

"Mom, it's Jason."

Her heart thumped. She didn't expect his call so soon. Even though Jack told her he'd call, this seemed almost too good to be true.

"Jason, it's good to hear from you again." Did she sound normal enough? Unsuspecting? "I feel spoiled having just talked to you two days ago."

Female laughter mixed with tears erupted in the background.

Amy.

"Mom …" He let out an excited squeal. "We're pregnant!"

She high-fived an invisible hand over her head. "Oh, Jason!" She *had* to act surprised. She wasn't about to let on that she expected the news. After all, an angel told her. What better source for truth? Still, it felt fantastic hearing it from Jason's lips. "That's wonderful news!"

"Yes. We just had it confirmed. Amy's almost two months along. And ..." He sounded like a giddy girl. "There's something else."

More? How much more could she take?

"Yes?" Her pulse raced. She had to sit down.

"I got the contract in Knoxville. We'll be moving after the New Year."

Jack could've mentioned this little tidbit. No wonder he'd said she wouldn't be alone. "You'll be living in Knoxville?" She fanned her face. This was worse than hot flashes.

"Yes. We plan to get a house on the east side so we're even closer to you. We want you in our child's life as much as possible."

"Jason, you don't know how happy you've made me." She blubbered like a baby.

"We needed this, Mom. All of us. And, if it's a boy we want to name him Jack."

She shook her finger at the ceiling.

You knew this, didn't you?

She wouldn't let on to Jason that she knew a little Jack would soon be born. She needed to go to the mall and start shopping for boy baby clothes. And little stuffed animals. And baby furniture for a nursery. And maybe she should start one of those early college savings funds.

So much to do ...

"Mom? You still there?"

"Uh-huh. I'm here. Oh, Jason, your dad would be so proud. I guarantee he's looking down on you now and smiling."

"You think so?"

"I *know* so. Never doubt it for a minute."

They talked longer than they ever had over the phone. And after Jason rambled on for a great deal of time about what the doctor told them and when the due date was, he put Amy on the phone, and she retold everything. Traci let them talk until her hand went numb, and she had to say goodbye.

In less than a month, they'd be here. Then right around the fourth of July, a new Jack Oliver would be brought into the world. How could she have ever thought she'd want to miss this? Heaven could wait a little longer ...

* * *

"Vivian?"

Damn, I think I woke her up again.

"Traci, it's six a.m."

"Sorry."

"What's wrong?"

"Well, I think I may have to get a new agent."

A large amount of shuffling on the other end of the phone filtered through the line, then a much more alert Vivian breathed hard into the mouthpiece. "Why? What did I do wrong?"

Traci giggled. "Nothing. I've decided I don't want to write romance novels any longer."

"You've lost your mind."

"Nope. Things have changed a bit. I'm going to be a grandma."

Vivian shrieked. "That's wonderful!"

"Yep. Amy's due in July. So, I had an idea. I think I want to start writing children's stories. Something she and I can read to the baby."

"I see." Disappointment screamed through the line.

"Awe, c'mon, Viv. It'll be fun. I know you can sell them. So, what do you say? Fluffy animals?"

"I think I need more sleep. Call me back this evening, when you've had more time to think about it. Fluffy animal books won't sell as well as your romance novels."

"Really? You might want to check the numbers on that. Children's books do quite well. Anyway, I've made up my mind. So, let me know if you're still my agent."

"I'll always be your agent. Fluffy animals or buff men. Now, tell me goodbye. I need to sleep."

With a laugh, Traci ended the call.

Vivian would give it some thought, and in the end would see things Traci's way. They'd been through a lot together. This would simply be another step in their journey.

Traci's laptop beckoned her. Then, her eye caught the digital camera sitting beside it. She'd never looked again at the photo of Andrew. So, she powered it up and flipped to the correct frame.

Odd. All she could see was the tree. No Andrew. However, a strange light shone at the center of the photo in front of the tree. It had to be her angel made out of radiant light. No proof of a male visitor, but she didn't need it. She knew he was real. *Jack* was real.

She grabbed her laptop. A thought struck her as she remembered a conversation she and Jason had when he was a little boy. He'd asked her why a branch was sticking out from the side of a cliff, and why it hadn't grown in the forest with the rest of the trees.

What a great way to start a children's book. Maybe Vivian would approve of a talking tree branch rather than a furry puppy.

She grinned and typed.

Where Did I Grow Wrong?—A Twig Story
By Traci Oliver

"Ooh ... I like it."

She giggled at the catchy title. A good place to start.

Epilogue

"I think that was the best Christmas dinner I've ever had," Amy said. She leaned back in her chair and folded her hands over a perfectly flat abdomen.

Traci smiled at her daughter-in-law. Such a pretty girl. No one would ever know she'd given birth. *How did she lose all that weight so fast?*

"Your husband is an exceptional cook," Traci said. "Of course, I taught him everything he knows."

She couldn't imagine Jason's life without Amy. Not only was she lovely, she was kind and good. The perfect mate for her only son.

Amy's long blond hair was piled atop her head. She claimed it was easier with the baby. Otherwise, little Jack grabbed it with his tiny fists.

They were all sitting around the dining room table, unable to move after filling their bellies full. This was the first Christmas dinner they'd shared since Jason and Amy were married. Now that they lived in Knoxville, Traci had become spoiled with their frequent visits. She was grateful they didn't pack up the baby and head to Connecticut for the holidays to see Amy's parents. They decided to switch up each year, and luckily Traci was first on the rotation.

Jason lifted his wineglass. "I'd like to toast to life and all its many blessings." He turned to Amy, who held the baby in her arms. "I love you." He kissed her on the lips, then leaned down and kissed Jack on the top of his head. Then, he looked at Traci. "You too, Mom." He extended his glass toward her.

Traci held up her own glass, clinked it against his, and then Amy added hers.

"I love you all," Traci said, and then looked upward. "And you too, Jack."

The baby gurgled a happy little sound. His bright green eyes glistened.

"He must've thought you were talking to him, Mom," Jason said, with a grin.

She stood and reached for the baby. "Well, I was. I love both of my Jacks." She perched his plump little body on her shoulder and patted his back.

Content beyond words with her grandson cuddled against her body, Traci meandered to the front window. Snow drifted through the cold night air. In the background, Amy and Jason continued to chatter and laugh, but Traci's full attention lay on the precious gift in her arms.

"It's date night," she whispered in his ear. With a glance at the clock, she confirmed they had another thirty minutes before that magic time.

Her visitors no longer made appearances. Still, every Friday night at eight minutes past seven, warmth covered her like a blanket. As though Jack stood beside her and embraced her with angel's wings. The same feeling she'd felt last year at Christmas Mass after singing "Silent Night."

She didn't have to be looking at the clock to feel it. She could be anywhere, and it came to her. It had to have been Jack that night in the church.

Baby Jack grabbed a fistful of her shoulder-length hair and tried to put it in his mouth. Yep, five months old—almost six. Fully able to grab and learning how to crawl.

She gently freed herself from his grip, then sat with him on the sofa. It appeared he'd have Jason's dark hair but had Amy's green eyes. He was undoubtedly the most beautiful baby that ever lived. Regardless of the fact she was his grandmother, she swore it to be true.

She rested him longways on her lap and allowed him to grasp her index fingers. Much less painful than her hair.

"Your grandpa loves you very much, and he's watching you right now."

Jack kicked his feet and grinned. Could a five-month-old understand her?

"You're a smart boy, aren't you? And just you wait ... Grandma has all kinds of stories to tell you."

The Christmas tree shimmered in the corner of the room. Traci chuckled, thinking about who had helped her decorate it last year. And even though her time with Jonah had been fun, this year was one hundred times better.

Her heart had stopped aching some time ago, and she felt alive again. Her first children's book had been released right before Christmas, and sales were doing better than expected. Vivian had succumbed to the fact that Traci was no longer a romance writer and happily continued to represent her. She'd even admitted she liked the book.

"Hey ... Mom?" Jason wandered into the living room with a frame in his hand. "What's the deal with this photo?" He lifted the picture and ran his finger around the center.

"Oh. I took that last year. I thought the tree looked nice."

"But, what's that light in front of it? It looks like the photo was damaged. Why would you frame it?"

Should she tell him the truth?

"Your dad ..." She stopped. There was no way she'd go into detail about how she'd played dress-up with his dead father.

Jason and Amy sat in the other half of the L. They both stared at her, waiting ...

"That is," she went on, "I knew your dad would be proud of me for putting up the tree. So, I framed the picture to remind myself I was healing. He always wanted me to be happy. I didn't care that the print got a bit ... *overexposed*."

"Hmm ..." Amy said. "I didn't think digital photos could get overexposed."

"Oh, but they can," Traci replied. "Honestly."

"That's kind of weird," Jason added, and tipped the framed picture from side to side. He then set it on the coffee table. "If it reminds you of Dad and it helps, then I'm glad you framed it."

She nodded and smiled. Everything around her reminded her of Jack, and now all the memories made her happy.

Amy picked up the copy of *Where Did I Grow Wrong?* from the coffee table. She ran her hand over the picture on the cover—a cute little branch with a spider's web woven through it. "Do you miss writing romance?"

"No. Not really. I'm glad I wrote mine and Jack's story, and it seemed like a good place to end my romance-writing career. And now ..." She rubbed her hand over Jack's belly. "I have fun little stories to write." Of course her voice changed into baby talk, which prompted Jason to roll his eyes and shake his head.

"Did you talk to me like that?" he asked.

"Yes, I did." Even though she answered her son, her words and tone were focused on the baby. "And I did this, too." She lifted his little shirt, then blew on his belly, prompting a giggle.

Amy added a giggle of her own. "I'm glad he has you. I never knew either of my grandmothers. And with my folks so far away ..." Her smile disappeared.

"You'll see them soon," Traci said.

"No, we won't. It's a long ways away, and we can't afford the airfare right now. Besides, I'm not ready to travel with the baby."

There'd been one more Christmas surprise Traci held back. Now seemed like the perfect time to reveal it. "You won't have to travel. I decided we needed everyone here for New Year's, so I sent them tickets. They'll be here next Wednesday."

Amy let out a squeal, then jumped from the sofa and hugged Traci's neck. It startled Jack and his little body jerked. He let out a whimper that turned into a squall.

Jason also hugged her, but then took Jack and rocked him in his arms until he calmed. "Thank you, Mom."

"My pleasure." She stood and excused herself from the room. "I'll be right back."

She glanced over her shoulder at them. Their elation lit the room brighter than the tree.

Are you watching, Jack? They're so happy.

She hesitated before shutting her bedroom door. And she *never* locked it. Maybe she was afraid of being whisked away with Jack somewhere she wouldn't want to return from. And little Jack needed her. Even more so, she needed little Jack.

After lifting the lid to her jewelry box, she dug down into the secret compartment and pulled out John Martin's note. She read it a final time.

Traci,
Forgive my rudeness.
I am forever indebted to you for my creation.
With Sincerity,
John Martin

Physical evidence? Yes. But she didn't want anyone to find it. *Ever.* She wouldn't want to burden Jason with that kind of mystery. It wouldn't be fair to him. With her luck he might think she'd cheated on his father. Either that or she was totally insane and wrote notes to herself supposedly written by fictitious men. Neither scenario would be a good one.

She crumpled it in her palm, then returned to the living room.

"Is everything okay?" Jason asked. He swayed with Jack in his arms.

"Yep." Traci moved to the fireplace and knelt down. With a flick of her wrist, the wadded paper fell into the flames. "I feel fantastic."

"Mrs. Oliver?" Amy nodded to the book. "Would you mind reading to little Jack?"

All these years, and she still couldn't get Amy to call her *Traci*. "I'd love to."

She settled onto the sofa. Amy and Jason took their places beside her with Jack propped up on Jason's lap, chewing on his chubby little fist.

Traci took a deep breath, opened the book, and began to read.

"Just try a little harder. You can do it." The soft voice inside of him urged him on. "You're almost there!

"He was the tiniest of all twigs—not really even a twig yet—just barely a sprout, pushing his way through the hard ground into the world."

She stopped. Warmth flooded over her. Her eyes shifted to the clock, though she didn't need to see it.

Eight minutes after seven.

A smile covered her face.

I love you, Jack.

Acknowledgments

Thank you for sharing this journey with me!

The idea for this story came to mind one night when I went to bed and laid my head down on my pillow. I closed my eyes, but couldn't sleep. I lay completely still as thoughts tumbled through my brain until I had the entire book plotted. I opened my eyes only one time to look at my clock, right before I finally fell asleep. *5:00 a.m.* Two hours later, I jumped out of bed. Tired, but motivated!

When I told my husband my idea, he looked at me as though I'd lost my mind. But then he grinned and told me that people often like things that are a little *weird*. So, he didn't have me committed and encouraged me to write it. Thus, *A Golden Life.*

As unusual as this story might be, I poured my heart and soul into it. Truthfully, I bared myself, and those who know me well will affirm that. I kept a box of tissues close to my desk because I could never get through my read-throughs without needing more than one.

I thank God that unlike Jack, my husband, Rick, is alive and well. He encourages me every day with love and support. Without him, I know I couldn't be the writer I am. Thank you, Ricky, for your unending love, and for being my hero.

I'd also like to thank my son, Nathan, for all the rein-forcing nudges he's given me since I first started writing. I don't know how many times he's said, "You can do it, Mom," but he's been a great pick-me-up whenever I've needed it. He's a gifted artist who understands the impor-tance and *need* of positive encouragement.

Though a great portion of this book is fiction, there are also real places and people that I mention. At the top of that list is Kasey Schroeder. I met her a number of years ago on one of my many trips to Gatlinburg with my husband. Angelic Whispers is a real store, and one I encourage you to visit. And no, this is NOT a paid en-dorsement. This comes from my heart. Kasey's shop is just like I described it, and I own many pieces of jewelry that she crafted by hand. You should pay her and Miss Ginny a visit. You won't be disappointed, and you'll be sure to be greeted with a smile. Thank you, Kasey, for al-lowing me to add you and your shop to my story. You in-spired a great deal of it!

As for the technical side of things, I'd like to thank Tr-ish Milburn, who squeezed me into her busy editing schedule, and Jesse Gordon who also managed to fit me into his calendar and formatted this book. Rae Monet, my cover designer, was a real trouper on this one! I had something specific in mind that didn't quite work out. Lesson learned: leave the art to the artists! I absolutely love the finished product and am overjoyed she stuck with me.

I don't think I've ever been so excited about writing a book. Something about this one had me in manic mode. Along with my husband, I shared the idea with some of my author friends from Music City Romance Writers. I'll never forget them telling me to get it written. If I remember correctly, I finished the first draft in less than a month's time. Like I said, *manic*. Thank you to Monica McCabe and Dana Sieders, who read my original draft and gave me excessively helpful feedback and ideas on how I could improve the story. Also Joy Dent, Cindy Brannam, Caitlin Fryer, Charlotte Margolis, Tina Reid, Jennifer Gatlin, and Jackie Coleman put up with my never-ending rambling about this idea. They even graciously read it somewhere along the way through my edits and revisions.

On one of our trips to Gatlinburg, my sister, Julie, and her husband, Doug Wieringa, went with us. I told them my idea for this book and they seemed genuinely intrigued and enthusiastic about it. Because I wanted a man's perspective, when I completed one of my first drafts I asked Doug if he'd be willing to read it and give me feedback. He didn't hesitate and agreed to it. The feedback he gave me helped me look deeper into Traci's feelings, and I believe that in-depth look added an extremely important factor to the overall story. Thank you, Doug!

In addition, I'd like to thank my dear friends, Susan Tucker and Kellie Thompson, who listened to my idea while we had lunch one day. Though I hated revealing the end to them, when they wiped tears from their eyes, it touched my heart and gave me another boost of encouragement. Another friend, Julia Jones, always listens quietly to my ideas, then gives me a smile and a 'go for it.' Absolutely priceless. Thank you, Julia!

I've been blessed to have friends who've agreed to be Beta readers whenever I need them. They willingly read whatever I write. Their feedback is always invaluable! Thank you to Birgit Barnes, Bobbie Bauer, Mary Ann Brooks, Diane Gardner, Kim Gray, Shawndrae Johnston, James McCormick, Stacy O'Brien, and a new reader, Rachel Reppond.

My mom read an early version of this book. She told me it made her cry. But I think that's a good thing. Unfortunately, loss is a part of life, but I believe in all my heart that we have something fantastic waiting for us on the other side: The love of a Heavenly Father who will embrace us and welcome us home.

Other books by Jeanne Hardt

THE RIVER ROMANCE SERIES

Step back in time to 1850 and travel along the Mississippi River in the *River Romance* series!

Marked
River Romance, Book 1

Cora Craighead wants more than anything to leave Plum Point, Arkansas, aboard one of the fantastic steamboats that pass by her run-down home on the Mississippi River. She's certain there's more to life out there...*somewhere.* Besides, anything has to be better than living with her pa who spends his days and nights drinking and gambling.

Douglas Denton grew up on one of the wealthiest estates in Memphis, Tennessee. Life filled with parties, expensive clothing, and proper English never suited him. He longs for simplicity and a woman with a pure heart—not one who craves his money. Cora is that and more, but she belongs to someone else.

Cora finally gets her wish, only to be taken down a road of strife, uncertainty, and mysterious prophecies. When she's finally discovered again by Douglas, she's a widow, fearing for her life and that of her newborn child and blind companion.

Full of emotions, family secrets, and the search for true love, you'll find it's not just the cards that are marked.

* * *

Tainted
River Romance, Book 2

Despite her new position as manager of the *Bonny Lass,* Francine DuBois doubts her abilities. After all, the only skill she's ever been recognized for is entertaining men and giving them pleasure. But she'll never let her insecurities show in the presence of the new captain. He's too young to be a pilot and he'll never measure up to his predecessor. However, just below the surface, there's something about him she can't ignore.

Luke Waters may be young, but he's determined to prove he's more than capable. He'll show everyone he's the best pilot the Mississippi River has to offer. His only problem - the new crew manager. His religious upbringing taught him to frown on women of her profession, so how can he bring himself to overlook her way of life and give her the respect a workable relationship requires? Especially when he can't stop dreaming about her.

Which is worse? A tainted past, or a tainted opinion?

* * *

Forgotten
River Romance, Book 3

Rumor has it, the war is about to end. But that doesn't stop Billy Denton from running away to enlist. He's lived a privileged life on the Wellesley estate, where slavery is seen as a necessary means to operate their textile production. Believing no human should be enslaved by another, he's willing to fight—and even *die*—to change the future of the woman who holds his heart.

Living and working at the estate is all Angel knows. When Billy tells her he's joining the Union army, she begs him to stay, fearing she'll lose her best friend ... the only man she's ever loved. She'd rather remain a slave, than have him harmed in any way.

Angel attains freedom, but time passes and there's no sign of Billy. In her heart, she believes he'll come home to her. Their love may be forbidden, but can never be forgotten.

Holding on to hope ... Angel waits.

THE SOUTHERN SECRETS SAGA

A little more than six years have passed since the end of the War Between the States, and life in Mobile, Alabama isn't easy. Many loved ones were lost and folks simply want to piece their lives back together again.

But one thing hasn't changed ... The ability to love.

Follow the lives of five families. Many secrets will be kept, and some will be painfully revealed.

* * *

Deceptions: Southern Secrets Saga, Book 1

Claire Montgomery is twenty-five and single. After years of listening to her mama caution her about men, she's determined to stay that way. However, when Dr. Andrew Fletcher arrives in her little town, she's smitten.

Andrew tends the elite at Mobile City Hospital, but also cares for the poor Negroes in a less desirable part of town. Despite criticism from the hospital administrator, he's determined to stand by his principles and help anyone in need. Regardless of the color of their skin.

Andrew proposes marriage. Claire agrees and moves with him to Mobile, where they begin making plans to wed. Her world crashes around her when she discovers a letter that reveals a painful truth. Knowing she can't marry him, but not wanting to cause him pain, she holds the secret and runs away, only to discover she's carrying his child.

Every decision made changes the lives of those she loves. Secrets and lies become a way of life, and she finds that in protecting her child, she's lost sight of her values and endeavors to find them again.

ALSO BY JEANNE HARDT,
ANOTHER SOUTHERN HISTORICAL!

From the Ashes of Atlanta

After losing his Atlanta home and family to the war, Confederate soldier, Jeb Carter, somehow wakes up in a Boston hospital. Alone, desperate, and with a badly broken leg, he pretends to be mute to save himself from those he hates—Yankees.

Gwen Abbott, a student at Boston Women's Medical College, is elated when she's allowed to study under the guidance of a prominent doctor at Massachusetts General. While forced into a courtship with a man she can scarcely tolerate, her thoughts are consumed with their mysterious new patient. If only he could talk.

Two strangers from different worlds, joined by fate. Perhaps love can speak without words and win a war without a single shot being fired.

jeannehardt.com
facebook.com/JEANNEHARDTAUTHOR
amazon.com/author/jeannehardt

Made in the USA
Charleston, SC
25 November 2015